THE TRADE

GRIDIRON LEGACY BOOK ONE

BY AVA SUTTON

COMPASS PRESS

Published by Compass Press

Visit my website at avasuttonbooks.com
Cover Designer, Enchanting Romance Designs
Illustrator: Chloe Ball, @chloscribbles
Developmental Editor: Jeannine Colette, www.jeanninecolette.com
Editor: Jovana Shirley, Unforeseen Editing, www.unforeseenediting.com

ISBN-13: 979-8-9946341-5-8

A NOTE TO MY READERS:

Liam and Alie's story was always meant to be told from the very beginning. Because of that, it was important to include *Snow Blitz* at the start of *The Trade*. It's more than a prequel—it's the moment that sets everything in motion.

Their connection, the events that take place, and the emotions that follow all begin on that one snowy night in New York City. Sharing that first part of their journey ensures their story unfolds the way it was meant to—completely, from beginning to end.

Thank you for reading and stepping into Liam and Alie's world.

**If you have read Snow Blitz and would like to skip ahead, you can begin at Chapter 11.*

For Jeannine

You have championed for a Liam book since day one. This one's for you.

PART ONE

CHAPTER ONE

TWO YEARS, FIVE MONTHS AGO

LIAM

Why am I standing on a rooftop in the middle of winter, freezing my balls off? I did not sign up for this. I thought coming to some posh wedding meant we would at least be, you know, comfortable. I'd take the heat and humidity of New Orleans over this.

I came up to New York City for one of my college teammate's weddings. Brandon had been my roommate when I transferred to Michigan after I left Walker. He and his new wife live in New York since he plays for the Titans, so they got married at some fancy hotel in Midtown during a bye week.

Coming up here also gave me a good excuse to escape a little drama of my own. Last week, I'd broken it off with someone I had been seeing because I needed to stay focused on football right now. Too bad for Sabine, she'd thought our relationship was more serious than it was ever going to be.

Her texts have been coming in more frequently over the last few days, including two today, so, yeah, I'll probably have to change my number when I get back from New York. I have a feeling Sabine won't leave me alone otherwise.

Trying to warm myself up, I take a hefty gulp of my Macallan 18. Sure, there are heating lamps placed strategically around the rooftop with a glass wraparound to cut the wind, but it's still fucking cold. It was only supposed to be a short cocktail hour up here, and then we'd go to the main dining room for dinner, but I've been standing in this same spot, under one of the heaters, for close to an hour. If I had been better prepared and maybe worn a thicker coat, I wouldn't be acting like a pussy about the whole thing.

Glancing around, I take in the all-white wedding theme. Even we, the guests, were asked to wear white. It almost feels like we're in a white-out blizzard ... inside a snow globe ... that you can't get out of because it also started snowing about ten minutes ago.

Fuck, I'm trapped in this snow-globe world and starting to feel claustrophobic now.

A few of my old college teammates from Michigan are hanging around, but almost everyone brought a date, except me. They've tried to include me, and I can carry on a conversation with the best of them, but I'm just not feeling it tonight. I'll probably duck out after we eat.

They're great guys, but I miss my guys from Walker. We're on our own paths now, too, but we try to see each other now and then. Especially Archie Griffith. He's my best friend and the one I talk to the most.

My friends are either in the league now, too, or will be soon. And they're all falling in love. Not only are they falling in love, but they're getting married and—in Archie's case—having babies.

I pull out my phone because, now, I really miss them. Damn, I'm feeling sappy. I take a quick selfie and send it off to Archie, Beck, and Casey.

Liam: Wishing you guys were in NYC with me this weekend.

Beck: Aren't you at a wedding?

Liam: Well, yeah, but it's kinda boring.

Casey: Dude, I can't travel right now. We had a game today. You know this.

Archie: Sorry, buddy. I have a game tomorrow, and Emma is studying this weekend, so I'm on baby duty. Heading down to the ranch for a bit so Em can have a quiet house.

Liam: You guys suck. You should have come with me.

Casey: You love us.

Liam: Unfortunately. Assholes.

Archie: Have a good time. Maybe get laid or something. One of the bridesmaids?

Beck: Text us later. Charlie just got here and says hi.

Liam: Tell Little King I said hey.

Beck: Soon-to-be Linson.

Casey: Still a King right now.

Liam: Fine. I'll send you pictures of all the fun things I'm doing in New York. Without y'all.

Archie: Fun things to do ... you mean pussy, right?

Liam: Any girl I meet in New York tonight will strictly be a hookup.

Archie: Don't do anything I wouldn't do. HA! Text me later, Pitzy.

I laugh, then drop my phone into my pocket. When I look up,

I see the bundled-up bride standing next to a woman with long, dark brown hair in an ankle-length, bright red coat. I'm guessing she didn't get the all-white memo. Then I see my buddy Aaron Muldoon walk up to her. He places a hand on the small of her back, and when she turns her head to look up at him, I almost drop my whisky glass.

I've seen some beautiful women in my life, but she is unbelievably stunning, and I can't even see her whole face yet. But then they turn and walk away from the bride, and I get to see her head-on. She's got hair that looks like silk, with piercing blue eyes, a perfectly symmetrical nose, and her lips ... fuck me. They're full and painted in bright red lipstick that matches her coat.

They're walking toward me now, and he leans down to say something to her that makes her laugh. I'm done for. By the time they reach me, I've managed to pick my jaw up off the floor and compose myself enough that I don't look like an idiot.

"Sup, man? How's it going? Good to see you." Aaron reaches his hand out and pulls me in for a bro hug.

"Muldoon, good to see you. How's New York treating you?" I ask him, but glance her way.

"Good, good. The season's been—" Aaron stops talking when he looks behind me. "Oh shit, I gotta go say hi to someone. I'll be right back." Aaron looks at the woman as he walks away.

"Okay then. No problem. I'll just stand here by myself, freezing, but cool, cool." She tucks a piece of her hair behind her ear.

"Right?" I chuckle. "Whose idea was this? I mean, it does look incredible, but these heating lamps aren't doing a whole lot to cut the chill."

She straightens her arms and holds her hands out. "Picture this...New York City, it's snowing, love and magic are in the air, but I feel like I'm standing in a cryo chamber."

"Ha! Pretty close to the truth there. You ever been in one?" I tilt my head toward her.

She nods, smirking. "Oh, yeah. I'm a fan, but this is, like, really kinda crazy."

"It really is. I was just thinking about leaving after dinner. My hotel room is calling my name. I'll need a good thaw out after this. Until then, a stiff drink helps." I lift my glass to my lips and take another pull of my whisky.

"Whatever you have in that, I might need some to warm up." She tips her head toward my glass.

"Do you want some of this while I go get you a drink?" I hand it out to her.

"Hmm ... risky, taking a drink from a stranger. But you look like a trustworthy guy, and Aaron seems to know you, so why not?" She takes my offered glass and sips. "Nice. Macallan. Eighteen?"

My mouth drops open, and then I shut it so I can form words. "You know your whisky?"

"Mmm. I do. My father is a big fan. I also love a good brandy." She hands it back to me. "So, are you here on the bride or groom's side? Guessing the groom since you know Aaron?"

"Groom. I know Brandon from Michigan. Think I was more of a courtesy invite than anything else. We were roommates, but not incredibly close."

She laughs a warm sound that blends with the music. "I came as Aaron's plus-one. His girlfriend missed her flight, so I said I'd keep him company. That said, he's more interested in working the room and catching up with people."

I smile. "Yeah, he's always been a social guy. Always the life of the party. Even when it's freezing."

She grabs my drink from my hand and lifts it slightly. "The whisky helps." She takes a sip, and I take it back from her, lifting it in my own cheers. "To questionable decisions and good whisky."

She laughs again, and there's a devilish twinkle in her eyes. I'm mesmerized by them until lights begin to brighten behind her in various shades of red, blue, and purple. I move to the side to see where they're coming from.

"It's the lights at Saks," she states, and I arch a brow. She further explains, "The holiday lights show at Saks Fifth Avenue. The sparkling wonderland of lights and music that graces the building's facade every ten minutes." There's a pause in her voice when she realizes I have no idea what she's talking about. "I forgot you're not from here."

I grin. "Midwestern boy. Kansas born and raised. How did you guess?"

"I hear the hint of twang. Have you ever been to New York City in December?" She rubs her gloved hands together.

I shake my head. "I have not. And unfortunately, I'm only here for the weekend and spending the better part of it in my own snowglobe of New York City instead of exploring it."

"Too bad because a guy like you could get into a lot of trouble in this city."

I'm just about to say something when a woman wearing a headset starts to speak. "Excuse me, everyone. Can I have your attention, please? Thank you so much for your patience tonight. There was a minor water issue that we're working to resolve. We should be able to go in shortly. In the meantime, we'll be bringing more appetizers out for you to enjoy. And don't forget to grab a drink at the bar." She waves her hand, then spins around and walks over to the bride and groom.

I glance over at this angel in red, and she meets my gaze.

"I have an idea," she says, grinning.

"Oh, yeah? What's your idea?" I move in a little closer to her.

"How invested are you in staying here?"

I mean, is this a trick question? "Uhh, not very."

"I … " She starts to say something, then stops.

"I … " I prompt her.

She laughs. "I was going to say, do you want to get out of here? Let me show you what a Manhattan Christmas is like."

Fuck. Yes. "Absolutely. But I don't even know your name."

She tilts her head to the side. "Let's go with … Vixen. And you can be … Blitzen."

"What? Why?" I chuckle.

"Because it's fun and the holidays are magical." She holds out her hand to me. "What do ya say, Blitzen? You wanna go make some Christmas magic with me?"

I place my hand in her small one. "Lead the way, Vixen."

CHAPTER TWO

LIAM

When we get to the elevator, she drops my hand and presses the button for the lobby.

"So, where are we going?" I ask her.

"Well, since we're already at Rockefeller Center, we can take a minute to admire the tree, if you haven't yet." She looks at me, brows raised.

"I didn't even know it was here." I shrug.

"Right, right. So, we'll do that first. It's, like, a must on the list." She pulls out her phone and taps something that I can't see.

"You really aren't going to tell me your name?" I place my hand on her lower back and scoot in closer to her. I can smell her perfume; it's light, but it smells like the roses in my mom's garden.

"Nah, I don't think I will. And don't tell me yours."

"Are you a felon on the run or something?"

"Maybe, maybe not. Honestly, I just want to have mindless fun tonight."

"Life's been crazy lately?" I ask, but actually, it's like a statement of my own.

Between traveling, workouts, game play, game strategy, contracts, deals, managing time with friends and family … I've been a little stressed myself.

"You could say that the real world can get a little intense sometimes. Let's just have a good time together tonight. I never get to see the city from a tourist's view, so this will be fun for me. Let's live in the fantasy." She reaches around her back and takes my hand in hers again just as the doors to the elevator open.

"Okay, let's live in the fantasy." I squeeze her hand, and she looks over her shoulder at me and winks.

When we walk out of the building, we're facing St. Patrick's Cathedral. I know it from every movie set in Manhattan, but I only glance at it as she pulls me down 5th Avenue and toward those lights I saw from the rooftop. Saks Fifth Avenue is blaring "Diamonds in the Sky" while an incredible light display moves across the block-wide department store.

When we stop walking, Vixen places her hand on my chin and turns my face away from the music, and I'm instantly staring at a postcard.

Down an alley of lighted angels is the Rockefeller tree with the iconic building standing grand behind it. Television doesn't do it justice. It really is pretty incredible. I would say it stands at least seventy to seventy-five feet tall, with what looks like millions of glittering, colored lights.

"What do you think?" she asks.

I shrug. "I thought it'd be bigger."

Her bottom lip pokes out, and I grin, showing her I'm just messing around with her. She gives me a light shove in the chest.

We make our way through the crowded concourse and around the upper ledge that looks down at the ice-skating rink below us, with families and couples spinning around the loop. Some sections are almost mob-like, so I pull our joined hands toward me, forcing her to my side in a protective stance. I don't want to lose her, and I most certainly don't like the way some of the men stare at her as we walk by. She may have a firecracker personality, but she's a vixen in heels, and almost everyone we pass has taken notice.

It isn't lost on me the way she snakes a hand behind my suit jacket and clings to me as we walk to the base of the tree. When I finally release her, she still stands close to me.

"So, Vixen, are you a born and raised New Yorker?"

She looks up at me and smiles. "Both sides of my family have been here for generations. And other than my time in college, I've lived here my whole life, and I'll probably die here."

"Well, that's kind of morbid, especially standing here in front of this beautiful tree." I chuckle.

She smacks my stomach playfully. "I guess you're right, but I just mean, I love my city. New York is the greatest city in the world."

"You aren't biased or anything, right?" I laugh and put my arm around her waist. Sure, I'm a flirt, but I don't usually feel so at ease with anyone so soon. But there is something about her that just makes me want to touch her.

"Okay, funny guy, let's keep going. Christmas magic awaits!" She takes my hand in hers again. "Oh, wait. Let's take a selfie. Are you good with that?"

"Totally, but I want you to send them to me too."

"I will at the end of the night. Deal?" She releases my hand and pulls her phone out of her pocket.

"Deal," I say.

I lean down so my head fits in the frame and wrap my arms around her waist from behind. She tilts her head toward mine, and with the tree perfectly placed behind us, she snaps a picture. We're both smiling, and we look like a candy cane with my white outfit and her red coat. And now I want to be twisted up with her like a candy cane, in the warmth of my hotel room.

"Okay, let's roll," she says. We link our hands and start walking down 50th Street. "Are you cold?"

"Nah, I'm good. It's warmer down here than it was on the rooftop. My body temperature usually runs hot. Are you good?" I ask her. "You're in fancy clothes."

"Yep, I'm good." She lifts up her long coat and reveals ankle-length red pants.

"Huh, I assumed you had a dress on under that coat."

"I'm not a fan of dresses. I'm too antsy for dresses. I like to be able to move around without worrying I'm flashing my ass at everyone, you know?" She smirks.

I chuckle and nod. "I get it. I hate it when I flash my ass at strangers. I mean, I have a nice ass—don't get me wrong—but I'm selective on who I want ogling it."

"I bet that happens to you a lot. I can't see what's under your coat, but if it looks anything like the rest of you, it must be nice." She winks at me.

This girl.

I love that she's not timid or shy, and she's not trying to impress me. She's very … real.

"I think you're flirting with me, Vixen."

"I just might be, Blitzen," she teases, making us both laugh.

"Are you gonna tell me where we're going next, or is it a surprise? I don't know where I'm going, so pretty much everything will be unknown to me. I've only seen some things on TV or in movies."

We get to 6th Avenue and make a right, crossing the street toward the lights of Radio City Music Hall. There's a crowd of people standing outside the building.

"Is there a show tonight?"

"Yep, the *Radio City Christmas Spectacular*. I know you've heard of the Rockettes back in Kansas. But that's not where we're going. I could probably find a way to get us tickets, but I don't think you're the kind of guy who wants to sit down for two hours when you can rock around the city. Unless you really want to see the show?" She looks up at me questioningly.

"I'll go wherever you take me. I'm a pretty easy guy. I'm letting a snow-kissed angel drag me around a city I could get lost in, so I'll just keep holding your hand." I squeeze her hand and smile down at her.

"Snow-kissed angel. I like that." She returns my smile, and I swear her eyes sparkle.

When we reach the corner in front of Radio City Music Hall, we cross the street again. There's a large fountain with giant ornaments sitting in the water.

"Let's take our next few selfies here. We'll get one with the ornaments behind us, and then we'll get another one with the theater behind us." She looks around, then seems to find a spot.

"Okay, sounds good. Do they do the ornaments every year, or is it different every season?" I ask, looking around at the various sizes in the fountain.

"Every year. They're kind of iconic. You can't do Christmas in New York without posing with the city's biggest balls."

I raise an eyebrow. "Big claim."

She smirks. "Hey, it's tradition. And selfies are the perfect tourist memento. You don't just remember what you saw; you remember who you were with when you saw it."

I grin. "So, basically, photographic evidence that I met a snow-kissed angel and her giant balls?"

She bursts out laughing. "Careful, Blitzen. That caption writes itself."

I move to stand behind her again and wrap my arms around her waist, and this time, I rest my chin on her shoulder. "Ready."

To a passerby, we probably look like a couple who's been together for a while. We're definitely not acting like strangers. She seems just as comfortable with me as I am with her. That has to mean something. Sexy, unpredictable, and funny.

What are the chances that I meet my dream girl at a wedding? In another city. In a different state.

"Okay, let's move over there to get a better shot of Radio City behind us." She points to an area a little farther down the fountain pool.

"Yes, ma'am." I take a minute to appreciate the sway of her hips as she walks.

We take another selfie, and then she taps out a text on her phone. "How do you feel about ice skating?"

"Ice skating?" I thumb back toward Rockefeller Center. "You mean where we just—"

"Ugh. No. That's a tourist trap that will have you standing in line for two hours for a ten-minute skate. I have somewhere better, and we don't have to wait in line."

"Uh ... I could do that. Although it's been years since I've been on skates. Not really a big thing where I'm from. I'm not sure the dress socks I'm wearing or the heels you're wearing are going to work with the skates though." I point to her shoes. "Or that I'm dressed like a human snowflake in a white suit."

"It would be an issue if you didn't fill that suit out so well."

I smirk, and she rolls her eyes.

"Please don't fake modesty with me. We've known each other far too long for that."

"You mean, what, thirty minutes?"

"Our friendship is eternal." She sways playfully from side to side, then lifts a hand toward the street. "Oh! We're making a stop first. Come on. My driver's picking us up on the corner."

She takes my hand, and I thread my fingers with hers. Even though she's wearing gloves, I can still feel the heat from her hand.

"Your driver? Can't we just grab a cab?" I ask her.

"Nah, it'll be faster for my driver to get us."

We continue walking, and a three-person jazz band is playing Christmas carols. A saxophonist, a drummer, and a bass player are jamming to "Let It Snow." It's an upbeat melody, the kind you'd hear on a Michael Bublé album. I tug on her hand toward the jazz trio in front of a pair of towering candy canes wrapped in glittering lights, and she looks up at me.

"Dance with me?" I might not be the most romantic guy, but I'm feeling this with her, and honestly, I just want to hold her again. But this time, I want to look in her eyes while I do.

She snickers—half in protest, half surrender—and I pull her into me. I wrap her arms over my shoulders, and then I wind mine around her waist, moving in closer. We sway on the sidewalk, moving together to the music's lazy swing. Her heels slip once as I move to spin her and bring her back. She laughs, seemingly at the absurdity of this moment—at strangers embarking on an adventure in the city, yet stopping to dance for no reason at all.

I swing her again and dip her this time. When I pull her up, we're so close that our noses are practically touching. I can still smell the whisky and mint on her breath, and it's making me want to taste her lips.

"Still want to go ice skating?" My eyes flit between her eyes and her mouth.

She nods and swallows. "Uh, yeah. But … I think we'll make a stop first."

I raise a brow at her innuendo.

She laughs. "Looks like I found someone on the Naughty List. Get your mind out of the gutter. I'd say you really need to get on the ice and cool down."

"Hmm, you think I'll like it, do you? Even though I haven't been on skates in years?" I smirk.

"I think you'll hold your own. You look pretty … athletic to me."

Our eyes meet, and the corners of her mouth tug up.

She doesn't seem to know who I am, but she knows I'm friends with Aaron, so her guess is right. I'm just surprised she isn't saying anything about it or asking me how Aaron and I know each other.

"In fact, I am pretty athletic. But I still need you to hold my hand until I get used to it." I move in just a little closer. I'm an inch away from taking her lips when a horn honks loudly next to us, drowning out the music.

She pulls away. "That's our ride. We should get going." Her hand comes up, and she tucks a piece of hair behind her ear.

"Okay, yeah. Onto the next adventure." I follow her to the waiting car.

CHAPTER THREE

LIAM

We travel just a few blocks and pull up to a building that says Bergdorf Goodman a few minutes later. We probably could have walked to get here faster, to be honest. There are some Christmas decorations in the windows that look like something out of an old-fashioned movie.

"We're going shopping?" I ask her.

"We're going to run inside for a few essential items." She scoots closer to me so we can get out on the same side of the car.

"Are they still open?" I look out the window and then turn to her. "I'm actually staying at The Plaza, which I think is right down the street. I can just run to my room and change."

"The clock is ticking to get some socks and a pair of gloves for you." She pushes me a little. "Open the door. It's time to scoot."

"Okay, let's do it." I exit the car and hold the door open.

I take her hand as she climbs out of the car.

"Thank you, Blitzen. Let's go get what we need to continue

our night of fun." Her eyes are sparkling again, and she acts like she's walking into a candy store.

"You like to go shopping?" I chuckle.

"Sure, but I'm more excited about what comes after the shopping. Okay, let's split up and go get what we need and meet back here in ten minutes. Does that give you enough time to find everything?" She turns to face me.

"Just tell me where I need to go, and I'll get it done. I'm a guy, so the first pair I see will work." I hold out my hands and smile.

"Right, okay. You go that way." She points behind me. "I'm heading this way." She throws a thumb over her shoulder.

We both take off quickly, and I make my way to the men's department and spot the accessories. I pull a pair of light-gray wool socks off the fancy table, then move to the next section, where hats and gloves are displayed. I'll skip the hat, but I grab a pair of gray leather gloves. Considering I'm wearing all white, I feel like the gray will blend in a little better than black would. I mean, I'm no fashionista, but I can practically hear my mom's voice in my head, leading me to the gray. I guess I'll find out soon enough if I made the right color choices.

I don't know what I'm doing here. Bergdorf, of all places. Holiday chaos, lights flashing, music on the speakers. I left a wedding an hour ago. A wedding. The kind of thing I usually bail on before dessert. And now I'm in Midtown, chasing after a woman I barely know. That's not me. I don't chase. I don't … do this.

Commitments have never been my thing. Never wanted to owe anyone anything. First, my focus was on college and football, with any free time devoted to my friends. Now, my pro career is my top priority. Not that Vixen is looking for a commitment. Actually, this spontaneous night in New York is exactly what I look for in a woman. And yet I'm already wondering what will happen at the end of this night. What will happen tomorrow …

I should walk away—catch a cab, get back to the hotel, and keep the night simple before I have to head back to New Orleans tomorrow. But there's something about this girl. About this night. The spark in her eyes, the way she laughs and almost dares me with her experiences. I'm not going anywhere.

I move over to the sales associate, who is looking at me like she wouldn't mind seeing me naked.

"Is this all for you today, sir?" she asks.

I pull out my wallet and hand her my black American Express card. "This is all. Thanks."

"Thank you for shopping with us, Mr. Pitz. Come back and see us soon." When she hands me my bag, her finger grazes the top of my hand.

This woman is pretty, but nothing compared to my angel in red, who is probably waiting for me in the lobby.

I nod and smile politely, then turn and rush back to meet my Vixen.

As I turn the corner, I spot her. My Vixen. She really is the most beautiful woman I've ever seen, and it's a privilege to spend this time with her. I mean, seriously, how did I get so lucky? This gorgeous stranger rescued me from the most boring wedding I've ever been to and is taking me around her city during one of the most special times of the year. I'm slightly worried this is a dream.

She's removed one of her gloves so that she can take the tag off of the red earmuffs in her hand. There's a black-and-red plaid scarf draped over her arm too. There's a bag sitting by her feet, which I'm guessing holds socks because it's about the same size as my bag, which has my socks and gloves.

"Hey, did you get what you needed?" She nods toward the bag in my hand.

"Yep, I'm ready." I hold out my arm, gesturing for her to lead the way.

Once she puts the earmuffs on her head, which look abso-fucking-lutely adorable, she winds the scarf around her neck.

"We'd better get out of here, or they might just lock us in for the night."

I shudder. "That would be my worst nightmare. Let's go."

"You don't like the idea of that, huh?" She giggles.

"Um, no thank you. What if the mannequins come alive? Have you ever seen that movie? My mom used to put it on sometimes when I was little. Freaked me out."

"I can't say that I have seen that one. You're too funny." She pushes the door open, and we walk back out into the chilly night air. It stopped snowing a while ago, but it's still freezing.

"So, how do we get to the rink?" I ask her.

"Well, it's a bit of a walk, and time is ticking, so we'll just grab one of these rickshaws to Wollman Rink."

She leads us over to a rickshaw that looks like Christmas literally threw up on it. "All I Want for Christmas Is You" by Mariah Carey is blasting from the small speaker the driver has attached to the back of his seat, facing the bench seat.

"Are you taking rides?" she asks the driver.

"Yes, I am. Where you headin'?" he asks her in a thick New York accent.

"Can you take us to Wollman Rink?" She steps onto the platform and sits on the bench seat.

"Yep, that'll be twenty." He turns and looks at me. "You gettin' in or what?"

"Right. Yes. Getting in." I hesitate, eyeing the wheels like they're about to file a complaint with OSHA. The frame creaks when I shift my weight forward. I mean, sure, I'm fit. I'm an NFL quarterback. But I'm also six foot three and two hundred fifteen pounds of solid muscle. Not exactly rickshaw material.

Still, I climb in—gingerly—half expecting the whole Christmas cart to collapse under me.

"Come on, Blitzen. Don't be scared." She waves her hand toward herself, motioning me to sit with her.

"I'm not scared as much as I don't want the tires to pop when

I get in." I chuckle, but lift myself up and into the seat next to her.

"Buddy, this ain't nothing. You in?" The driver turns his head to the side, waiting for my answer.

"Yep, ready." Vixen places her hand on top of mine and curls her fingers under mine.

I look at her and wink. "This should be … fun."

She laughs. "Yes, it will be. We'll be at the rink in no time. Are you ready to have your mind blown with my ice-skating skills?"

"One hundred percent ready for it. You aren't some professional figure skater or something, are you? You gonna embarrass me on the ice?" I let go of her hand and wrap my arm around her shoulders and pull her in closer to me.

Her head tilts from side to side. "Not exactly, but … "

"But … " I prod.

"I did play ice hockey from the time I was seven through college. I was a left wing." She lifts her shoulder and looks at me out of the corner of her eye.

"Wow, that's pretty amazing. So, you'll definitely embarrass me on the ice then. Awesome." I nod.

"You'll be fine. I'll hold your hand the whole time. I promise you, I won't let you fall," she whispers as she leans in closer to me. Then she places the softest kiss on my cheek.

I try to turn my head to meet her lips, but the rickshaw goes over a bump, leading us into the park, and she grabs on to the side.

"A little bumpy." She turns her head, but I can see the pink coloring her cheeks.

"So, Vixen, what's your favorite thing about Christmas?"

Her eyes soften, and for a second, the teasing slips away. "Hmm. I think it's that feeling you get when you walk outside, and the air smells like snow, and everyone's pretending life's a little more magical than it really is."

"That's surprisingly deep for someone who just calls herself Vixen," I tease.

She shrugs. "I contain multitudes."

I grin. "For me, it's the food. My mom makes these ridiculous sugar cookies, shaped like footballs. The frosting's terrible, but … it's kind of tradition."

"Football cookies. That tracks," she says, laughing. "Let me guess … you're one of those guys who turns Christmas dinner into a competitive sport?"

"Only if there's mashed potatoes involved."

"Good to know," she says, smiling.

I lean back and nod toward her. "All right, your turn for a tougher one. Least favorite thing about Christmas?"

"Oh, easy." She lifts her gloved finger like she's making a dramatic declaration. "Those inflatable yard decorations. You know, the ones that collapse into sad plastic puddles during the day? Terrifying."

I laugh. "You're anti-inflatable? That's bold."

"They just … stare at you when they're half deflated. Like Frosty's seen things."

"I feel like that's a personal story," I say.

"It might be," she says, mock serious. "You?"

I think for a moment. "Gift wrapping. I cannot for the life of me fold corners properly. It always looks like I let a raccoon do it."

She laughs, head tipping back. "A big, strong guy like you, taken down by Scotch tape. Tragic."

"It's humbling," I say. "I've learned to lean into the *I tried* aesthetic."

She grins. "That's what bows are for. They distract from the chaos."

"Noted. I'll add bows next year. Maybe even a little glitter."

"Careful," she warns. "Glitter's a commitment. Once it's on you, it's forever."

I have a feeling I'll feel the same way about her when this night is over.

CHAPTER FOUR

LIAM

Wollman Rink glows like a Norman Rockwell painting with its white ice and soft, golden lights strung around the perimeter, and the dark silhouettes of the city rising behind the trees. The night is crisp, the kind of cold that nips at your nose, but doesn't bite.

But none of it touches the heat that hits me when I look at her. She stands there in that red coat, cheeks flushed from skating and laughter, breath puffing in small clouds. The lights catch in her hair, turning her into something warm and bright against the winter night. And, yeah … even if it were below freezing, that sight alone could thaw any man straight through.

She's skating circles around me, and it's not that it's hard to do since my skating skills are not top-tier. Sure, I can throw a football for seventy yards and work my way around three-hundred-pound linemen, but I cannot for the life of me find my balance on these skates. In my defense, the skates we rented aren't the best. The blades are dull and well past needing to be replaced. But I'm letting this little Vixen pull my ass around, looking like an idiot.

"You're doing so good. I think you're ready to go on your own now, don't you?" She tries to let go of my hand, but I squeeze hers tighter.

"I'm not so sure I'm ready for that yet. You can't leave me." There might be a slight panic to my tone, but I don't even care. I brace my legs and stand stock-still.

She belts out a laugh, dropping her head back. Once she catches her breath, she looks at me. "You got this. You're an athlete. I have faith in you, Blitzen."

"I don't know. I feel pretty unsteady—" What she just said stops me. "Wait. You know I'm an athlete?"

She opens her mouth, then closes it. Her gaze meets mine, and a slow smile forms on her lips. "I mean, you have all that"—she gestures to my body—"going on. And I can't even see the whole thing under the jacket."

"Uh-huh." I slide myself closer to her, and with a confidence in my balance that I don't quite have, I reach out and slide my hand around her neck.

"And you don't look hot-girl fit."

"What the hell is hot-girl fit?"

"A body that looks good but lacks cardiovascular endurance." She lifts a brow. "Aesthetic only. No stamina."

I bark out a laugh. "Zero stamina? That's what you think of me?"

"I don't know," she says, pretending to inspect me like I'm a questionable produce item. "You look like you could run a mile, but you also give off strong needs-an-inhaler-after-climbing-stairs energy."

"Oh, that's rude." I tighten my hand at the back of her neck just enough to draw her a fraction closer. "Very rude, Vixen."

"Truthful," she counters, but her voice dips, betraying her.

"And what energy do you give off?" I ask.

She pretends to think. "Hot-girl fit with exceptional emotional intelligence."

I snort. "That's not a category."

"It is if I say it is."

"You realize," I say, leaning in until my forehead almost touches hers, "you're talking a lot of smack for someone who's currently one slip away from landing in my lap."

Her gaze flicks down, just for a second. "Please. If I wanted to be in your lap, I'd already be there."

My pulse stutters. "Is that right?"

She shrugs, all faux innocence. "I mean … you're the one holding my neck like you're about to make a move."

Oh, I am. Very much.

But before I can deliver a clever comeback—or actually act on the gravitational pull between us—her skate slides just a hair.

She grabs my jacket with both hands, eyes wide. "Okay, nope! Too close! Blitzen, stabilize me!"

I try. I really do.

But she's clutching me, and I'm overconfident, and suddenly, we're both wobbling like newborn deer on ice.

"Don't fall," she warns.

"You're the one—"

She yelps, I overcorrect, and we end up chest to chest, her breath warm against my chin, our skates locked in a doomed tangle.

We freeze.

Her hands are fisted in my jacket.

My hand is still on her neck.

Her nose brushes mine. "If we fall," she whispers, "you're going down first."

"Gladly," I murmur, "but maybe not on the ice."

Her eyes flare just before she shoves me—playfully, barely—just enough to untangle our skates.

"Focus, athlete," she says, cheeks flushed. "We're here to skate, not flirt."

I grin. "Pretty sure we're doing both."

She groans, but she's smiling. "God help me, you might have the stamina after all." She shakes her head and looks away.

My hand falls, but I bend my head to try to catch her eye. "Come on, Vixen. Tell me what you really think of me. No bullshit."

"I'll tell you this." She purses her painted red lips and puts her hand on my shoulder. "I like your face. You have a sweet smile and an air of confidence that I'm into. Your eyes are mischievous, which should be a warning sign, but I find myself wanting to know more about you rather than walk away. You're fun to hang out with, and you follow along with me, even when you don't know what my plans are. You roll with it, which tells me you're easygoing and able to adjust your plan when needed. So, I guess what I'm saying is, I'm pleasantly surprised by how my night turned out."

For a second, something warm hits me right in the chest.

Who the hell is this woman?

I've dated confidence before. I've met spontaneous. But I've never met someone who's both those things and somehow still impossible to predict. Someone who can make the entire room blur out just by looking at me like she means every damn word. It's … unnerving. And addictive.

A smile breaks across my face. "Okay, Vixen. I like you too. And I couldn't be happier with how my night turned out."

We're locked in a stare—one of those rare moments where everything goes quiet—and I swear something shifts. Right when I think she feels it too, "Jingle Bell Rock" blares through the speakers. She breaks eye contact, releases my hand, and pushes off, skating away from me backward with that smug little smirk.

The moment snaps in half.

"Hey! You can't just leave me here on my own!" I shout over the music.

She lifts her chin and laughs—light, teasing, like I didn't just hand her a piece of something real. "You got this, Blitzen. I believe in you! Come on. Follow me!" she shouts back and waves her hand toward herself.

And just like that, she turns my quietly emotional, chest-tight moment into a chase.

Damn her.

But I go after her anyway.

"I can't believe I'm doing this. I'd better not hurt myself, or Coach will have my ass," I mumble as I start to shuffle my feet.

"Just go for it! If you go too slow, you'll definitely fall. Slide and glide, my friend." She spins, then takes off at a speed that makes me a little nervous.

"Fuck. Okay, get yourself together, Pitz. You look like a pussy out here." My little pep talk is enough to get my glide on. One foot, then the other. Okay, this isn't so bad. I think I can do this.

"Look at you go! I knew you could do it." She spins around me again, then skates backward, watching me move.

"I don't understand how you can skate like that. Aren't you scared you're going to run into someone?" I'm kind of nervous about it, honestly. There's no way I can get to her safely if she gets hurt.

"You mean, like this?" She swerves and wiggles her hands in the air.

"Ha-ha, funny girl." I'm trying to be serious, but I can't help but laugh.

She looks so happy and carefree.

I stand here, just watching her.

And it hits me—hard enough to knock the air out of my lungs.

Is it actually possible to fall for someone after only a few hours?

I used to give Archie so much shit for that—swearing he'd lost his mind when he and Emma clicked on day one.

But now … yeah, I get it.

And I don't want to get it.

Because I'm not that guy. I don't do commitment. I don't choose romance over football or my family or … anything really. This night was supposed to be fun—one night, no expectations, no complicated aftermath.

Yet here I am, wanting things I shouldn't want.

Wanting to be in her space.

Wanting her in mine.

Wanting to know her—really know her, every sharp edge and soft part she hides behind the jokes.

It's ridiculous.

It's dangerous.

And if I were the kind of guy who let relationships matter, I already know exactly where I'd be headed with her.

Unfortunately, I'm not that guy.

So, why does it suddenly feel like I could be?

Her long brown hair is flying behind her as she speeds around the rink. She keeps turning her head to find me, a smile on her face. And those eyes, glittering. She really is stunning.

And she looks like mine.

My feet are moving of their own accord now in her direction. I want to get to her and wrap her in my arms.

"You coming to get me, Blitzen?" She starts to giggle.

"I am." But I'm actually not because I windmill my arms, trying to keep my balance, but my feet slide out from under me. "Fuck!"

I land flat, not just on my ass, but completely laid out. I somehow manage not to hit my head on the ice, thankfully preventing a concussion.

"Holy shit, are you okay?" Ice sprays all over me as she comes to a stop next to me. When she bends down, she puts her hands on either side of my face. "You good?"

"I don't know," I whisper. "Maybe you should check my head."

"Did you bump it?" She places her hands under my head, and I take the opportunity to take hold of her waist and pull her on top of me. "Oh! You little sneak. Are you even hurt?" She braces one hand on the ice beside my head, the other on my chest, holding herself above me.

"I'm so hurt." I pout my lip and give her my best puppy-dog look.

"Uh-huh. Where?"

She's basically straddling me at this point, in the middle of the rink. But I couldn't care less if people are watching us. Or worse, filming us.

"Here?" Her finger runs up my chest, and even through the fabric of my coat and suit, I can feel it.

I've lost my voice, so I just shake my head and swallow.

"What about here?" She traces my lips with her gloved finger. The leather is smooth on my mouth, but I want more.

Wrapping my hand around her wrist, I tug her in closer to me. "I think you should kiss it and make it better."

"You do, huh?" She's a breath away now. It wouldn't take much for our lips to meet.

The speakers crackle, and a calm, overly cheerful voice echoes across the rink. "Ladies and gentlemen, this is your last song of the skate session. Please finish your laps and exit the ice when the music ends."

"I guess that's our cue to leave," I say, brushing her lips with mine.

"Sounds like it." She sits up, straddling my hips, then swings one of her legs to meet the other so she's kneeling next to me. "Do you think you can get up on your own?"

"Probably not in a pretty way, but, yeah, I'll manage." I'm slightly irritated that our moment was interrupted. Again. But I smile instead because I know that just because our time here is up, our night doesn't have to be over. "Hey, you getting hungry?"

I maneuver myself so I'm on all fours, which isn't a graceful look, but I just need to get on my feet so I can get to the side and pull my way back to the bench to remove these demon slicers.

"Starving." She holds out her hand to me as I manage to stand. "I know just the place."

CHAPTER FIVE

LIAM

She's nibbling on her bottom lip as she looks at the menu. If New York feels like some sort of Christmas caricature art, Serendipity feels like stepping into a daydream. It's a mix of retro kitsch, whimsical fantasy, and vintage charm. Pastel-pink walls, Tiffany-style lamps hanging low over every table, and a collage of quirky antiques and old-fashioned clocks. It's as cute and vibrant as the woman sitting across from me. But not nearly as sexy.

"So, you said this place is known for its frozen hot chocolate?" I ask her.

"Mmhmm. It's so yummy. You have to try it." She sets her menu down and wiggles her eyebrows at me. "It's practically orgasmic."

"Orgasmic, you say?" I hold up my arm. "I'll take two, please!"

She drops her mouth open, entertained by my nonsense.

"Do you want one too?" I tease, smirking.

She clears her throat. "Why, yes, I think I do."

The waiter comes by to take our order since he probably saw my raised arm. "Are you both ready to order?"

"Yes, I'll take the bacon mac and a frozen hot chocolate." She hands him her menu. "Oh, and can I also get a glass of water?"

He nods, then looks at me. "And you, sir?"

"I'll have a cheeseburger, hold the tomato, but can I get some extra pickles?" I look at him, and he nods. "Great, and I'll have a frozen hot chocolate too."

"I'll get that right in for you." He takes my menu and walks away.

"So ... Vixen, tell me about you. I know you're from New York and that you know my buddy Aaron. How do you know him?" I ask.

Her earmuffs are sitting in front of her on the table, and she takes them in her hands and starts to twist them back and forth. I can't tell if she's nervous or just needs something to do with her hands.

"I'm from New York City. I know Aaron because our families have been friends since we were babies. Or before that really. Our dads went to college together and stayed in touch. Then, when his family moved to New York, we spent a lot of time with them. He's like a brother to me." She looks up at me from under her long, dark lashes.

"Do you have any siblings?" I want to know everything about her.

"I have an older sister, and we're pretty close. She's just finishing up her sports medicine residency, so she'll be around more now."

"Where did you go to college?" I reach out my hand and take one of hers in mine.

"I just graduated from Boston College in May, and I'm back here now full-time. I'm considering getting my master's, but I'm not really sure I want to." She lifts a shoulder.

"Boston, huh? I haven't been there either. Do you like it better there or here?"

She leans across the table to get closer to me. "Don't tell anyone … " She puts her delicate finger on her lips. "I like Boston better."

I gasp. "You do? Wait, why would that be a secret?" I laugh.

She tilts her head back and forth. "You know … the rivalry between the Red Sox and the Yankees. Tale as old as time, my friend."

"Ahh … baseball. Gotcha."

"New York will always be my home though."

The waiter returns to the table with her water and two large bowls, each with what I assume is the frozen hot chocolate, topped with whipped cream. Definitely not on my food plan, but I'll indulge anyway. It looks amazing.

"Thank you," she says as he sets hers in front of her.

"Thanks, man." I look up and smile at him.

"My pleasure. Your food should be out shortly." He turns and walks to the table next to ours.

"What was your major in college?" I lift the straw from my drink, dragging the tip slowly across the whipped cream, and bring it to my mouth, letting a dollop cling to my lips. I glance up, and she's watching me—mouth slightly parted, eyes tracing the motion like she's memorizing it.

"Uh, what? What was the question?" She tucks a piece of hair behind her ear.

"Your major? What do you want to be when you grow up?" I chuckle.

"Excuse me, sir, but I'm very grown up." She winks at me, flirting again.

"Oh, I'm well aware of that." I laugh. "But what do you want to do with your degree?"

She takes a sip of her drink, sits back, and releases my hand. "Well, my degree is in business management. So, manage … things." She looks off to the side, not meeting my eyes.

"That's cool. Do you have any jobs lined up yet, or are you already working?"

"I have a job, yes. I work in my family business actually." She looks back at me with a smile.

"That's awesome. And lucky. What's your family business?" I take a drink of the most delicious concoction I think I've ever tasted. I'm not sure I can ever drink regular hot chocolate again after this.

"My family is in the sports business." She takes another sip of hers.

"You're kidding?" I sit back in my seat and set my hands on the table.

"Nope. I mean, we have other businesses, too, but our parent company is sports-related."

Makes sense. She's in the sports business, she's good friends with Aaron, and she was at the same wedding I attended. I could pry more, learn more about her—her name, where she works—but I'm not going to. Not tonight. This little game I'm playing—trying to figure out if she knows who I am—is too much fun to ruin with facts.

Part of me would be disappointed if she did know. Ever since becoming a pro football player, I've been warned more than once to watch who I spend time with. Mainly women. It's a harsh reality that some people only want to get close to you because of your status. That's why I've stayed away from getting too close to any woman. I hate that thought. Especially since I have friends who've found real, genuine relationships with amazing women.

As my agent reminds me of often, they met their girls in college when they were still mildly famous. Now, apparently, I'm a "somebody," and I have to be careful.

But tonight, none of that matters. Tonight, not knowing who she really is—her name, her job, whether she even knows my name—is exactly what makes this dangerous little game addictive. It's just skating, just teasing, just laughter. No expectations. And for once, I can enjoy it without thinking about what comes next.

Before she can say more, the waiter brings our food to the table. He sets hers down in front of her first. Her mac and cheese is piled high with bacon chunks resting on top. It's bubbling over the sides, and it looks delicious. Then he sets mine down in front of me. My burger sits on a big pink dish, with French fries taking over half the plate.

We both thank him, and he leaves the table.

"Enough about me. Tell me more about you, Blitzen. Where are you from?" she asks me.

I smile as I remove the tomato—since they forgot to keep it off—and the bottom part of the bun, setting them to the side on my plate. Then I put the lettuce on the top bun, and with my fork, I place the burger patty on it. When I look up at her to answer, she's holding her fork but watching me.

"You a picky eater?" She smirks.

I laugh. "Ha. Not really. I just try to limit my carbs, and I want a few fries, so I'll sacrifice half the bun."

"Ah, okay. So, your hometown?"

"Right, yes. Well, you know I'm from Kansas, but I live in New Orleans now for work. I have an older brother, and I was somewhat of a surprise to my parents, but I'm close with them. I still call my mom every day." I chuckle. "I'm a Sagittarius. Umm … what else? Oh, I went to college at Walker University, then transferred to Michigan for my last year, which you probably figured out since I know Aaron." I lift my brows and look at her.

She nods as she chews her food, then swallows. "Yes, I … figured that it was college."

"Yeah, it was my last year. If you don't already know, which I suspect you do because of the company we were in, I play football." I raise my brows, looking at her.

She nods and smiles. "Let's just keep it at that, okay? Don't tell me anything else about your career. I want to know the man under the helmet." She winks.

"You do, huh?" I chuckle. "Okay, sure. What else do you want to know?"

She purses her lips and puts her finger on her chin. "So, you must have just had a birthday since you're a Sagittarius. Happy belated birthday." She lifts her water to me in cheers. "Um, were you happy or sad to leave Walker and go to Michigan?"

"Yes, it was on December 10, and thank you. As for my transfer, it was the hardest decision I've had to make so far, honestly. My friends at Walker are like family to me." I pull in a deep breath. "Don't get me wrong; I have some good buddies from Michigan. I mean, I wouldn't be here if I didn't care about them, but it's just different." I shrug.

"I get that. I don't have a ton of close friends, but my sister and I are really close, and like I said, Aaron is like a brother. It was hard being away from them when I was at college."

Even though she has said it twice now—that they're like family—I have to know if it's ever been something more. "Have you and Aaron ever dated?"

Her head drops back, and she lets out a deep belly laugh. "Oh God, no. It's never been like that between us."

"Okay, good to know. I just want to make sure that me being here with you won't cause any problems if y'all are *close*, close."

"Ew, no. I mean, he's a great guy, but I have never seen him as anything more than a friend." She takes another bite of her food.

"But you don't have a boyfriend, do you?"

"Blitzen, I wouldn't be here with you if I did." She gives me a flirty smile. "You don't have a girlfriend, do you?"

I shake my head. "No, I don't have a girlfriend."

I'm not gonna close down an opportunity with this girl by explaining that my job is a priority right now because if I have a chance with her, even for one night, I'm not blowing it.

"Good. I'm glad to hear it." We stare at each other, smiling.

"Are you ready to move on to our next adventure?"

"Vixen, I'll go anywhere with you."

I reach for her hand again, and she places hers in mine.

CHAPTER SIX

LIAM

We walk out of the restaurant, and she slips her gloves back on, smoothing the leather over each finger with slow, precise movements that feel far more intimate than they should. I leave mine off—the cold feels good on my hands—and she reaches for one without hesitation. Her leather-covered fingers lace through mine as she makes a right onto 60th Street, tugging me along like she already knows where she wants us to go.

I should feel ridiculous, walking beside her in an all-white suit, like I'm about to headline a Vegas magic show or pose for a boy-band comeback album. But I don't. Maybe it's because she keeps looking at me like I'm something worth looking at. Or maybe it's the heat simmering under my skin, just from being near her.

We walk another block, the city humming around us, before curiosity gets the better of me. Or maybe the tension does—thick, steady, impossible to ignore.

"So," I say, "be straight with me. Why the red?"

She laughs—low, warm, the kind of sound that strokes

against my skin without ever touching me. "Since Aaron invited me at the last minute," she continues, "he forgot to mention the dress code. I didn't know it was an all-white wedding until we were already walking in. All red was what I had."

"It's a bold choice."

"I'm an old-school kind of girl." She lifts one shoulder in a slow, confident shrug. "If I'm going to stand out, I'm going to commit. That said, I'm bold, but I didn't love taking attention from the bride. That wasn't the intention."

It's the first time tonight she sounds even slightly unsure. It makes her seem more real. And somehow more dangerous.

"Is the fish-out-of-water outfit the real reason you wanted to leave the wedding? Because you in that red coat against a terrace full of white felt like … fireworks waiting to happen."

"Partly," she adds, her pace slowing as her gloved fingers tighten around mine. "More than that … I wanted to leave with you."

The words land somewhere low and warm in my chest. "Why me?"

She gives me a long, deliberate look—slow, lingering, like she's memorizing me. "Well … it might have had something to do with you showing up, dressed like"—she gestures at me with a lazy flick of her leather-clad fingers—"a very charming marshmallow."

I groan. "Terrific. Exactly the look I was going for."

"A handsome marshmallow," she corrects, stepping just a bit closer. "The kind you don't toss in cocoa. The kind you … savor."

Her tone dips on the last word, and I feel the pull of it in my stomach.

"You want to savor me?" I ask, poking my chest with a finger, my voice rougher than it should be.

She nods. "I wanted to walk through Manhattan at Christmastime with a handsome stranger who could make me forget my senses for a few hours." Her breath rushes into the air between us. "And maybe … a few hours more."

She steps just close enough that the side of her body presses against mine, her coat touching my suit. It's nothing overt. Just enough to make my pulse quicken. Just enough to make me imagine her without the coat, without the gloves, without the distance.

"Where are we going next?" I look down at her as she looks up at me.

"We're heading back toward Central Park. I thought we could take a carriage ride. Have you ever been on one?"

"I've ridden a horse before, but never in a carriage." I bring her gloved hand up to my lips and kiss the back of her hand. "Hey." I stop walking and face her. "Thank you for doing all this with me tonight. It's seriously the most fun I think I've ever had."

"Really?" She smiles and tilts her head.

I nod. "I swear."

"I'm glad. I'm having a good time too." She turns, and we continue walking.

We can hear another street musician somewhere nearby, playing jazz music. There's a comfortable silence between us as we walk.

Right before we cross the street to the park, we see a vendor selling various Christmas trees, some decorations, and a display stand with ornaments hanging from it.

"Hang on a sec. Let's look and see what they have. You should definitely get something to remember this night in Manhattan, right?" She looks up at me, and the reflection of the lights in her eyes makes them sparkle.

"For sure, but I think you should too. I don't want you to forget my handsome face." I wink at her.

"Oh, there's no way I'd forget your face or this night." She takes an apple ornament off the hanger and turns toward me. "I'm really glad we were both cold and bored."

"Me too, Vixen. Me. Too." I take her other hand in mine and pull her in closer to me. "Have I told you how beautiful you are?"

"Tell me," she breathes.

I slide my hand into her hair and step in closer still. "You're beautiful in a way that blindsides a guy. Not just because of your face—though that alone could ruin me—but because you're vibrant and unpredictable, like the whole season is wrapped into one woman. You've got that Christmas kind of magic … the kind that pulls a man in, warms him up, and makes him want more. It's the kind of beauty someone doesn't forget."

"Hey. You gonna buy that, lady?" the vendor interrupts us.

Still holding my gaze, she answers him, "Yep. I'll take this one and this one." She pulls away from me and holds out an ornament of the Rockefeller tree.

"Which one is mine?" I point to her hand.

"The apple is yours. The tree is mine—because that's the first time I noticed the green in your eyes, and they shimmered in the light of the tree, and I didn't want to look away." Her teeth graze her lip.

"And I get the apple because you're—"

"Bold, bright, and impossible to ignore." She lifts a shoulder.

"I was thinking because you're too tempting not to want to take a bite out of."

I let out a groan, and she smiles, then ducks her head and walks over to the vendor.

"That'll be thirty," the guy says.

"I'll get it." I walk over, pull out forty bucks, and hand it to the guy.

"Oh, wait, one more thing." She grabs a Santa hat off another stand.

"Twenty," the vendor says.

"Twenty? You've got to be kidding me." She puts her hands on her hips and huffs.

"I got it. Here you go, buddy." I hand him another twenty.

"Keep the change. Merry Christmas." I nod, then reach for her hand. "Let's go, my little Vixen."

As we walk, she starts to laugh. "You just got ripped off. We could have gotten that same hat at Duane Reade for half that price."

"Ah, who cares? And you picked it up, not me!" I wrap my arm around her waist and tickle her side.

She giggles and squirms away from me. "No tickling!"

"Okay, let's go find this carriage." I wrap my arm around her again, and we continue to walk.

"Oh! There's one!" She points to an all-black carriage with a red seat bench and a gorgeous black horse. There are white lights attached to the carriage and along the harness. We walk over to it, and she asks the driver, "Are you taking rides?"

"I sure am. Hop on in." He waves his arm toward the carriage with a wide smile. "I'm Frank, and I'll be your driver tonight." He looks at me. "Hey, don't I know you?"

I don't really want to be rude, but I also don't want to be talking about football the whole time with the driver, so I just smile and wink at him. "Thanks for the ride."

I guide her over to the step and hold her hand. "My lady."

"Thank you," she says, then places a kiss on my cheek before she climbs into the carriage.

I can feel the heat from her lips, even after she pulls away.

Once she takes a seat, I climb up and settle beside her. I drape my arm along the back of the bench, hand resting on her shoulder, and pull her a little closer, letting her lean into me. I think I hear a quiet sigh, but it could just be the horse's hooves clopping over the pavement. Either way, it hits me—I love having this woman in my arms.

Her warmth presses against me, soft and solid at the same time, and the faint scent of her wraps around me. My chest tightens in that way that makes me want to hold her tighter, to feel her even more. Everything else—the cold, the noise, the moving horse—blurs into the background. Frank rattles off the route he's taking around the park, but I barely register the words.

All I can focus on is her—the way she fits perfectly against me, the subtle weight of her body molded to mine, the heat of her skin against my arm. My pulse jumps every time she shifts just enough to brush against me, and a low, dangerous thought slides through my head.

I don't want to let go, not now, not ever.

After we're on our way and Frank leaves us to ourselves, I tug her to me and set my hand on her leg. "Are you cold?" I place a kiss on the top of her head.

"A little, but you're keeping me warm." She leans her head back to look at me.

"Can I tell you something?" I ask, looking between her eyes and her lips.

"Yes," she breathes.

"I've never wanted to kiss someone as badly as I want to kiss you." I inch my face closer to hers.

She reaches her hand up to my face. "So then, kiss me." Her hand holds the back of my neck, and she pulls me toward her.

I don't care that Frank is with us or that people passing by can see us. I need to taste these cherry-red lips.

"Are you sure?"

"If you don't kiss me, Blitzen, I'm going to kiss you—"

Before she can finish what she's saying, I press my lips to hers. Her mouth is soft, warm, and impossibly sweet, and I want more than just a taste—I want all of her. I trace the seam of her lips with my tongue, and when she parts, I slide inside, feeling my tongue brushing against hers. She tastes like a danger I want to keep indulging in.

She twists against me without breaking the kiss, and I lift her legs, draping them over mine. Her body molds against mine, every curve pressing into me, every movement setting a fire in my chest. My hand slides along her thigh, cupping her ass cheek through the layers, feeling the heat radiating through her clothes. I want her skin to skin, but even this—layers and all—is enough to make me ache.

Her hand snakes up the back of my head, running through my hair, pulling me deeper. Our tongues slide and tangle together in a slow, hungry rhythm. I feel her pulse in the subtle pressure of her hands, her hips shifting on the seat, the faint tremor in her body against mine. Every touch sparks something feral in me, a tension that makes my hands clench and my pulse pound.

Time ceases. Frank rattles off directions in front of us, but I don't hear a word. I don't care. All that exists is her, the way she melts into me, and my need to want more.

Finally, I lean back slightly, resting my forehead against hers. My chest rises with the burn of desire, hands still lingering on her body, reluctant to leave. "Come back to my hotel with me," I say, voice deep, certain, a command disguised as a promise.

She pulls back and looks around, then back at me and nods. "Okay." Then she slams her mouth on mine again.

We kiss until my lips feel swollen, but I don't want to stop. I never want to stop.

A throat clears. "Hate to interrupt you lovebirds, but we're almost back to our departure area."

I pull away from our kiss and turn toward Frank. "Actually, can you drop us off in front of The Plaza?"

"No problem, sir." He nods his head.

I look back at her, and she's biting her lip, watching me, but she has a soft smile on her lips.

I take my thumb and press it against her lip and tug it free from her teeth. "That's mine to bite."

She touches her tongue to the tip of my thumb.

"Fuck. Yes," I groan.

The carriage pulls to a stop, and Frank steps out of his seat and waits for us to disembark. I step off first, then turn and reach for her, grabbing hold of her waist and lifting her off the carriage. When I set her down, I get into my pocket for my wallet and hand Frank three hundred-dollar bills and shake his hand.

"Sir, I'm so sorry to ask, but can I get your autograph?" Frank leans in.

I glance at him, heart skipping a beat. *Shit. Keep it calm. Keep it casual.* "Yeah, sure. Do you have something for me to sign?" I pat my pockets. "I don't have anything on me."

He pulls out a notepad and a pen from a pocket in his coat and hands them both to me. "I really appreciate it. My grandson, Michael, is a fan. He won't believe it when I tell him I had you in my carriage tonight."

I take the notepad and lean slightly away from her, keeping my head low. Scribbling quickly, I sign my name and add a little note to Michael.

She leans over to watch, curiosity written all over her face. "What's this about?" she asks softly, tilting her head.

I slide the notepad back to Frank without looking at her. "Just a little fan moment," I murmur, keeping my tone casual, almost teasing, letting the mystery hang.

Frank smiles wide, eyes sparkling behind his glasses. "Thank you, Mr. Pitz. Michael will be thrilled."

I nod with a smirk, then shake Frank's hand. "No problem."

Her lips twitch with a smile, but she doesn't press. I drape my arm around her shoulders, feeling her warmth against me, her subtle shiver under my touch.

She looks up and smiles. "Come on, Blitzen. I'm cold and ready for you to warm me up." She shakes off my arm and takes my hand in hers, and we walk into The Plaza.

CHAPTER SEVEN

LIAM

As soon as we get into the elevator to go up to my floor, I put my hands on her hips and gently push her to the wall. "I can't wait to get my hands on you." I probably sound desperate, but I am, so I don't give a fuck.

"Me too. I can't wait to see what's under this coat." She grabs the lapel of my jacket and tugs.

I bend down and kiss her, slow and deep.

The elevator doors open, and she breaks the kiss and looks to the exit. "This is us?"

I look at the room numbers on the elevator sign and nod. "Yep, this is us."

She doesn't wait for me. She just walks out and then stops and spins around to face me. "What's your room number?"

"Twelve fifty-five." I point to the left. "This way."

She starts to walk down the hall toward my room, but I swoop in behind her and pick her up and carry her the rest of the way in my arms.

"What are you doing?" She laughs.

"I can't wait. I want you in my room as soon as possible." I move quickly down the hallway.

She leans in and starts kissing and sucking on my neck, making me groan.

When I get to my door, I set her on the ground, and I pull out my key card and tap it. Once it clicks, I push it open and hold the door for her to enter.

As soon as the door closes, I'm on her. I step up behind her and move her hair to the side, dropping kisses on her neck and up to the soft spot behind her ear while we walk toward the bed. "You smell so good. Like fresh roses."

She turns in my arms when we get to the bed. She pulls off her gloves one by one as I start to unbutton my coat. I lay it on one of the chairs at the foot of the bed and take her gloves from her hand and set them with my coat. I reach for the buttons on her coat, and we lock eyes.

Her smile is wicked when she reaches for my suit jacket. I'm unbuttoning her coat while she unbuttons my jacket and pushes it off my shoulders. When I get to her bottom button, she wiggles her arms free and drops her coat on the floor.

She kept her coat on, even in the restaurant, and now I know why. The top of her outfit is sleeveless and hugs her tits just right, then curves down her body. The pants flare at her ankles. I never knew pants could be so sexy. And it's all red. Like the color of her lipstick.

I make quick work of my shirt and tie, and then I kick off my shoes.

She takes a seat in one of the chairs to remove her shoes, but I kneel in front of her. "Let me."

"Okay," she says, leaning back in the seat.

Fuck me, even her feet are perfect. I remove both of her heels, then lift one of her legs and kiss her ankle. I set her foot back down on the floor and stand. I reach for her hands and pull her up from the chair.

She turns and faces the bed and sweeps her hair over her shoulder, giving me access to the back zipper. "Unzip me?"

"Fuck yes."

I'm so jacked up that I fumble with the small zipper for a minute until I get a good grip. Then I practically rip it off while I make my way down her back. As the zipper parts, I see a lacy red bra and, lower, a lacy red thong to match. When the zipper hits the end, she reaches around to the back and unfastens her bra, and it drops to the ground.

Am I holding my breath? I think I might be because I feel like I'm about to pass out from anticipation.

When she turns, I see the most perfect pink nipples. I slide my hands around her waist just as she grabs the button on my pants.

"You're so fucking beautiful, Vixen. How did I get so lucky to spend the night with you?"

"You're not too bad yourself. Your body is insane. The abs … Jesus H. I can't wait to run my tongue over them."

She pushes my pants down my legs, and I step out of them. We're facing each other, and we can't hold back any longer. Our mouths collide, and I grab the backs of her thighs and lift her so her pussy fits directly over my hard-on in my boxers.

I walk to the side of the bed and lay her down without breaking our kiss. I drift a hand to the top of her thigh and make my way to her center. She's soaked through the lace, and I push it aside and run my index finger through her wetness. I pull back and look into her eyes. "This is all mine."

"Yes," she moans. "Yours."

I kiss her lips again, but don't deepen it. I shove my boxers off, bend down, and kneel on the floor, grabbing the tiny strings of her thong and pulling it down her legs, revealing the prettiest pussy I've ever seen. It's perfectly pink, just like her nipples, with a thin strip of trimmed hair, and she's glistening. For me.

I drape one of her legs over my shoulder and grab under her thigh and spread her open to me. I can't wait another second to taste her, so I bend my head and run my tongue from her hole to her clit. She's just as sweet as I thought she would be, and I feel like I'll never get enough of her. I could actually die between her legs and be thankful she allowed me to.

I lean in and press my mouth where she wants me most.

The sound she makes—low, broken, helpless—nearly undoes me. It shoots straight through my chest, straight through every place I've ever tried to keep under control. I grip her thigh harder, anchoring her to me because for a second, I'm not sure I can stay steady under the force of wanting her.

She tastes like heat and surrender and something dangerously close to addiction.

I don't even try to slow down. I can't. Not when she arches into me, not when her breath comes in uneven little gasps, not when she keeps whispering my name like it's been pulled from somewhere deep inside her.

Every sound, every shiver, every press of her hips—it feels like it brands itself into me.

I tighten my hold on her, pulling her closer, sinking into her completely.

And the way she responds … God …

It's enough to make me forget every line I swore I wouldn't cross.

"Oh God, that feels so good." She takes my head in both of her hands, holding me to her as I lick, suck, and devour her pussy.

I move my hand from her leg and push my middle finger into her, thrusting it in and out as I flick her clit with my tongue. Her hands fall from my head, but I see her grip the comforter by her sides. And when I look up her body, her back is slightly arched, and her head is tilted, eyes closed, mouth open, panting. She looks like a goddess.

When I start to feel her pulse around my finger, I suck harder on her clit and move my hand faster, creating more friction as she comes.

"Yes, just like that," she moans. "Don't stop."

As if I could. I want to taste her cum on my tongue, and I want to lick up every drop.

When she starts to come, she tries to close her legs, but I don't let her. I hold both legs in place as she rides it out.

"Oh my God. Fuck. Feels. So. Good."

I'm so focused on her pleasure that I don't even realize my own orgasm building. I mean, fuck, my hand isn't even on my dick, and I blow. Just from making her come.

When she starts to come down, her body relaxes, and I release her legs, climbing up her body, kissing every inch along the way.

"You're so fucking perfect. And the way you look when you come had me coming all over the carpet, and I'm still rock fucking hard."

I kiss her on the lips and then slide my tongue into her mouth. She moans when mine reaches hers, no doubt tasting herself.

"I need you inside me. Like, right now." Her hands reach around my back, and she runs them up and down, stopping at the top of my ass. "Fuck me, Blitzen."

She tilts her hips, trying to angle herself so the head of my cock is at her entrance. I push forward just enough that when she moves her hips, my dick pushes inside of her. We both moan this time. I thrust in a little deeper, then deeper again, until I'm completely sheathed by her pussy.

"You're so fucking tight. Am I hurting you?"

She shakes her head. "Don't you dare stop."

"Not a chance."

I start fucking her, slow at first, and then both of us begin to lose control, and our rhythm gets a little sloppy as we edge near our orgasms.

"Look at me," I murmur.

Her lashes lift, just barely, but enough.

One glance, and I'm gone.

She looks wrecked in the most stunning way. Her hair spilled across the pillow, her skin flushed, her breath catching every time I move even slightly. I've never wanted anything more in my life than to keep her right here, trembling.

Her fingers tug at my hair. A deeper sound breaks from her throat, soft but desperate, and I feel the answering pull low inside me, tightening everything.

I move my mouth against hers again. Slow, deliberate, claiming her inch by inch. Not explicit. Just undeniable.

Her whole body responds, arching, tightening, her toes curling against my back. I hold her steady, not letting her escape the intensity building between us, not letting myself escape it either.

She says my name again … shaky, breathless.

I've never wanted to hear anything more.

Her hand slides down from my hair to my cheek, thumb brushing my skin. A gentle touch, but somehow more devastating. There's trust in it—so much quiet, unspoken trust— that it nearly undoes me.

I lift my head for a fraction of a second, just long enough to kiss the inside of her wrist—gentle, reverent, a promise more than a touch. She shivers violently, grabbing the pillow with her free hand, breath hitching like she wasn't prepared for tenderness in the middle of all this heat.

"Don't stop," she whispers, and there's something raw in it. Something honest. Something that pulls me closer, deeper.

"Come for me. Strangle my cock, baby. I can't hold it much longer."

I drive into her faster and faster as she presses her nails into my back. And fuck me, is that a turn-on.

"Yes," she pants. "Harder. I'm so close."

I reach down between us and rub her clit in circles—because I'm gonna blow at any second, and I'm a firm believer that a lady comes first. "You close? I'm losing control."

She nods. "Kiss me."

I tilt my head and kiss her deeply, my tongue twirling around hers. When she wraps her lips around my tongue and sucks, I'm done for. My balls start to tingle, so I rub her clit faster, trying to get her there with me.

When she breaks the kiss and cries out, I feel her pulsing around my cock, and I explode into her.

I rest my forehead on the bed next to her head as we catch our breath.

"Goddamn, that was hot," I say breathily.

"So hot," she breathes. "When can we do it again?"

She turns her face to mine, and we both smile.

"Give me five." I place a kiss on her shoulder and then pull out of her and lie on my side, facing her.

She sits and then turns to me. "Be right back." Then she walks into the bathroom.

While she's in there, it hits me. *I didn't wear a fucking condom.* Fuck. I've never *not* worn a condom. *Shit.*

I move up the bed and lean against the headboard as I wait for her to come out. I don't bother to cover up because I do intend to get inside her again as soon as possible. And I really don't want her to cover up either.

She walks out of the bathroom with pink in her cheeks and a satisfied smile. That I put there. When she reaches the bed, I pat the spot next to me. But instead of sitting next to me, she climbs on top of me and straddles my waist. My dick is pretty happy about it and decides he doesn't need five minutes after all.

Her hands rest on my chest, and she leans down to kiss me. As the kiss deepens, she starts rubbing her bare pussy up and down my hardened cock.

I grip her waist and pull back enough to speak. "Baby, as much as I love this, um, we didn't use a condom."

She stops moving and sits up. "Oh shit. Right."

"I'm clean!" I blurt out. "I've never had sex without a condom."

"Okay, good. I'm clean too. I'm sorry. I just got lost in the moment, I guess. I'm on the pill, too, so we're good."

I nod. "So, yeah, then we should be okay." I'm not sure who I'm trying to convince, but my cock is winning the battle.

CHAPTER EIGHT

LIAM

My dick might be broken. After three rounds of my being buried deep inside the prettiest pussy I've ever seen and a top-notch blow job that left traces of her red lipstick on my cock, we both fell asleep.

She's lying on my chest right now, and my arm is wrapped around her, holding her to me. I've never actually slept with someone like this. I don't really like to be touched when I'm sleeping. It makes me too hot. But with her, I could get used to this.

Her hair fans out across my shoulder and onto the pillow. It looks and feels like silk, and against her creamy skin, she looks a little like Snow White, but with long hair.

Thing is though, I'm not ready to say goodbye to her. I've never felt like this about anyone. Ever. I wouldn't say I'm a player. Okay, maybe I am a little, but I've never had a girl who's made me want … more.

I'm not sure anything can come of it with me living in New Orleans and her here, but my season is almost over, and a lot of the guys have houses in different places in the offseason. And I'll have time to travel, so maybe I should take a shot.

I kiss her head and start to stroke her back. "You awake?"

She hums. "I am now." Her hand on my chest starts to drift toward my growing cock.

"Keep touching me like that, and I'm gonna start thinking I made Santa's damn Naughty List." I pause for a beat and grin. "And honestly? Feels worth it."

As much as I want to bury myself inside her right now, I want her to know that last night was special. And I kind of want to see where her head is. I don't want to embarrass myself by going for something that doesn't have a chance.

"Yeah? I kinda like you, so I guess we both win." She kisses my chest as her hand snakes under the covers, and she takes my erection in her hand and starts stroking it.

I groan. "That feels so fucking good. You keep that up, and I'll forget what I wanted to say."

She looks up at me. "Oh, sorry. Did you want to say something? Is this the part where we say goodbye and *thanks for the memories*?" She laughs, but it's forced.

I kiss her to stop her from thinking the worst. "I'm not ready to say goodbye. That's actually what I wanted to tell you. But I don't want to freak you out." I take hold of her waist and pull her up so she's straddling me.

She sits up, and in one of the sexiest moves I've ever seen, she twists her hair and works it into a knot at the top of her head. Seriously, why is that so sexy?

"You won't freak me out. What's up?" She places her hands on my chest.

"Well, I just wanted to say thank you again for the most amazing night. I've never met anyone like you, who I felt so comfortable with right away. Like, completely drawn to you." I run my hands over the top of her thighs. "Is that cheesy?"

She bites her bottom lip and smiles. "Cheesy? No, not at all. I like it. And I like you." She sucks in a breath. "I had a great night with you too. It was unexpected, but that's kind of the best part, right?" She tilts her head to the side and lifts a brow. "You, Blitzen, were a very nice surprise." She bends down and kisses me on the lips.

I wrap my hand around her neck and deepen the kiss. We break apart, panting.

"So, I'm not the only one thinking we had a connection?"

"No, it's not just you. I feel it too. But I'll be honest with you. This isn't something I was looking for, and I'm not really sure what we can do about it since we don't live near each other. Do you have any ideas?"

"Well, I might. I mean, if you want to see if the magic goes beyond Christmas, I would love to see you again."

She sits up again and traces the muscles on my chest and down to my stomach. "I would love to see you again too."

"Good."

We smile at each other.

"So, your idea?" she prompts.

"One of my best friends and his fiancée did long distance while she finished school. I mean, we could try it and see how it goes." I really want her to say yes.

"Hmm … I'm not opposed to trying it. Maybe we keep it light until we spend more time together and see how it all works out? No pressure." She takes my hands in hers.

"Right, no pressure. We see where it leads us." I repeat, smiling. "I have to warn you though: I have no idea what I'm doing. I've never tried to have a relationship. But most of my close friends are all hooked up, so I think they're good examples." I laugh. "That probably sounds stupid."

"Not at all. Tell me about them." She rolls off of me and lies on her side next to me.

I turn toward her so I can look at her. "What do you want to know?"

"I don't know. Just tell me about them. You've talked about them a few times, so I assume they're important to you. So, if we're going to try this on for size, I should probably know about the people in your life." She props her head on her hand.

"Well, they're my favorite people in the world, so I could probably talk about them all day." I smirk. "The three I'm closest to are Beck, Casey, and Archie. We all played together at Walker and were roommates. Beck and Charlie—Casey's twin sister—are getting married this spring. Casey and his girl, Noelle, finally got their shit together last year. They were best friends, but we all knew it was something more."

"Oh, I love that." She smiles. "The way you talk about them ... your face lights up."

"Yeah, I love these guys. Archie is my best friend. He and his wife, Emma, are the ones I spend the most time with. They have a little girl, Lainey, who is the cutest thing ever." I tuck a stray strand of hair behind her ear.

"Are they around our age?" She runs her hand up and down my arm.

"Yep. Archie and I are the same age, and I guess Emma is, too, actually. Funny story ... they hooked up one night at a party, and she got knocked up. It was a whole thing because she was on scholarship for golf, and Arch was entering the draft after the season, so it wasn't ideal timing. I still can't imagine being a dad right now. It's wild to me. I mean, don't get me wrong; he's the best dad, but the thought of having a kid right now ... " I shiver.

"You don't want kids?" she asks.

"Oh, no, I absolutely do, just not anytime soon. My schedule is crazy, and when I have kids, I want to make sure I'm present for them, if that makes sense?" I raise a brow.

"Yeah, it makes total sense." She nods.

"Archie is lucky because he plays near his hometown, so they have a lot of help from his parents, and her parents also moved there too. So, it works for them. I'm sure you know who he is. He's kinda hard not to know. He's got a loud personality." I chuckle, thinking of him.

"I might know who he is." She smirks. "But I don't know him personally. He seems like a fun guy though."

"He is. And he's the same in person as you see on TV. One of the best guys I know."

"I'm happy you have friendships like that. They're hard to come by. I only have a few close friends, too, but my sister is my best friend. Speaking of … I have to meet her for lunch today. What time is it anyway?" She turns and looks for her phone.

It's not on the nightstand beside us, and I have no idea where mine is. She gets out of bed and pulls out her phone from her coat pocket.

"Oh shit! I have fourteen missed calls between my sister and Aaron. I probably should have said goodbye to him last night when we left. He likely called my sister, looking for me." She lifts her phone to her ear and listens to one of the messages.

"Do you need to go now?" I sit up and turn my body to the side of the bed.

"Uh, yeah, I should get going soon. It's almost ten. I need to go home and change. Should probably shower too." She sets her phone down and gives me a wicked smile.

I walk toward her and wrap my arms around her waist, lifting her. "How about we shower together?"

"I don't think I have time for that, but … I could be persuaded to fuck you again."

"Persuaded, huh?" I bark out a laugh. "I accept that challenge." I walk us back to the bed and lay her down, then brace my weight on my arm as I climb over her and settle between her parted legs.

"You'd better make quick work of it though. I gotta go, Blitzen."

Our faces are practically touching, and she wraps her arms over my shoulders and closes the distance with a kiss. I suck her bottom lip into my mouth, and she moans. Then I make my way to her neck and down to her breasts. My hips start to rock of their own accord, my dick sliding right through her pussy, as I suck one of her nipples into my mouth. The crown of my thickening cock rubs against her clit, and she grabs my hair and tugs my head, forcing me to look at her.

"If you don't put that gorgeous dick inside me, you're going on the Naughty List." She tilts her hips, trying to put me inside of her.

"But I've been a very good boy this year." I drop my mouth to hers and slip my tongue inside just as I thrust into her, making her moan.

Our pace turns frantic as our hips grind against each other. My open mouth is hovering over hers, our breaths becoming more rapid with every stroke.

"Don't come until I say. I'm nowhere near ready to be done with this pussy." I touch the tip of my tongue to hers. "I can't get deep enough." Even to my own ears, I sound more in control than I actually feel. "I want to fuck you so hard that you'll be thinking about me for days."

"Yes, please," she pants.

To tease her and to hold off my own orgasm, I slow my pace and pull out completely, then rub my cock against her clit. Once. Twice.

"Do you feel what you do to me?" I slam back into her pussy —hard and to the hilt. "You drive me crazy." Kiss. "Make me feel like I've lost control." Kiss. "I'm not ready to leave you. Want to stay inside you."

"Harder. Fuck me harder." Her hands slide down my back, and she takes hold of my ass, squeezing. She might even leave a bruise.

I hope she does.

"Goddamn, you feel so good. Made for me." My pace quickens because my dick is fully in charge now, chasing euphoria.

"Oh God, I'm gonna come. Liam!" she cries out.

It's not lost on me that she just said my name, but I'm not gonna ruin the moment by calling her out on it.

"Come, baby. I'm gonna leave my mark on you, so I need you to get there." I reach between us and circle her clit with two fingers.

We're both becoming so frantic, and I really don't want to blow before she does. I lean down and take her mouth in a wet, searing kiss. It's hot and dirty and just what she needs to push her over the edge. I feel her pussy start to strangle my dick.

"That's it. Come for me." I kiss her through her peak, and then I pull out just as my orgasm hits.

I push up on my arm and take my cock in my other hand, pumping until hot ropes of cum shoot out onto her stomach. "Fuck me, that's hot."

She releases my ass and brings her hands to her belly and starts to fucking trace her fingers through my cum, spreading it around and up to her breasts, circling her nipples. Then she reaches down to her belly button, where some more of my cum has pooled, and she swipes her finger through it and brings it to her lips and sucks it into her mouth.

"Holy fucking shit. You might make me erupt again, just seeing you suck my cum off your finger." I pull on my cock one more time, squeezing every last drop onto her. "You truly are meant for me. I'm one hundred percent convinced. I can't ever let you go now."

I shift my weight and lie down by her side. She's still tracing my cum on her body, so I cover one hand with mine and follow her pattern, rubbing it into her skin. Branding her. Marking her as mine.

She looks at my face and gives me a satisfied smile. "I feel like jelly now. I'm not sure I can actually move to leave."

I lean over and kiss her softly. "You're so beautiful. Let me go get you a washcloth to clean my mess off of you." Even though I don't want to. "You can still join me for a quick shower, you know?" I wiggle my brows at her.

She laughs. "If I get in the shower with you, there's no way

I'll make it to lunch on time. I still need to go home, remember? I can't show up in last night's clothes."

I kiss her one more time, then get off the bed. Walking to the end of the mattress, I grab my pants, fish out my phone, and see that I also have some texts from our group chat, including one from Archie. And one from Sabine. I'll reply to everyone but her later. I'm not wasting time with my Vixen right now.

I set the phone down on the table between the two chairs at the end of the bed. "Be right back." I walk into the bathroom and get a washcloth and wet it.

When I get back to the room, she's sitting up against the headboard, watching me, smiling. Her hair has fallen out of her bun, and her cheeks are slightly pink. And she looks thoroughly fucked. Goddamn if that doesn't make me proud.

I sit on the edge of the mattress and wipe my cum off her stomach and move up to her breasts. "You look so pretty, painted in my cum. I hate to wash it off."

She starts to laugh. "Yeah, but it'll dry soon, and no one likes that. Might be a little uncomfortable on my way home too." She winks at me.

I finish cleaning her off and then fold the washcloth and set it near the foot of the bed. "Are you gonna tell me your name before you leave? If we're planning to see where this goes, I can't call you Vixen forever." I take her hand in mine.

"Hmm … I guess you're right. Besides, it's not really fair, is it? Since I know your name." She puts her finger on her chin.

"Exactly." I lift our hands and kiss the back of hers.

"Alie. My name is Alie." She leans forward, closer to me.

"Alie. That's pretty." I meet her in a quick kiss, then pull back. "I'd better get in the shower, or I might miss my flight. Give me five, and we can walk out together?"

"Let me use it before you get in."

She scoots to the side and stands, then walks toward the bathroom. Once she closes the door, I stand and grab my bag from the closet that has my clothes. I pull out a pair of boxers, joggers, a T-shirt, and a sweatshirt. I hear my phone buzz on the table and walk over and pick it up again. This time, it's my mom. I'll answer her later too.

When Alie walks out of the bathroom, I nearly drop my clothes and take her to the bed again. She passes by me and starts to pick up her clothes off the floor.

"Hey, wait for me, yeah?" I lift my brows.

She nods. "I'll wait for you, but hurry up, Liam." A smile breaks out on her face.

"My name sure sounds good, coming from your lips." I smile back at her and walk backward into the bathroom. I don't bother shutting the door.

CHAPTER NINE

ALIE

I pull my red pantsuit over my hips, the fabric sliding into place as easily as the knot forming in my chest. If I didn't already have plans today—and Liam didn't have to get back to New Orleans—I would've stayed tangled up with him in that bed until the very last possible second. Being wrapped around him felt dangerously easy.

Through the open bathroom door, I watch him step into the shower. Steam billows around the shape of his broad shoulders, the water carving paths along his skin until he disappears behind the fog.

A smile tugs at my lips. Never in my life did I imagine I'd spend the night with him—Liam Pitz, one of the hottest new quarterbacks in the league.

Of course I knew who he was. I always know the players; it's impossible not to when you work in the business and your father owns the New York Titans.

But I didn't go to the wedding last night, searching for him. I went because Aaron needed a plus-one and also insisted I get out of my slump.

It's been a rough few months. My ex blindsided me in the fall, breaking up with me after pretending to care for nearly a year. It turned out he wasn't interested in me at all—just in getting close to my father. Another baller looking for a good time, as Dad put it. I learned the hard way that Grant girls need to tread carefully.

Dad made me promise, no more athletes. Not for a while. Not until my judgment wasn't clouded by heartbreak or loneliness.

So, no, I didn't walk into the wedding, plotting to fall headfirst into the arms of a rookie quarterback.

In fact, Dad's warning has played in my head on repeat my whole life: *Rookie athletes have terrible reputations. Money, women, partying, football—it's their entire world.*

And when Liam told me he wasn't ready for a family, none of it surprised me. It fit exactly what Dad had drilled into us: *Do not get mixed up with a man whose entire future depends on keeping his life uncomplicated.*

But then Liam smiled at me. Really smiled. And once we started talking about ridiculous things, like being in a Christmas snow globe, something in me cracked open. He wasn't trying to charm me because of my last name. He didn't even know my last name. For the first time in a long time, someone saw me, not the Grant legacy or the Titans heiress. He looked at me like I was just a woman in red, making him laugh. And once we were talking, I didn't want it to end.

Maybe that's why I let myself fall into his bed. Against my better judgment. Against every warning I'd ever gotten.

I don't know what I expected when I woke up here this morning, wrapped in his arms, listening to the low, sleepy rumble of his voice. But for a second—just a second—I wondered if this could be something more.

"What have I gotten myself into?" I whisper.

As if on cue, Liam's phone buzzes on the nightstand.

"Hey, Liam!" I call. "Your phone is ringing."

"It's fine, just ignore it," he says over the rush of water.

I try. I swear I do. But it keeps buzzing, persistently enough to draw my attention to the screen. When the name flashes across it—Sabine—my breath hitches. A woman's name. Elegant. Familiar in a way that sends a quick, sharp sting up my spine. Jealousy flares, then fizzles, leaving humiliation simmering beneath it. I shouldn't care. I have no claim on him. But the truth is, a tiny piece of me already does.

The buzzing stops. I exhale and shrug into my coat. Then the phone lights up again.

Scott Jackson.

I know him. Everyone in football knows him—one of the top agents in the business. Liam's agent.

> Scott Jackson: No can do. You're in New Orleans for at least two more years, per your contract. Put in the work and keep them happy with their decision to make you one of the highest-paid rookies in your class.

Two years in New Orleans.

Two years far away from New York.

Far away from me.

The small, reckless hope I didn't want to name flickers and dims.

Another buzz.

> Sabine: I didn't sleep at all last night. I need you.

My throat tightens. Another buzz.

> Sabine: I took a test this morning. I think I might be pregnant. The doctor said Tuesday is the earliest they can confirm. I want you with me … I shouldn't have to do this alone.

A wave of nausea rolls through me. Another buzz.

Sabine: We can tell my family when you come home with me for the holidays.

The air in the room shifts—thick and heavy, pressing down on my ribs. This isn't a pleading ex. This is someone who speaks like she has a right to him.

Someone he made promises to.

My hands tremble as I stare at the screen.

Every warning my father has ever thrown at me roars to the surface at once. *Rookie athletes. Unreliable. Immature. Too many women. Too many blurred lines. Too many complications.*

The room tilts.

This is not a fling he forgot to mention.

This is a man with someone waiting for him in New Orleans … someone who expects him at a doctor's appointment.

Someone who talks like he belongs to her.

And I … I'm the girl he met at a wedding. The girl in red, who he flirted with for one magical night. The girl who let herself believe he saw her and not her last name.

Then I see a notification from Archie Griffith, and because I have to add insult to injury, of course, I scroll up to see it.

Archie: Since I didn't hear back from you last night, I assume you got that pussy.

I am such an idiot. Everything inside me recoils at once. The memories of my ex. The warnings from my father. The constant fear of being used. The reality is that Liam lives in another state and now may have a child with someone who sounds very much like his girlfriend.

A painful, familiar thought slices through me. *I was stupid to believe, for even a second, that he could want me for me.*

I look toward the bathroom door, steam drifting out from it, and every instinct inside me fractures. I should wait. I should ask. I should let him explain. But humiliation grips me tight. Fear grips me tighter.

My phone buzzes from somewhere in the room. I grab it instinctively and shove it into my pocket, only for something small and hard to clink against it.

I pull it out. The ornament. The tiny Christmas tree we bought last night after wandering through Manhattan like two idiots high on winter air and each other.

It feels unbearably heavy now.

I set the ornament beside his phone—both are symbols of two worlds I can't be a part of. The world where he lives in another state and has other … complications, and the fantasy we created last night. None of it can be my reality.

My feet carry me to the door, even as my heart tries to root me in place. I pause with my hand on the handle, staring back at the bathroom. I almost call his name. Almost ask him what all this means. Almost choose to trust him.

But believing in people is how I got hurt last time. And I can't—will not—go through that again. Not with someone I could fall for. Not with someone whose life, career, and complications exist so far outside my reach.

I swallow hard, open the door, and whisper, "Goodbye, Blitzen."

Because if I say it any louder, I'll stay.

And staying might break me.

CHAPTER TEN

LIAM

I hear a door close, and I look out into the room and don't see her. I wipe the water off my face and clear the glass shower door to see better. "Alie?"

No response.

"What the fuck?" I turn off the water and grab a clean towel from the bar next to the shower. "Alie!" I yell out louder.

I don't bother drying off, but I wrap the towel around my waist and run into the room.

She's gone.

I jog over to the door and pull it open. The hallway is empty. "Goddamn it!"

How is this possible? She said she would wait for me. I know I didn't imagine what happened last night and again this morning. I step back into the room, and the door slams behind me.

I look around the room, looking for any sign of her. Maybe she had to leave and she left me her number. But the only evidence of her being here are the rumpled bedsheets and the

Rockefeller Christmas tree ornament she picked out last night that sits next to my phone on the small table.

"Fuck." I sit down in one of the chairs and lean my head back, resting it on the cushion.

Maybe I was just a fling to her after all.

CHAPTER ELEVEN

ONE MONTH LATER

ALIE

Ten days late. I'm never late.

How could this have happened? I've religiously taken the pill since I was sixteen.

After a proper freak-out, I had my assistant run to the drug store to discreetly grab a pregnancy test—or five—so I could rule out what I suspected to be true.

So, after chugging nearly a gallon of water, I take the first test and wait for the results.

I pace my small bathroom in my office as the timer on my phone winds down to zero. I close my eyes and take in a deep breath. As I exhale, I open my eyes and look down at the long white stick resting on the counter next to the sink.

Two pink lines.

"Oh. Fuck." *This can't be happening.*

I close my eyes and brace my arms on the sink to hold myself up. I inhale deeply, trying to wrap my head around how this is possible. I'm an analyst, for fuck's sakes. The numbers are not supporting this outcome. *Pregnant.*

A knock on the door startles me, and I bump the test into the sink.

"Alie, it's me. Let me in," my older sister, Presley, says.

I don't even bother to compose myself before opening the door.

"Pres," I start and then immediately start to cry.

"Okay, so I take it, the test was positive?" She wraps me in her arms and rubs my back.

I can't even speak through my sobs, so I just nod.

"Alie, we got this. I will be with you every step of the way. Let's just take a second to figure out a game plan and how we're going to address it with Mom and Dad. And you need to tell *him*, of course." She pulls back and looks at me, but keeps her hands on my shoulders.

I sniff and reach for a tissue on the counter. "I just don't understand how this could have happened to begin with. You know I've been on the pill forever."

"Well, let's trace your timeline. You think this is from your little rendezvous with Liam Pitz the week before Christmas, right?"

I nod.

"And you remember taking your pill the morning after?"

I think back to that morning, and memories of us having sex —again—flash through my mind. Yeah, nope, I did not. Definitely got distracted by his magic dick.

"I … didn't, no."

"Aliette Grant, I think you have your answer on how this happened, then, yes?"

"In my defense, I would have taken it if he hadn't distracted me. Then I saw those texts, and I just panicked and left. By the time I got home, changed, and met you for brunch, it had completely slipped my mind. I feel so stupid." I grimace. "Do you really think one missed pill would do it though?"

"Not necessarily, but you know that shit is only ninety-nine percent effective. Are you absolutely sure it was just one day?"

I start crying again. Those few days after, I was in a haze. I couldn't stop thinking about him, and I was crushed that I could be so wrong. I'd thought maybe we could actually try to be something.

"You know what? It doesn't matter. What's important now is making sure you're taking care of yourself and the baby. When are you going to call him?"

I shrug. "Well, I could call him if I had his number."

"You don't have his number?"

"No, Presley. I ran out of there like my ass was on fire. I didn't stick around for his number."

"Al? You in here?" Aaron, my best friend and one of our players, shouts from outside the bathroom.

"Shit. I have to tell Aaron." I cover my face with my hands.

"He'll know Liam's number, right?"

I pop my head up. "Yes! He should."

I run my hands over my face, doing my best to wipe away the tears and the overall distress the last ten minutes have brought. I move around my sister and open the door.

"Hey. What are you doing here?" I walk to him and hug him.

"I just came to see what my favorite girl was up to. You wanna grab some lunch?"

"Are you done for the day?"

"Hi, Presley." He nods at my sister when she walks out of the bathroom.

"Hello, Aaron." She sits on the edge of my desk and crosses her arms.

She's known Aaron for as long as I have, since our parents are good friends. For some reason, though, she's never really cared for him, and I don't know why.

"Uh, yeah. I just wrapped up in the weight room, and I'm starving."

Glancing down, I look at his leg. "Your knee holding up?"

He had an injury in college and occasionally has some pain when he's training hard. We're getting ready to go into spring camp, so he's been building up the muscle around it to strengthen it. We took a gamble, drafting him, knowing he had this injury, but our family ties made it a little … complicated to not draft him.

"Doing good. I'll be fine, Al." He wraps an arm around my shoulders and tugs me into him.

"Aaron, you should go have one of the trainers check you before you leave, but first, we need your help with something," Presley says.

"Pres." I glare at her.

"What's up?" He tips his head up when he looks at her.

"Alie needs Liam Pitz's number." She cuts to the chase. My sister is anything but subtle.

"Why? He's a dickbag," he huffs.

After my night with Liam, I told Aaron the very basics of our time together. He knows that I saw texts from Liam's best friend, Archie Griffith, and a text from a woman, but that's pretty much all I told him. He doesn't need to know details about my sex life. Although things are about to get a little more personal.

"Whether he's a dickbag or not, she needs his number." Presley stands and takes my hand in hers and squeezes gently.

"Alie, what's going on?" He puts his hands on his hips and tips his head when he looks at me.

"Well…" I swallow. The words feel stuck in my throat, so I look at my sister pleadingly.

"She's pregnant," Presley announces.

"Pregnant?" He looks confused.

Me too, buddy.

"Yes, as in they had intercourse, and now she's carrying a child," she says sarcastically. "Do you need me to explain further?"

I love my sister, but she can be a little blunt.

"I got it, Presley. Thanks." He glares at her. "And it's Pitz's baby? You're sure?"

"Aaron, yes. You know I don't sleep around, good God." I

break out of my sister's hold and move around my desk, where I have a full Google search of Liam Pitz pulled up, take a seat, and I quickly close out of that tab before my sister can say anything else in front of Aaron.

"Right, sorry. That's not what I meant. But you're sure it's his and not Derek's?"

Derek was the guy I dated in the fall, but we ended things weeks before I met Liam.

"I'm one hundred percent sure." I lean back in my chair, holding onto the armrests.

"So, give his number to Alie," my sister suggests.

"Right, yeah." Aaron takes his phone from his pocket and taps a few times. "Okay, done." He looks up at me, then looks back at his phone again.

I look at my cell and wait for the shared contact. It doesn't come through. "I didn't get it."

Aaron shrugs. "I texted him. Trust me when I say that guy is a world-class player. Before I let you talk to him in your … condition … I'm going to feel him out first."

Presley straightens up. "Aaron, you don't have to—"

"I got this." His tone is direct, but his attention is on his phone, like he's reading a text.

"Did he answer already?" I ask, sitting up straight.

"Uh, no. It came back, saying *failed to send*."

"Surely, you can find out if he's gotten a new number." Presley looks exasperated. "Or we can just call the team and get it. Who's his agent?"

"No." His voice is calm. Too calm. "I'll take care of it. There's no need to get his team involved and definitely not his agent in a personal matter right now."

He straightens, pacing once behind my desk, like he's thinking three moves ahead—always three moves ahead.

"You're not just some girl who had a wild night," he continues gently. "You're the legacy of an entire franchise. A billion-dollar brand built on discipline and image." He exhales like this is a burden he's willing to carry for me. "If this leaks before we control the narrative? It won't be a sweet human-interest story. It'll be headlines. 'Empire Princess Pregnant After One-Night Stand.' They'll reduce you to a punch line."

He rounds the desk and lowers himself in front of me, squatting so we're eye level. Intimate. Grounded.

His hands close over mine.

"You and I both know how these teams operate," he says softly. "If you call him, it doesn't stay between you two. It goes to his agent. His PR people. Their lawyers. Suddenly, it's out of your hands." His thumb brushes over my knuckles in reassurance. "Let me handle it quietly. Directly. I can protect you from the circus."

His eyes hold mine—steady, unwavering.

"I'll be here with you through this, okay? Anything you need, just say the word, and I'm here."

I know he's trying to comfort me, but everything just feels wrong. I need a minute to come to terms with all this. I feel overwhelmed, and a whole lot freaked out.

A baby wasn't part of my plan right now. And definitely not with my holiday fling.

PART TWO

CHAPTER TWELVE

PRESENT

LIAM

When my agent called me with the news that New York offered me a contract for three years, forty million guaranteed, I couldn't get on the plane fast enough. As much as I appreciate the fans in New Orleans and the organization, I just never felt like the city was the best fit for me. So, when they fired the offensive coordinator (OC) after we lost in the playoffs, I took my out. Thank God my agent had added that little caveat to my contract.

In New York, I know I can be an asset to this team. They've had a losing record for the past two years, and they're equally hungry for a change in leadership on the field. And I'm the perfect guy to fill the role.

Not to mention, I know a few guys on the team, and, hell, my best friend's little brother just got drafted by the Titans in the NFL Draft last week. Aston Griffith will be one of my teammates, and I couldn't be happier. He's like a little brother to me, too, so it'll be fun playing with him.

I'm meeting with team management today at the training facility in New Jersey. Since I got an apartment in Midtown

Manhattan, in the Hell's Kitchen neighborhood, and my car hasn't arrived from New Orleans yet, the team sent me a car.

As we exit the Lincoln Tunnel, entering New Jersey, I turn around and see the city behind us. I snap a selfie and open my group text with my buddies from Walker University.

Liam: Bright lights, big city, bitches.

Casey: Look at you, Rookie of the Year. Is that a gold necklace?

Beck: He's gotta spend that money on somethin'.

I am, in fact, wearing a gold chain, but I know they're just playing with me. I won NFL Rookie of the Year at the end of my first season, and they're still teasing me about it. And they both have high-paying contracts. None of us is hurting for money—that's for sure.

Archie: My guy. City looks good on you.

Liam: I agree. I think this was a great move for me.

Archie: You're gonna light that place up.

Liam: You know it. When does Aston get in?

Archie: Uhh, I think next week sometime. He's home right now, getting all his shit organized. With Ace going off to a different team, this is gonna be a big change for them. They've never lived apart, so you'll need to keep an eye on him for me. Aiden's home, too, so we're getting some quality family time in.

Liam: I don't think Aston is the one you need to worry about. Ace will tear it up in Florida.

Casey: I was just about to say ...

Beck: Nah, Acer will be just fine.

Archie: They'll both be fine. So, you just have a meeting today and a tour, or what? I assume Scotty boy is with you?

Liam: Yeah, I guess so. Scott is meeting me there. I think I need to meet with the medical staff, too, and get some initial weigh-ins and tests done for baseline numbers. Probably looking at being here most of the day.

Archie: Coach Andrews is a good coach. I think you'll work well with him.

Liam: Yeah, and Tully is one of the best OCs in the league, so hopefully, we'll have a winning season this year.

Beck: I gotta run, boys. The boss is calling. Her pregnancy cravings are out of control.

Casey: Feed my sister before she gets hangry.

Archie: I need to run, too, but text me later and let me know how it went.

Liam: We're about to pull up to the building anyway. Talk to you guys later.

I close out the text thread and pocket my phone as we pull up to the entrance.

I see my agent, Scott; the general manager, Tom Gardner; and Coach Andrews waiting for me just outside the doors. When I start to open my door, the driver stops me.

"I'll get the door for you, Mr. Pitz."

I wave him off. "I'm good. Thank you for the ride."

"I'll be here to take you back into the city when you're done for the day. They'll notify me when you're wrapping up."

"Thanks." I hold out my hand.

"Name's Joey." He shakes my hand in return.

"I'll see you later then, Joey."

"We're lucky to have you here, sir." He gives me a broad smile.

"I appreciate that. I'm excited to be here." I nod, then exit the car.

"Hey, buddy." Scott leans in for a one-armed side hug.

"Hey, Scott." I give him a few sturdy taps on the back.

"Liam, how was the ride in?" Tom asks, reaching for my hand to shake.

"Faster than I thought it would be." I chuckle.

"Depends on what time of day you head out, but now the traffic isn't too bad. When you head this way on game days, make sure you check the traffic reports." He smirks.

"I'm always early to the field anyway, so it shouldn't be a problem." I turn to Coach. "Good to see you, Coach."

"Pitz." He nods with a smile. "We're ready to get the ball rolling."

"So, let me give you a rundown of what we're doing today. We're going to meet with the owners, some members of the management team, and staff. Then we'll give you a tour of the facility and take you down to the trainers so they can get your vitals and baseline numbers, if you're okay with getting started today. Lunch will be brought into our meeting with management, so I hope you're hungry." Tom glances over his shoulder at Scott, then back to me and smiles.

"I can always eat. And it sounds like a full day, but I'm ready to get started."

"Excellent. Mr. Grant is looking forward to meeting you and spending some time with you today. You've spoken on the phone, right?"

"Yes, he called me after I signed my contract. Same day I spoke with you actually."

I look around as we walk. There are photos of past and present players lining the hallway in a mural-type display. Trophy cases with playoff awards reflect the dynasty of this organization, and—I'll be honest—I have chills right now. This is one of the oldest teams in the league, kept within the same family, and they wanted me.

"Right." Tom breaks my thoughts. "Here we are then."

He opens a glass door, and I notice about ten people sitting around an oblong table. Most of them are men, but there are three women also. One of them is sitting next to James Grant, the owner, and the other two are sitting to the left of him. The woman closest to him is wearing team gear, like one of the medical staff would wear, but she resembles the older woman, so I'm guessing there is a connection. And she's kind of glaring at me, clearly not impressed. The other woman has her head down, and her hair hangs around her, so I can't see her face.

James stands and walks toward us, hand out in greeting. "Liam Pitz. It's a pleasure to meet you. We're looking forward to watching you take our team to the show this year." He chuckles, but he's not kidding. "Good to see you too, Scott."

"Sir, Mr. Grant, thank you for the opportunity. I'm excited to be here." I shake his hand and smile, nodding at some of the others around the table.

"Call me James. We're a pretty laid-back bunch. Let me introduce you to my family first. Then we'll get to the rest of the suits," he says with a smile.

I glance to the women, now guessing these ladies are members of his family.

Scott is already talking to some of the guys at the table, so I follow behind James without him.

"This gorgeous lady is my wife, Kate." He wraps an arm around her when she stands to shake my hand.

"Liam, it's so nice to meet you finally. I've been hearing all about you these last few weeks." She has a smile that lights up a room and looks vaguely familiar.

"Thank you, Mrs. Grant. Hopefully, the chatter will die down now that I'm here."

"Like my husband said, we're a laid-back family. Call me Kate," she says, taking her seat.

James walks to the other two ladies. "This is my oldest daughter, Presley. She's the lead physician on staff, so she'll be taking you down later for your intake numbers."

Presley doesn't stand. I wonder if it's me or if she's like this with all the players.

She doesn't even fully turn her body.

She just looks at me from where she's seated, one ankle crossed over the opposite knee, pen poised mid-air, like I've interrupted something more important.

Her eyes drag over me—slow, assessing—not in admiration. In evaluation.

I can't tell if she's sizing me up or stripping me for parts.

"Nice to meet you, Presley." I nod, but she continues to glare at me.

"Hmm."

That's it.

No smile. No handshake. No attempt at warmth.

Her attention drops back to her tablet, as if I've already been categorized and filed away.

James clears his throat like he's trying to smooth the moment over. "Presley runs a tight ship."

Yeah. *Tight* is one word for it. What the fuck is her deal?

"And this one here with her nose stuck in the books is my youngest daughter, Aliette. She's the mastermind behind the finances. Alie is our director of football administration—or salary cap manager, if you will." He chuckles.

When Aliette finally looks up, I nearly fall over. It's her. My Alie. The woman I've been thinking about for two fucking years. The woman who walked out on me without an explanation or any trace.

All these years, I tried to get information about her. Looked up every Allison, Alessandra, Alice, Alissa, Alexa … and here she is. Aliette.

I tried to get her number from Aaron, even came to New York and met up with him, but he told me she wasn't interested and eventually stopped replying to my texts. Asshole.

Alie stands. "Mr. Pitz, welcome to New York." There's a slight hitch to her voice.

So ... I guess she's pretending not to know me. Awesome.

I hold my gaze on her, willing her to look me in the eye. "Please call me Liam." Christ, I sound like I'm going through puberty. She does look at me then, just briefly. Long enough to acknowledge I spoke. Long enough to make my pulse misfire.

She gives me a closed-mouth smile and takes her seat.

Her expression mirrors Presley's in structure. Composed and unreadable. But the energy is different.

Where Presley makes no effort to hide her disdain, lets it sit openly in her stare like a warning sign, Alie keeps hers tucked away. Controlled. Contained. Guarded.

Like she's protecting something. Or someone.

Her fingers lace together in her lap. Her shoulders square. Calm. Professional.

But her eyes flicker once—quick, almost imperceptible—like she's measuring how much of herself she's willing to give away.

Presley looks at me like she's already made a judgment.

Alie looks at me like she's afraid she might.

And somehow, that's worse.

The rest of the introductions around the table are made as I'm led to my seat next to Scott at the other end of the table. I can't tell you who any of these people are because my head is spinning.

My Alie is Aliette Grant. Essentially, she's one of my new bosses. I knew there were family members involved in the organization, but funny enough, I've never seen pictures of Alie or her sister in the press. There must be a reason for that, although I never looked into the family in depth. Most of the information I got about the Grants and the Titans was from my agent. He failed to mention the daughters' roles in the company though.

There's no way I'm gonna let her get out of telling me why she ran off on me two years ago. I just need to get her alone.

I lean toward Scott. "You didn't tell me his daughters were on the staff."

"Don't even think about it, Pitz," he grits out with a smile.

"Too late. I know one of them."

"Pitz, I'm telling you, don't fuck this up." He looks down at the binder in front of him and opens it. "Gentlemen, shall we sign some paperwork?"

I look away from Scott, back down at Alie, and see her speaking closely with her sister. Presley looks up and catches me and places her hand on Alie's arm.

Alie doesn't look at me, but instead picks up her pen and flips through some papers in her own binder.

"Let's get to it. I have a date tonight with my lovely wife, and we need to get back to the city before traffic becomes a problem." James leans over and kisses his wife's temple.

I notice she doesn't make a move to leave, so she must also be involved in the team's inner workings.

Scott hands me a pen.

"Thanks," I mumble, then open my own binder.

The meeting goes by in a haze. Lunch is served, but I don't eat a bite. And as soon as we're done, Alie takes off without a goodbye. Joke's on her though. She won't be able to run from me forever.

CHAPTER THIRTEEN

ALIE

When I get back to my office, I go right into the bathroom, close the door, and lock it. I'm not prone to getting panic attacks, but I might just have one today. I grab the sides of my sink and hang my head down, taking deep breaths in and out. Seeing him again was everything and nothing like I'd expected it would be. I didn't expect him to look so happy to see me. Makes me wonder if he remembers everything about that night the way I do.

I turn on the faucet and splash some water on my face, trying to cool down the flush in my cheeks. I need to get control of myself because I'm going to have to deal with him on a regular basis.

A knock on the door doesn't surprise me, but I'm also not in the mood to talk to anyone right now.

"Alie, it's me. Open up," my sister says from the other side of the door.

"Give me a minute," I tell her.

"Come on, Alie. I just wanna make sure you're okay. I have to go back downstairs and get everything set up for his testing."

I dry off my face. Take another deep breath, then straighten my shirt and open the door.

"I'm fine, I promise. I'm not gonna lie—it was a lot to see him. But I've been preparing for this for the last few weeks, so it'll be okay." I suck in a breath. "I'll figure out a way to deal with this." I'm not sure if I'm trying to convince myself or my sister.

"Okay, but I also need to find a way to work with him because I'm about to tear into him. I still can't get over the fact that he wanted nothing to do with you and the baby, and now you're gonna have to look at him all the time. What happens if he sees the baby? And Alie, you know Mom and Dad are gonna realize this out soon enough. Seraphina looks exactly like him—not just her eyes, her smile, and her hair color, but some of her mannerisms. Like the little dimple she gets when she smiles is identical to his." She reaches for me, but I move to my desk.

If she hugs me right now, I'll probably start to cry, and I hate to cry, dammit.

"No, I know it's gonna be hard to keep this a secret for too long from Mom and Dad anyway. And he might not want to have anything to do with her, but I guess it's inevitable. He's gonna see her around the complex. He could very well see her in the nursery today."

Thankfully, we have a nursery on-site. My family has always supported on-site child care, so I can pop down to see her anytime I want.

I pick up the picture of my daughter off my desk. It's from her first birthday in September. Her chubby little cheeks are smeared with pink frosting from her cake. She really does look a lot like him. I never told my parents who her father was, but Presley is right. One look at them, and anyone could figure it out, especially now that he's here.

I knew this was a possibility when discussions started about bringing him here, but in all honesty, he is what's best for our team. I can't let our past or our daughter compromise the role he has here. We need a winning season.

"I won't say anything to him out of respect for you, Al. You need to clean up your own mess, but it's gonna be hard for me to bite my tongue, so if I can make a suggestion … I think it would be best for everybody involved if you have a private discussion with him sooner rather than later. We're all going to have to work together, and we'll likely have to address that Seraphina is his daughter publicly." She sits in the chair across from me and leans on the desk, arms crossed.

"I don't see any reason to announce that publicly. She has our last name." I set the picture back on my desk.

"Well, if that's how you feel about it, what are you gonna do if he changes his mind and decides he does want to be involved with the baby? Wants her to have his name?"

"I think … it's a little too late, don't you think, Pres? He made that decision when he found out I was pregnant. He's had time to come to me to ask me about her, and he never did. He was too busy with football and who knows what else. He could have a girlfriend for all I know. But I guess I should notify our attorney what's going on. Just in case we need him." The thought makes me sick, but I try to act like I don't care.

"Maybe, but you know that the text message from that girl in New Orleans had to be fake. Pretty sure you would know by now if he had another baby with someone else. Well, maybe not if he didn't want anything to do with that baby either." She shrugs. "I don't know. As much as I don't like him for not wanting to be a part of Seraphina's life, I think there might be more to the story here, and I think you owe it to your daughter to find out. It's not a bad idea to let the attorney know, but I don't think you should do anything until you talk to Liam."

"I'm just not sure I can do it today. I have a lot to think about for work, and Liam Pitz will have to go on the back burner for the rest of the day. I have more contracts to review. And I have to turn in all the numbers to the board by Friday. I really don't have the time to deal with my private life right now, so for my sake, I'm hoping that I have a little bit of time before I have to deal with him one-on-one." I drop my head back onto my chair.

"Okay, but I'm telling you, Alie, you need to do it as soon as possible. We need to know how to handle this as a family because, in some way or another, Liam Pitz is going to have to come to terms with the fact that he has a daughter and that his daughter is part of *our* legacy." She reaches for my hand that's resting on my desk.

"You're right; I will, I promise."

She clears her throat. "Can I play devil's advocate a little bit here, Alie?"

"I guess if you must. You don't listen to me anyway."

"What if he does have a change of heart and wants to be a part of her life? What are you gonna do about that?"

"If Liam wants to be in Seraphina's life? That's what I wanted when this all started. I want my daughter to have a father. That's not an issue though. He didn't want her the last year and a half, so he certainly won't want her now."

"He could. And what if he wants you too?"

"That's ..." My breath hitches at the thought. "Wouldn't matter. He's the most selfish man I've ever met."

Presley tsks. "Because the way he was staring at you in that boardroom today ... if I didn't hate him so much, I would've been turned on just by the way he was looking at you. And as much as I hate to admit it, that man is even more gorgeous in person than he is on television or any photo I've seen. You are one lucky bitch to have seen that man naked."

"Presley, honestly! Don't talk about him like that. He's one of our players and your niece's father."

"Oh, come on. You can't tell me that you didn't see him and want to drop your drawers."

I smile. "I mean, okay, I'll admit he's even better looking now than he was the last time I saw him, if that's possible, but I cannot entertain the thought of being with him again. It would be a distraction for me personally, but even more so professionally. This is strictly a business relationship, even though he's Seraphina's father."

"Okay, well, just a reminder: he does not have a *no fraternization* guideline in his contract, so really, if he wanted to go after you and you consented, nobody could stop him."

"Trust me. I am not going to fall for Liam's charms, no matter how gorgeous he is."

"You could fuck him and leave him. Tie him up, then walk away, leaving him in an incredibly embarrassing position for someone to see."

"Presley!" I admonish and yet find myself laughing.

She may be a straight shooter, but she has one twisted mind.

"I mean, I suppose Dad could technically fire him if he wanted to, but then we'd have to pay out his contract, and it'd get ugly, and as much as he loves us, I don't think he would do that, even for you." She grimaces. "You know what I mean."

"Dad doesn't like ugly press, but he does love me, and he loves Seraphina more, so let's just take all of this one day at a time and try to contain the problem the best we can."

"The problem being Liam?"

"Yes, Presley."

"Liam, the problem or the savior of the Titan dynasty? I wonder which one Liam Pitz will turn out to be." She releases my hand and taps her chin.

"Get out of here. Go do medical things. Go take his blood pressure and sweat samples or whatever it is you do down there."

She stands, laughing. "Okay, so you won't be upset if I see him naked, right?"

"I'm serious, Presley. Get out of here."

"I'm going, I'm going, but for real, you're sure you're not gonna be upset if I see him naked?"

"Presley."

"Okay, fine. I'm going, but I'll let you know if he looks as good as what you said the night after you had sex with him." She giggles and waves.

"Get out of here!" I throw a pen at her as she walks out the door, then slump back in my chair.

I can do this.

I can be around Liam Pitz and do my job effectively.

I can be around Liam Pitz without caring what he does in his personal time.

I can be around Liam Pitz and try not to see my daughter in his face.

Let's see how long that lasts.

A few hours later, I wrapped up my day and picked up my daughter from the nursery, and we went home to our apartment in the city. We live in the same building as my parents on Central Park West.

When Seraphina was born, I decided to move out of their penthouse, but I wanted to stay close, so I accepted the unit a few floors down from them as a gift. I'm not one to take handouts, but after months of their insistence, I finally accepted the home under one condition—no more handouts.

Seraphina and I spend most of our time at my parents', but it's nice to have a space of our own. Even though my parents were shocked by my pregnancy, she is the apple of their eyes, and of course, she's spoiled rotten by them, but I'm trying to raise her as normally as I can.

After grabbing something to eat for myself and feeding Seraphina her dinner, I gave her a bath, which is her favorite. Now we're in her room, and I'm reading her a bedtime story. She chose *Guess How Much I Love You*. It's one of her favorites. Sometimes, she even wants me to read it twice.

Not tonight though. She tends to get chatty at night, and tonight is one of those nights. It's like she has to purge whatever energy she has left from the day.

"I pwayed trucks."

"Did you play with a friend?"

"Pwayed with Efan."

"You mean Ethan?"

"Yes, Efan."

"Right, okay." I just smile and nod this time, not bothering to correct her. Besides, it's cute.

Just like she did as a baby, she likes to hold pieces of my hair while we chat and cuddle. She twirls it so tight sometimes that I get knots, but I don't mind because I know it won't last forever. It's the little moments like this that make all the worries of my day go away. The love that I have for her is indescribable.

She pauses her story about trucks and sits up. "Mommy, I need ball."

I twist my body to see if it's behind me, and luckily, it is. She can't sleep without the pink football stuffed toy that Aaron got her when she was an infant. "Got it." I reach over the guardrail on her bed and hand it to her, and then she tucks it close to her chest.

She lies back down, takes a piece of my hair again, and continues her mumbled story.

I have one arm tucked under the pillow, and my other gently rubs her back. Her little pajamas have pink footballs on them too. They're from my dad. I've tried teddy bears, baby dolls, and blankies, but she cannot go to sleep unless she has her football in her hands, and she loves her football pajamas. Her two favorite guys are my dad and Aaron.

Throughout my pregnancy and when she was born, Aaron stood by my side. He was supportive in every way a best friend could be, and he loves my little girl. And though Aaron and I have never been together romantically, we are often together. To an outsider, we look like a family when we're in public. He's even been called her father, and he doesn't correct them. Instead, he just says thank you. I also remain quiet, not wanting to explain, and let him assume that role, but at home or at the facility, he's Uncle Aaron.

He's had his share of problems this year. He was injured last season, and it was career-ending. Luckily, his rehab progressed quickly, and even though he's no longer able to play football, he is still involved in sports. He recently took a job as an agent with one of the top agencies here in New York, so we still get to see him all the time. Right now, though, he's out of town, working with new clients, and it's the NHL playoff season, so he's been traveling around, watching the games of some of his athletes.

I'm sure he's heard about Liam's trade, and I'm kind of surprised that he hasn't asked me about it yet. It's been all over the news.

Seraphina's eyes start to get heavy, and she yawns, pausing her story about Ethan and the trucks. Everything that weighs on me about how to handle and work with Liam eases when I watch my little girl fall asleep. The moments with her, being present with my baby, are what give me purpose and pure happiness.

I lie next to her for a few more minutes to make sure she's fully sleeping and study her little face. She really does look so much like her dad, and my stomach clenches. I just don't understand how he couldn't want to be a part of this beautiful baby's life. She's my world. Even through the hardest times, when she was a baby and not sleeping through the night, I was grateful that I'd been given this gift of being her mama.

I lean down and kiss her on the forehead and breathe in her

sweet scent. Her dark brown, silky hair is starting to get a little wave to it, just like Liam has, more and more every day.

I continue watching her as she sleeps, peaceful and content. When her breathing falls into a rhythm where I know she's out for the night, I brush my fingers through her silky, soft hair and tuck her close to me because I have a feeling our world is about to change.

CHAPTER FOURTEEN

LIAM

Alie left yesterday before I could find her office. And her sister was professional but a bit standoffish with me during my medical examinations, and I'm still not sure why. I'd never even met her before. I tried to be friendly and engaging, but she only answered me with short responses. So, after I was done for the day, I came back to my apartment.

Tonight, I'm watching *SportsCenter* and scrolling Instagram, looking for any trace of who Aliette Grant is, but it's like she's a ghost, like she doesn't exist. There are a few news articles mentioning her, along with pictures of her from when she was young, but not many. It's like her family has hidden them from the public eye, and I can't say that I blame them. They're a football dynasty. I can't imagine the kind of press and pressure that can put on a family, let alone a child, but Alie and Presley both work for the organization now, and there's still no trace of any picture of Alie at football games or press. But I do see Presley in a few pictures.

Alie has an Instagram profile, but it's set to private, so all I can see is her profile picture. I try to search for her sister and get the same result, so I text Aaron asking him to give me Alie's number again. The message is delivered, then marked as *Read*, but he doesn't respond. Even though he told me she wasn't interested in me and to let it go, I'm gonna ask anyway.

I imagine I could get her number from Scott, but if I ask him for it, he'll ask questions that I don't have answers for, and besides, I don't really want him to know everything about my night with Alie two and a half years ago.

I literally searched for this girl for months when I got home. I texted Aaron back then, too, and nothing. So, I came to New York in an effort to find her, which finally got a response from him. We planned to meet for a drink, although he didn't stay. He just showed up to tell me she didn't want to have anything to do with me and I needed to let it go. That was it. No explanation as to why. Just dropped that bomb and left.

Once I got past the point where I accepted that she didn't want to be with me, I tried to move on. Football became the only true relationship that I've had in the last two years. My entire focus, all my time, all my energy, went to playing. My first year in the league, I felt like I needed to prove myself, and I did. My second season, it was even more important to establish myself and try to develop more chemistry with my team on the field.

My OC and I got along great, and it was the same with the coaches. The best part about being with the Saints was that their run game was one that I could get on board with. We had a similar style to what we had run at Walker, so I was comfortable and familiar with it, and it was easy to adjust to their style of play.

On the personal side of my life, every time I tried to meet a woman, I just didn't feel like the chemistry was there, and I'm not saying I was a complete saint, but it was very few and far between when I actually tried hooking up with anyone. Because every time I tried, all I could see was her.

My phone dings with a text, and Archie's name pops up on the screen.

Archie: How did it go today?

Instead of answering him in a text message, I dial him, and he answers in his deep voice on the second ring.

"What's going on, brother? How did it go today?"

"Well, it was interesting. That's for sure," I huff.

"Oh, yeah? In what way?"

"Well, do you remember the girl I met in New York City a couple of years ago?"

"You mean the girl you hooked up with at that wedding and haven't stopped talking about since? Didn't you even go up there and look for her at one point?" He chuckles.

"I did, without success. I am not gonna lie and say that I didn't hope that I'd possibly have the chance to meet up with her or see her somewhere when I came up this way. So, let me tell you what kind of fuckery has been going on here."

"Uh, okay, this has to be good." He laughs. "You already get yourself into some trouble?"

"No, not exactly, but you're never gonna believe who one of my new bosses is."

"Who?"

"It's her! She's one of James Grant's daughters."

"No fucking way," he mumbles.

"I'm deadly serious. When I walked into that boardroom today, I almost passed out on the spot."

"Holy shit. Did she say anything to you? Did she recognize you?"

"Of course she recognized me, you asshole. I'm not that forgettable."

He laughs. "I'm just playing. What happened? What'd she say?"

"Nothing. That's the weirdest thing. She acted like she didn't know who I was. She welcomed me to New York, and that was about it. She wouldn't even make eye contact with me the rest of the meeting, and then she bolted as soon as the meeting was over." I shake my head even though he can't see me.

"Oh, that sucks, dude. Well, did you get to meet up with her after?"

"No, I had to go down to testing. Coincidentally, her sister is one of the team doctors, and she didn't seem all too happy to be dealing with me either. I don't know what the fuck I did wrong. Alie's the one who left."

"I know. It took a long time for you to forget it."

"I never forgot. But, yeah, now I've finally found her. And what are the fucking odds? She's literally my boss, and she likely negotiated all the numbers in my contract, so there's no hiding any information from her. She knows everything about me, and I know nothing about her." I laugh, humorlessly.

"Well, I'm sure you know something about her. You spent the whole night and the following morning with her, if what I remember is correct."

"Yeah, that's true, and I'd like to think that was the real her that I met that night in New York, but now I have no idea—because why didn't she tell me who she was when I met her then?"

"I mean, I'm really not all that surprised."

"Why would you not be surprised? I know she knew who I was. It wouldn't have changed anything about that night for me."

"Pitz, brother, she's the daughter of one of the wealthiest families in the country, and her family owns an NFL team. Of course she knew who you were, but can you also understand why she would want to remain anonymous?" He pauses. "She probably wanted to hang out with you for a night without any pressure of who she was, and maybe, just maybe, she wanted to see if she could have something real with someone, you know? I can't imagine the microscope she must be under. I mean, knowing what we have to deal with, being professional athletes, but growing up in a family like that? I'm sure it's a lot."

"Yeah, but that's the thing: she's not in the public. I have never even seen her anywhere. I can't find anything about her on social media either."

"I'm looking now, and I don't either, but I'm sure it's for a reason. Maybe she and her sister want to remain private because of all the family's notoriety."

"I'm gonna find out. I have to find a way to talk to her. To get her alone."

"Well, I hope you get the chance to, but like you said, tread carefully—she is your boss. And if she acted like she didn't know you in that meeting, there's a reason why she doesn't want her family to know you have a connection, you feel me?"

"Yeah, I feel you, and I get it. I understand why she's private and why she acted like she didn't know me in front of a room full of suits, but it hurt. It hurt my heart, man." I laugh, trying to lighten my sour tone.

"I hear ya. I'm not sure how I would have felt if Emma acted like she didn't know who I was. Shit, you remember I couldn't find her either, and we were on the same campus, so give yourself a break. You had a whole country and a city of millions of people to try and find her in. But you can look at it this way: everything happens for a reason."

"That's exactly what I was thinking. It is no coincidence that this all worked out this way. I know now more than ever that my coming to New York was the right choice."

"Who are you talking to?" Emma, Archie's wife, asks.

"It's Liam. Hey, Pitzy, hold on. I'm gonna put you on speakerphone."

"All right." I lie down on the couch.

"Hey, Pitz," Emma says.

"Em, how are you doing?"

"Good. Very pregnant," she humphs.

"Maybe you guys can try keeping off each other," I suggest.

"Nah, can't do that," Archie chimes in.

"Yeah, yeah. But you're feeling okay, Em?"

"I feel pretty good. We have a couple of months to go, so I won't start feeling bad until the last few weeks. That's always the hardest for me, especially with the two younger ones. Chasing after those two is a full-time job." She laughs.

"I bet. I have no doubt that my little niece and nephew are little hellions."

"Excuse me, but my Little Sunshine is not a hellion. Duke, on the other hand, that apple didn't fall far from the tree, if you know what I mean," Archie says proudly.

"Oh, yes, he already has a girlfriend, and he's in preschool," Emma says.

"Of course he does." I chuckle and shake my head.

"Darlin', he can't help it. He's got that swagger. It's that Griffith charm."

"Ha-ha. I know, as evidenced by being pregnant with our third child."

"That's right, baby. All mine."

It sounds like they're kissing now, so that's my cue to cut this off.

"Okay, guys, I'm gonna let you go. I have to get up early and go to the gym."

"Dude, Organized Team Activities don't start for another week and a half. Why are you working out already?" Archie asks.

"Because, unlike some of us, I'm on a brand-new team, and I have to prove myself. I have to prove my worth. I want them to believe that every dollar they've spent on me is worth it." I take a deep breath. "And I want to see who shows up because that always tells me a lot about their leadership and how hungry they are to win."

"Or how much they want that money." Archie laughs.

"True," I agree.

"All right, well, keep me posted on your little situation in

New York."

"What situation in New York? What's going on?" Emma asks.

"Remember that girl Pitz hooked up with in New York at that wedding a couple of years ago?"

"Yes, the one he couldn't find later?"

"Yep. Well, not only is she one of his new bosses, but she's also the team owner's daughter," he says, a little too cheery. Like he's enjoying this.

"No! You've got to be kidding me."

"I know, Em. I can't believe it."

"Did you just die when you saw her? What did she say when she saw you? I mean, obviously, she knew you would be there, but oh my gosh!"

"She acted like she didn't know who I was, other than their new player, and I didn't get to talk to her because she took off before I got done for the day."

"That sucks, Liam. I'm sorry, but there has to be a reason. You totally have to find her and talk to her," she says.

"I know. I'm gonna try to. I'll figure out a way to get to her so we can have a conversation. I just really want to know why she didn't want anything to do with me and took off after our night together. And why I couldn't find her. I was telling Arch that there's no online trace of her."

"Hmm ... well, find her and talk to her privately. Maybe even outside of work. Just be honest with her and tell her how much that night meant to you. And ask her what happened. Don't play games. Be direct and ask her why she left and didn't want to have anything to do with you." Emma suggests.

"Yeah," I sigh.

"All right, brother, we'll let you go. We've got two kids looking for some dessert, and then Mommy and Daddy need to get their dessert."

"Archie, stop it, dude. I don't need to hear that shit." But I say it with a laugh. He's never gonna stop oversharing.

He lets out a bold laugh. "Good luck. I'll talk to you tomorrow."

"Will do. Later." I disconnect before waiting for a response.

Then I toss my phone on the cushion beside me. I drop my head back, and I think back to one of the most magical nights of my life.

I really thought we could have something special, and I'd never felt that way about anyone before in my life. That feeling that my friends talked about when they knew they'd found their ladies? Never before Alie. So, when I came out of that shower and she was gone but had left the ornaments that we'd gotten together to remember our night, I felt played.

But now I think there's more to it, and I'm gonna find out what it is.

CHAPTER FIFTEEN

ALIE

Seraphina and I are going into the office today with my dad. Sera keeps him busy the whole ride there. He explains football and the differences between the offense and the defense, even though she already knows them—it's her favorite story from her Poppy. She can hear the same story over and over again, and she never gets tired of it, especially if it has to do with football, and it's even more exciting if it's her Poppy telling a story.

And me? I'm lost in thought, thinking about how I'm going to avoid Liam Pitz. I have a feeling he's going to be at the facility today. Just knowing he's there … well, I'm sure it's gonna be hard for me to concentrate. And I really need to get these reports done.

I knew when we took the trade for him that this could be a challenge, but after seeing him again, I think it's going to be harder than I expected.

"Okay, peanut, we're here. Let's get you to Miss Sandy." I grab her little Burberry backpack and my matching messenger bag.

"Today, we make cwafts," she tells us.

"Oh, that sounds fun. What kind of crafts are you going to make?" I ask her.

"Fowers."

"I love flowers." I tuck some of the flyaways behind her ear.

"Me too, Mommy. Your favowit?" She looks up at me.

"Hmm … I like a lot of different flowers. What kind of flower are you going to make?"

"Tuwip my favowit."

"I do love tulips, too."

"If der's blue, I make dat. Your favowit color too."

"Thank you, baby. That's so sweet. I can't wait to see it."

"Lunchey with me?"

I look at my dad and see him watching us with a smile, but there's also a curious look on his face that I can't quite read.

"Yes, I will come down and see you on your lunch break as soon as I can. I might not be able to stay the whole time, but I will definitely come and sit with you for a little bit," I tell her.

"Okay, see fowers too."

"I can't wait to see it."

"Poppy, wan one?" Sera turns to my dad.

"I would love a flower from my favorite girl." He touches her head.

The car stops, and we exit before the driver can get to the door. Then we walk into the building, her little hand in mine. My dad watches us with a smile on his face.

"She's the most precious little girl, isn't she?" he says.

"She sure is." I smile at him.

"You know, we never asked you any questions when you told us you were pregnant, and although it was a surprise to us, she has been a blessing to this family," he says, then clears his throat.

I'm not sure what to say to that. Is he fishing for information? "Thank you, Dad. She's definitely a blessing to me."

His phone rings, interrupting our conversation, and after he holds the door open for us, we go to the right as he goes to the left, but not before he stops to give my daughter a kiss on the head.

"Have a good day, peanut. I'll come visit you later today, okay?"

"Bye-bye."

He blows her a kiss and returns to his call as he heads toward his office.

I take Seraphina into the nursery and get her settled in with Miss Sandy.

"I have to go to work now, sweetie, but I'll see you later today. Okay?"

"Bye, Mommy!" She waves her little hand goodbye when I leave.

I walk through the main corridor to the other wing, heading to my office, and just as I enter the hallway, I hear the door to the building click open. I see Liam coming in, wearing gym clothes, with one of our other players, Brody Vaughn. Liam and I make eye contact, and I turn my head quickly and practically run into the wall. I look back over my shoulder to see that Liam is still watching me, so I turn and move faster.

How is it possible that he is so fucking hot? Seriously, he's just getting better-looking. It's not fair that men age like fine wine. I know I'm in good shape. I work out regularly and eat pretty healthily, but my body has definitely changed since having Seraphina. I wonder if he still sees me the same or if he can see the differences. I know I'm being silly. I'm sure he's barely looked at me, let alone notice differences from when I saw him two years ago.

When I get to my office, I pull my phone out of my bag and set it on my desk, then hang it in the closet next to the bathroom.

This morning, when I woke up, I saw a text message from Aaron, but I haven't responded to him yet because of the chaos of getting ready this morning. So, I pull up our message thread and read his note again.

Aaron: Alie. What's going on?

Alie: Aaron. Not much. What's going on with you?

The way he's worded this message is odd to me. I'm not sure what exactly he's asking me, but within minutes, he replies.

Aaron: What's going on with me? You know what's going on with me. I'll be traveling back and forth between Canada and Florida for the foreseeable future because these teams won't fucking beat each other within the first four games of the series. But that's not what I'm asking, and you know it.

Alie: No, I actually have no idea what you're talking about.

Okay, maybe I do, but I don't want to show my hand if that's not what he's asking.

Aaron: When did you guys decide to bring Pitz on board? I know you don't discuss business with me, but this is different, and you know it.

Alie: Well, there's nothing that's different because he's one of our new players, and that's it.

Aaron: That's it?

Alie: Yes, Aaron, that's it.

Aaron: I don't like this, Alie. We need to talk about this. Can you call me now?

Alie: No, Aaron, I'm at the office. I can't talk to you about this right now. I'll have to talk to you later.

Aaron: Call me tonight if you can.

Alie: I will try.

Aaron: All right, talk soon.

I don't bother to reply and set my phone down, then power up my computer. I just need to get lost in some numbers for a while. We have seven new players we acquired in the draft, and we have one more trade that we need to iron out, so that should keep me distracted from thinking about Liam for at least the next couple of hours. Hopefully.

After I have lunch with Seraphina, my curiosity gets the best of me, and I wander down toward the gym. I've tried my best not to think about him, but it's really hard, knowing he's in the building. I mean, I won't be mad if I get a glimpse of him. For all I know, he's already gone anyway. Most of the guys come in for a couple of hours, maybe eat, and then they take off. For my sake, it would be best if he was gone, but also, I do want to see him, even though I don't want to admit it to myself.

I casually walk by the windows to the gym, as if I'm going to my sister's office—so me being down in that area doesn't look suspicious. I don't even know why I'm worried about this right now. It's not unusual for me to be down here. I'm just being paranoid. When I look into the windows, as I slowly walk by, I don't see him, but I do see a couple of the other guys from the team. They see me, too, and wave, and I wave back, then continue walking to my sister's office.

When I get there, she's speaking with one of our trainers and reviewing a few nutrition plans.

"Hey, are you almost done, or are you gonna be a while?" I ask her.

"We're just wrapping up. Give me a few more minutes. You can stay." She gestures to her couch. "Take a seat."

So, I move from the doorway to sit on the small couch and wait as they finish.

"Okay, Kerry, thank you so much. I'll be back in the training room in about thirty minutes. I have to finish up a couple of things and check in with my sister here."

"Sounds good." Kerry waves at me before walking out.

My sister makes her way over to the couch and sits next to me.

"So, little sister, what are you doing down here, in the dungeon?" she asks with a smirk on her face.

"Nothing. I just finished lunch with Sera, and I wanted to come and see what you were up to." I turn toward her and prop my arm along the back of the couch.

She hums. "That's why you came down here? To see what I was up to?"

"Yes. Am I not allowed to do that?" I ask, shaking my head. I know she's on to me.

"Oh, you can. It's just not typical for you to come down here at this time of day to come chit-chat with me. You usually have your head shoved in your spreadsheets for most of the day, outside of having lunch with Sera." She laughs.

"That's not true. I come down here and see you all the time. Come on, Presley." I give her a pleading look. I don't want her to make me say it.

"I'm just giving you a hard time. So, you came to see me and talk about what?" She smirks.

"Nothing, jeez. I just came to see what you were up to and how your day was going."

"Aliette Grant, don't bullshit a bullshitter. I know why you're down here."

I try to act indifferent.

"Alie"—she places her arm on my arm—"if you're worried about what I think, or Aaron, or whoever else … don't. You have to do what's best for you. And Sera. Yes, I think the guy is a complete dick for what he did to you, but when I was working with him, I realized he was insanely charming. I get it; I see the appeal."

"What are you talking about? You, of all people, think he's Satan's spawn."

"That's kind of true. If he was Satan's spawn, that would make Sera the granddaughter of Satan. What I think of Liam is … not what I was expecting him to be."

"What do you mean?"

"It pains me to say this, but I can understand why you would want to see him. I wanted to tear into him so bad about why he wanted nothing to do with Seraphina, but I'm honoring your wishes and not bringing it up. That said, he doesn't seem like the kind of guy who would … " She drifts off, as if cautious about her words.

"What are you getting at?"

"I'm just saying that it's okay if you want to see him. That's all."

"I don't wanna see him," I say too quickly.

"Alie, he's the father of your daughter. Of course you want to see him. You have no choice, really. It's okay to do this on your own terms though. And it's natural to be curious about him. Plus, he is quite nice to look at." She tries to bite back her smile.

"Is that right?" I tilt my head and give her a *no shit* look. "Yes, well … I mean, I didn't come down here specifically to see him. I did come down here to see you, but if I happened to see him in the weight room, I would not have been upset about it."

"I see. You just wanted to see him lift weights?"

"Right. I need to make sure we made a sound investment decision."

"Ha! Okay, and were you curious about how much he could bench, or were you hoping to see him all sweaty and manly-looking?"

"Sweaty? Gross." Okay, maybe not gross. "Just ... you know what? Forget it. It's fine. I'm gonna go. I'm going back to my office." I stand and walk to the door.

"Don't leave." She laughs. "I'm just playing with you. I know he's still here, but if he's not in the weight room, he's probably cleaning up for the day. He's been in the gym for a couple of hours already so they could test his sweat and get some readings on him. If he's done with that, he's probably getting ready to leave soon, I would think."

"Right. Okay, well, I'm just gonna go, then." I point my thumb over my shoulder. "I'm gonna go up to my office."

"You go do that." She smiles as she stands.

"Yes, I'm gonna go, and I'm gonna do the work things."

"Sounds like a plan. You should go do the work things today. You know what? I'm gonna walk you up. I could use a little break."

"Okay, suit yourself."

When we start to walk out of her office, we run into Liam—because of course we do. He's changed into a pair of jeans and a T-shirt from his gym clothes.

"Well, well, well. Liam Pitz." My sister stops, crosses her arms, and looks from me to him.

"Hello, ladies. Nice to see you, both," he says, looking directly at me.

"You just get done with your workout?" she asks him.

"I did. Met some of the guys on the team too. All in all, a productive day." He's still looking at me.

"Excellent. And you saw my team before you showered, yes?" Presley goes into doctor mode.

He finally looks away from me to my sister. "Yes, ma'am. I believe they got everything they needed from me for today."

Then I'm met with his intense gaze—the kind that makes the butterflies swarm in my belly and my chest rise with a gasp. It's the same look he gave me on that wintry night of magic and Christmas puns and an insane amount of flirting that led to the hottest night of my fucking life.

"Make sure you hydrate and get some protein in the next thirty minutes." She uncrosses her arms and then looks at me. "Are you good? I'm going to run down to the training room to check on a few things."

I literally feel my eyes shoot up to my hairline. She can't leave me alone with him. "Um … " I can't seem to form words.

"Actually," Liam interjects, "is the marketing department that way? I'm supposed to stop by to pick up some promotional gear."

"It's not, but that is close to Alie's office. She can show you the way."

"That'd be great. Thanks."

My sister taps him on the shoulder, then winks at me as she walks away and mouths, *You're welcome.*

Bitch.

"We going this way?" He points in the right direction.

"Uh, yeah." I nod and swallow the lump in my throat.

"Ladies first." He smiles at me and gestures with his arm.

"Thanks," I whisper.

We walk silently, but it doesn't take long before he speaks.

"Alie, we need to talk."

"Do you have questions about your contract?" *Good Lord, what am I doing?*

"Nope, pretty solid there. You know why we need to talk."

"Hmm, not really." The flutters in my tummy are telling me to abandon ship and run down the hall and far away from him. Because I feel his body heat next to mine, and I can smell the clean scent of his body wash tickling my nose.

Instead of replying, he takes my elbow and opens a door to his right. He pulls me inside, then shuts it. And locks the door!

"What are you doing?" I gasp. I walk farther into the room, and my butt hits the edge of a table.

"I want to talk to you."

"You've had two years to talk. And you think now, here, is the best place to talk?" I look around the room and note we're in the offensive line meeting room.

Thank God most of the coaching staff is upstairs in meetings.

"Well, if I had your number, I wouldn't have to talk to you here." He walks toward me slowly, closing the space between us.

He's so handsome that it momentarily distracts me.

"You don't need my number."

"Alie, come on. We had an amazing night together, and then you just vanished. I want to know why."

"That's what you're hung up on? The fact that I didn't stay to greet you when you got out of the shower?"

His jaw flexes. He drags a hand through his hair—a nervous tell he probably doesn't even realize he has. He looks unfairly good when he's irritated. Broad shoulders tense beneath his T-shirt. Eyes dark and searching.

"Yes, actually," he says. No arrogance. No smirk. "Actually."

I fold my arms, pretending I don't notice the way he steps closer without meaning to. Pretending I don't feel the pull.

"We had this amazing night," he continues, voice lower now. "An incredible morning. And then you were gone."

"God, your ego is beyond what I imagined."

His head snaps slightly, like that landed somewhere deeper than I intended.

"It's not about my ego." His voice roughens. "I don't care about keeping score. I care that when I got out of the shower, you had left."

The air shifts.

He's not posturing. He's not teasing.

"I mean," he exhales, searching my face, like he's trying to find something he lost there, "we skated in the park. You were laughing so hard that you almost fell. We had that ridiculous dinner with ginormous milkshakes. That carriage ride …" His mouth softens at the memory. "You kissed me like you meant it."

My pulse betrays me.

"You didn't seem like a woman planning an escape."

I swallow. "It was just one night."

He steps closer. "Don't do that. Don't pretend it was nothing."

My defenses rise automatically. "I really don't want to talk about this right now, Liam."

"Why?" he presses quietly. "What did I do?"

His thumb hooks into the pocket of his jeans, like he's physically holding himself back from reaching for me.

I look away first.

"This is what he wants to know, why *he* was ghosted," I mutter under my breath.

"What?"

"Nothing."

"It wasn't nothing, Alie. I had just made you come, not once, but twice. Then I got up to shower, and you bolted."

"I don't think it was twice," I mumble, but I think he's right, if memory serves.

He chuckles and moves closer to me, and I realize I have nowhere to go. He would definitely catch me if I tried to move around him.

When he's a breath away, he braces one arm on the table next to my hip, and the other hand comes up to my face, stroking my cheek.

"You know I'm not lying."

I cannot form words.

"If you don't want to talk here, have dinner with me tonight." He moves in closer. So close that I can smell the mint on his breath.

I look between his mouth and his eyes.

"I can't."

"Why?"

"Because."

His head moves to the side, and his lips brush the corner of my mouth when he speaks. "Alie, have dinner with me."

I close my eyes and try to compose myself, but it's no use. The goose bumps are in full force, my stomach is flip-flopping all over the place, and it's taking all my strength not to reach out and touch him.

"Liam," I breathe.

"Say yes."

He pulls back and runs his thumb over my lips.

I should push him away.

But I don't.

"I gotta say, seeing you again … fuck. You're even more beautiful than I picture in my dreams." He traces my bottom lip.

I place my hand on his stomach with the intention of pushing him back, which is a huge mistake because I can feel every ripple of muscle through his soft, thin T-shirt. So, instead of moving him, my hand takes on a mind of its own and traces the ridges of his abs, making them contract.

"Alie, say it."

I draw in a slow breath and drop my hand.

I owe this man nothing. I owe him less than nothing.

And yet there are conversations I've had with him a hundred times in my head. Speeches sharpened to a blade. Questions I deserve answers to. A finale that includes several creative insults and a well-placed knee to the groin.

I'm supposed to be furious. Instead, I'm … stuck. Because the man in front of me isn't the villain I rehearsed for. And that's the problem.

"Okay, I'll have dinner with you, but I'll meet you somewhere."

"Let me make dinner for you at mine. That way, we can have some privacy to talk."

"Talk? Yeah, right. No, I'll meet you." I place my hands on his chest, and this time, I do push him back.

"Okay, you win. Tell me where and when. But you're gonna have to give me your number." He smiles, and it should be illegal. This man can get anything he wants with just a little tilt of his lips, including me, apparently.

"Give me your phone." I hold out my hand.

"Yes, ma'am." He smiles like he just won the Lombardi Trophy, takes it out of his pocket, unlocks it, and places it in my hand.

I open his messages, create a text, enter my number, and send myself a text.

"Don't make me regret this, Pitz." I hand it back to him.

"You won't. I just want to talk." He drops it back in his pocket.

We just stand there, staring at each other for a minute, until voices from the hallway startle me.

"Shit. We can't go out together. It'll look weird."

"Why weird? For all they know, we're talking business." He starts to move toward me again, but I hold out my hand before he can get too close.

"Nope. Stay there. I'll go first, and then you can leave five minutes after."

"Are you serious?" He smirks.

"Deadly." I turn and walk toward the door.

Before I can turn the handle, he calls out to me, "I'll be waiting for your text, Alie."

"Give me an hour, and I'll tell you where and when." I look over my shoulder to see him standing with his hands on his hips.

He just nods with that stupid, sexy smile of his.

I gotta get out of here before I lose control and climb him like a tree. But also … I need to make dinner plans, and … find a babysitter.

What the fuck am I doing? This is a really bad idea.

CHAPTER SIXTEEN

LIAM

Alie sent me an address for Blue Ribbon Sushi Bar in Columbus Circle and a time to meet after I saw her downstairs near the gym. I still don't know where I'm going, so I hired a car to take me to the restaurant.

She's not here yet, but she made a reservation under her name, of course, and the hostess showed me to a table in a private area in the back, which makes sense, being that I'm recognizable.

Minutes go by, and I wonder if she's gonna stand me up or if she'll actually show up tonight. I feel like there's something she's not telling me, similar to the strange reactions I get from her sister, and I'm gonna get to the bottom of it tonight.

The waitress comes over and offers, "Would you like to try one of our sakes, or perhaps a cocktail?"

I lean back in my chair. "Let me hold on that until my date gets here, but can you grab me a bottle of water, please?"

"Of course, sir. Would you like sparkling or still?"

"Still is fine. Can you make sure there's plenty of ice?"

"Yes, sir." She walks away to get my drink.

I take my phone out of my pocket and check for the tenth time to make sure she hasn't canceled on me, but there are no messages. I set the phone on the table in front of me just so I don't miss a message coming through. Not that I want to jinx it, but I also don't want to sit here alone all night.

The waitress brings the water to me, and just as she's setting the bottle down, I hear Alie before I see her. When I look up, I see Alie dressed casually in a short-sleeved sweater, a pair of jeans, and some heeled boots, with a small Louis Vuitton cross-body hanging across her chest. Her hair is tied back into one of those messy buns, and she's never looked more beautiful to me.

I stand to greet her. And as she approaches, I walk around the table to take both of her hands in mine, bringing her closer to me, and kissing her on the cheek.

"Hi, Alie."

"Hi," she says, smiling shyly.

I don't want her to be shy. I want her to be comfortable with me, like she was the night we met.

"Did you find this place okay?" she asks as I pull out her chair.

"Yeah. I had a driver bring me because I haven't gotten my bearings yet. My sense of direction is a bit thrown off."

She smiles, slowly, as she sits. "Good. I didn't want you wandering into Jersey by accident."

I push her chair in. "I feel judged already."

"You should. I chose this place very strategically." She slips her small bag onto the table and adjusts her watch. "It's exactly halfway between our buildings."

"You know where I live?" I say as I sit and pull in my chair.

"Yes," she says, tucking a loose piece of hair behind her ear, then adjusting her watch two more times.

"That's not fair. I wanna know where you live." I smirk.

"That feels like information you haven't earned yet."

My brows raise. "Oh, I'm earning points now?"

"You lost points," she counters smoothly. "You're in recovery mode."

Lost points?

The server comes to the table. Alie orders a sparkling water—then turns back to me.

"So, Alie, did you have a nice day today?" I fold my hands in front of me on the table.

"Is that what we're doing? We're gonna go with small talk and niceties?" she asks.

"Well, I figured we could ease in."

She laughs softly. "You don't strike me as a man who eases into anything. I don't see the point in being around the bush." She shrugs.

"Why are you nervous?"

"I'm not nervous."

"You just adjusted your watch three times."

Her mouth curves. God, I missed that mouth.

"Now that we're out of earshot of anyone who cares, can you tell me what happened that morning? I thought we'd agreed to see where it would go."

She's staring at me now, studying my face, as if she's looking for a lie.

"I had a change of heart." She bites the inside of her cheek.

"No, I don't think you did. I think you got scared or maybe didn't have as good of a time as I thought you did." I pause to read her face. "And instead of talking to me about it, you bolted. I think we both know I enjoyed myself that night. That definitely wasn't a lie a for me."

"I'm not a liar, Liam."

"Neither am I, Alie."

"Are you sure about that?" She brings her arms onto the table and crosses them, leaning forward.

"Yes, I'm sure about that. I don't lie to anybody. I have no reason to." I could be offended, but in all reality, we really don't know each other. But I'm going to change that.

"So, when you were in the shower and your best friend, Archie, texted and asked about your hookup ..."

"That night wasn't just a hookup for me," I interrupt. "I had no intention of hooking up with anybody that weekend. Meeting you was a coincidence, and like I said to you that night, I'd never felt an instant connection with somebody the way that I did you."

"So, if I called Archie right now, he would tell me that same thing?"

"If you called Archie now, he'd tell you how absolutely nuts I was about you. How I kept trying to find you after that weekend."

"Really?" she asks, head tilting to the side.

"Yes, really. I thought about you for months. I tried to call and text Aaron to get your number ... "

"Yes, I know you spoke to Aaron. I heard all about that."

"You heard about it?" I shake my head, confused. "That's what I'm saying. I called Aaron to get your number, and he ignored me. And then ..."

The air changes. Not dramatic. Not explosive. Just ... tight. Her eyebrows lift, like she's rerunning a play in her head and the outcome to the game doesn't match.

"Wait," she asks, baffled. "He didn't give you my number?"

"No, that's what I was going to say. By the time he did talk to me, he wouldn't give me your number."

I can see the fight happening inside her. The urge to unleash whatever version of me she's been living with.

Is that what this is about? Did Aaron say something about me?

My dedication to my career has made me push every woman away. Every woman besides Alie. If she had given me the time, I think I would have changed my plans for her. But she never even gave me a chance.

Now, she's here, and she's looking at me with her eyes narrowed, studying me, as if sorting through a narrative about me she's at war with.

I can't imagine the conclusions she must have drawn about me. I want to press her about them. Demand from her what she has believed all these years. Instead, I wait.

She crosses her arms and shakes her head. The war against me is winning.

"So then, Aaron's a liar?" She mumbles. "I don't know what to believe. What about Sabine?" She uncrosses her arms and leans back when the server brings her a glass of water.

"Would you like to order an appetizer or a drink from the bar?"

"You can bring us a bowl of edamame and a spicy tuna roll, and I'll take a nice Pinot Noir," Alie says.

"Very good. And you, sir?"

"I'll have the same." I honestly don't care what it is. I just want to keep talking to Alie.

"I'll be right back with those drinks and put your order in."

I nod and thank her.

"Okay, so now what about Sabine? How do you know who she is?" I shake my head in confusion.

"Well, she texted you, and it sounded like you had some unfinished business to take care of." She takes a drink of water.

"Sabine … I inhale and shake my head. "She was just trying to get a paycheck."

"So, every girl who gets pregnant just wants a paycheck?"

"She was never pregnant. It was a hoax. She wanted to be with me for appearances and my money. I broke up with her weeks before I even came to New York, but she wouldn't let it go. Then, when I got home from New York that weekend, she was waiting for me in my building. Long story short, it got out of control, and I had to file for a restraining order against her. I even had to change my phone number because she was harassing me."

"Oh God. Really?"

"Yes, really. It fucking sucked, to be honest."

"So, you didn't have the same phone number that you had when you were in New York?"

"No, I had to change it within a week of being home. And I had just finished my first season with the Saints, and I didn't want the situation to go public, so I took care of it. But why are you asking about my number?" I tap my finger on top of my phone that's still sitting on the table.

"It doesn't matter." She shakes her head.

"Oh, yeah, it does. It does matter if you're asking. So, I'll tell you again—Aaron blew me off. And, fuck, I didn't know your last name. I looked all over social media for you, and I couldn't find you. No Alie, Allison, Allesandra—nothing matched you." I lift my hands. "Honestly, Alie, I feel like you had an unfair advantage, knowing who I was."

"I did know who you were that night. You're right." She nods, watching me.

"That night with you was unlike anything I'd ever experienced. My buddies have talked to me about what it was like, getting with their wives, and it had never happened for me before, so it almost seemed like a myth." I laugh lightly. "But when I met you, I felt something that I'd never felt before. And I think you felt the same. At least, I thought you did. I hoped you did. So, do you have any other questions for me about that night?"

My question is met with silence. She doesn't smile. She just watches me.

The server wordlessly sets our drinks on the table and walks away.

Her fingers tighten around the stem of her glass. Her posture shifts, spine straightening, shoulders pulling back like she's fortifying something invisible.

Her eyes move over my face slowly. Assessing. Not soft. Not warm. Calculating.

Like she's comparing what I just said to something else she'd already decided about me.

I hold her gaze, waiting for her to call me out. To laugh. To accuse me of dramatics. She does neither. Instead, a small crease forms between her brows in confusion or maybe suspicion. For a second, I get the strange feeling I'm being measured against a version of myself I've never met.

And I have no idea which one of us is losing.

She shakes her head and sits back in her seat. "I don't know. I think it's a lot of information for me to process for one night. Let's just talk about something … lighter?"

There it is. The exit ramp of conversation.

I study her for a second longer. She won't meet my eyes now. She's focusing on the candle. The table. Anywhere but me.

She's not indifferent. Indifferent doesn't look like that.

"Lighter?" I say slowly, giving her the out she clearly wants. "Okay." But I can't shake the feeling I just said something that shook her, and I don't know if that's good or very, very bad.

"Tell me about your time in New Orleans."

"What do you want to know? I'll tell you anything."

She folds her hands around her glass. "Did you like living there?"

I huff a quiet laugh. "It was…a lot. That is one non-stop party."

"I can see that. I've only been there a few times for fun, and it was a whirlwind. But the food. Beignets, jazz … heaven." She has a small smile on her face, like she's trying to hold it in.

"Yeah, the food was top-tier for sure. And the fans were incredible. Very loyal and very loud. Sometimes a little terrifying." I chuckle. "It was good for me though. I feel like my time there helped me find my way in the league. Forced me to grow up a bit, if that makes sense."

She nods, her gaze dropping to the table.

"What about you?" I say, leaning back slightly. "Are you still terrorizing public skating rinks?"

Her mouth curves. There she is.

"I do not terrorize," she says. "I inspire."

"You dragged me onto the ice with zero warning."

"You're welcome," she counters. "I'd be back to my antics if it wasn't springtime, thawing the ice. That and I'm swamped with work."

"All work and no play, then?" I study her.

She lifts a shoulder and still eyes me like she's trying to figure something out. "Pretty much, yeah."

I don't want to press her if she's not willing to tell me more, so I turn the conversation back to football. "So ... Aliette Grant, what's it like, growing up in a football dynasty?" I smile, then take a drink of my water.

Finally, a warmer smile breaks across her face. "Well, it's all I've known, so I'm not really sure how to answer that, I guess. My dad can tell you the story about how his great-grandfather bought the team in the 1920's for what would be considered pocket change now." She smirks. "Not to mention, my mom's family has their own ties to football. So, it's just really what our life is. Holidays, vacations ... all revolve around the season, the draft, and playoff math."

"Wait, your mom's family too?" I ask, surprised.

"Yep. My mom's maiden name is Presley." She looks at me to see if I'm connecting the dots.

"As in the Columbus Bulls?"

"That's the one." She nods and shrugs.

"Oh wow. So ... Presley Grant. Big name to live up to."

"Presley has a big personality, so she carries it just fine." She laughs. "We're really only involved with the Bulls for annual board and shareholders meetings at this point anyway."

"And it's just you and your sister?"

She nods. "My dad was an only child, so it's all up to Presley and me to keep the Titan legacy alive. My mom's brother is more involved with the Bulls, and my cousins on that side are somewhat involved, but not like Presley and I are."

"Do you feel a lot of pressure, knowing that? Is it something you and your sister even want?"

"Of course. I love the game and everything that goes along with it. Well, not the publicity part of it, which is why my family has kept me and my sister sheltered from the media for most of our lives. But the whole infrastructure, the energy, the challenges ... I love it."

That explains why I couldn't find much online about her. Family privacy.

"Presley feels the same?"

"She does. I mean, medicine was something that was important to her, and she got to pursue that dream and incorporate it into the family business."

"Then I guess we're all pretty lucky to be doing what we feel passionate about."

She gives me a faint smile. "Yeah, I guess we are."

The server sets down our edamame and sushi, and for a second we both just stare at it like civilized adults pretending we're not sitting on top of unresolved tension.

She picks up her chopsticks with annoying elegance.

"So," I say, nodding toward her plate, "you're lucky I'm not allergic to fish."

Her brows lift. "Is that a thing?"

"It's absolutely a thing."

"Well then, I would've chosen pizza."

"That's insulting."

"To sushi?"

"To me. Unless it's the best pizza in Manhattan."

She smiles and pops a piece into her mouth, chewing thoughtfully. "You survived."

"Barely. Raw fish is a bold choice for a reconciliation dinner."

"Who said this is a reconciliation?" she asks lightly.

I ignore that. "You brought me to your favorite place. That feels strategic."

She shrugs. "You seemed like the type who could handle it."

"What type is that?"

"Adventurous. Slightly reckless. Mildly arrogant."

"Mildly?"

She tilts her head. "Fine. Moderately."

I laugh. God, I've missed this version of her.

She reaches for the soy sauce, dips carefully. "Besides, sushi tells you

a lot about a person."

"Oh, does it?"

"Mm-hmm. If you drown it in soy sauce, you don't trust the chef.

If you refuse to try anything raw, you don't like risk."

"And what does ordering spicy tuna say?"

She studies me like she's evaluating a case file. "That the person likes control. But also likes a little danger."

"That's wildly specific."

"I'm rarely wrong."

I take a bite and watch her over the rim of my glass. "So, what does ordering edamame say about you?"

She pauses just a fraction too long before answering. "That I know what I like."

Alie seems to be letting her guard down a little and I'm getting to see the woman I met two years ago. Fun, easy, Alie.

As we finish our food, a silence settles around us. Not awkward, just quiet.

When the server brings our bill, I hand her my card without looking at it.

Alie smiles. "Thanks for dinner."

"Happy you said yes to coming." I laugh lightly.

"Did you give me a choice? I thought it was more like, 'Say yes.'" She mimics my voice, sitting back in her seat, smiling, and crosses her arms across her chest.

"You didn't fight it too hard." I smirk.

She tilts her head and gives a subtle nod.

I get my card back from the server and put it back in my wallet.

"I should probably get going," she says, pulling her phone out of her bag. "Oh wow. Yeah, it's getting late."

I reach out to touch her hand. "Wait. Will you take a walk with me?"

She hesitates, but only for a second. "Okay, but not for long."

I stand and move around to her seat. "I'll take it." I hold out my hand to her, and she places hers in mine.

We walk outside into the cool night, the city still buzzing around us even though it's getting later in the evening. Our pace is slow, and our shoulders are touching, but she doesn't move away.

"This feels familiar." I look down at her and smile.

"What does? Walking?"

"Yeah. Walking with you specifically," I say, my voice certain.

She exhales slowly, tensing. "Maybe this isn't a good idea."

I stop and turn to face her. "Why not?"

"For the most minor of reasons, I'm your boss. Lines will blur, and things could get really … complicated," she mumbles.

I reach for her hands. "I don't mind complicated." I pull her in closer to me. "And I'm not going to ignore this connection between us."

"Liam …" She looks conflicted.

"Alie, let me ask you something. Did you have fun tonight? With me?"

She tilts her head to the side, still not pulling out of my hold. "I did."

"So did I. And I think we should do it again. And often."

"You know, you're kind of bossy." Her lips twitch.

"I think you like it when I'm bossy." I smirk.

"I'll think about it."

"Okay, I'll take it. But, Alie, don't make me wait too long."

She huffs, "Or what?"

"I can be relentless when I need to be. And I'm not gonna let you walk away from me again." A smile tugs at my mouth.

"Is that right?" She's staring at my mouth.

"Yep." I lean in and whisper in her ear, "And this time, I have an advantage."

"What advantage do you have?" She sucks in a breath, clearly affected by me.

"I know where you work now." I pull back, but still close enough that it wouldn't take much for me to kiss her.

A laugh bubbles out of her lightly. "Easy there, MVP."

We linger there, close. Both of us smiling. The moment stretches until I can't take it anymore, and I close the distance and take her lips in a soft, testing kind of kiss.

She doesn't pull away, so I deepen the kiss, winding my arms around her waist, pulling her in close to me.

Her hands slide up my chest, and she grips my shirt, as if she needs to steady herself. And I move one hand to cup her jaw, not wanting this kiss to ever stop. The sounds of the city fade around us, until all I hear is the rush of our breaths, both of us chasing the pull it seems we've both been missing.

When we finally break apart, she's a little breathless, eyes still closed, cheeks flushed.

"Alie"—I kiss her softly—"you good?"

I can't help but feel a bit smug.

"Yeah, um … yeah, I'm good." She opens her eyes and clears her throat and tries to pull away from me, but I don't let go. "I really should go."

I want to keep her with me. I don't want this night to end, but I also know that pushing too hard might just push her away.

"Okay," I whisper, but neither of us moves.

"Liam, seriously, I should go. It's getting late, and I have an early morning tomorrow."

"I'll walk you to the car, but, Alie, you need to let go of me so we can move." I smile against her lips.

"Right, yes." She releases my shirt and steps back. She pulls her phone out of her bag. After she taps out a few times, she puts her phone back in.

"I'll walk you to your car."

We both turn, and I place my hand on the small of her back. We walk quietly to where her driver has pulled up.

I open the door for her, and she turns to me. "Thank you for dinner."

"Thank you for meeting me."

Leaning in, I can't help but kiss her one more time. This kiss is meant to be a goodbye, but the heat sparks quickly. It's the kind of kiss that promises trouble. The kind that makes her take hold of my shirt again, tugging me closer.

She pulls back when her driver clears his throat, and she looks a little dazed.

Yep, I did that. Again.

"Good night," she says softly before turning and ducking into the car.

"Night, Alie," I say before closing the door. Our eyes meet through the window before the car drives away.

I stand there, watching her until I can't see the lights of her car anymore, and a smile tugs on my lips.

This isn't over.

Not even close.

CHAPTER SEVENTEEN

ALIE

By the time I get home, my head is spinning. Well, I suppose it's been spinning since he came into the building the other day.

Liam.

I open the door to my unit, and I see my sister pacing the room with Seraphina in her arms, her little head resting on Presley's shoulder. The sight hits me straight in the heart, grounding me.

Mommy first. Always.

I close the door softly and slide my boots off, setting them near the coat rack.

Presley hears me and turns toward me. "There she is," she says softly. "The woman of the hour."

Sera lifts her sleepy head and looks at me, immediately holding her arms out, her tiny hands opening and closing.

"Hi, sweet girl," I say as I cross the room and take her from my sister. She melts into me instantly, resting her head on my shoulder, warm, soft, content. And so perfect.

Presley walks with me over to the couch, sitting down first. "Okay, so spill."

"Can I at least sit first?"

"No, start talking."

I sigh and take a seat next to her, keeping Seraphina in my arms. My heart feels full yet heavy, all at the same time. Not to mention, I'm utterly and completely confused.

"Well, it was interesting."

"Interesting how?"

I glance down at my daughter, rubbing her back gently. "Being around him is, for lack of a better word, magnetic. He's got this pull about him that I can't explain." I let out a shaky exhale. "Like, even more so now than when I first met him."

Presley groans, "Oh shit, you're in love with him."

"What?! No, I am not." I roll my eyes. Even though the kiss he gave me … I can still feel it on my lips.

Sera squirms a little, so I pat her back as my thoughts race. Maybe she can feel my emotions going wild.

"I'm not quite sure how I'm going to be able to stay away from him, Presley." I look at her. "And how the hell am I going to work with him? I should have given this trade more thought, but he really is what's best for the team right now."

Presley's face softens. "You're not wrong. Work does make it a little messier."

"Messy? That doesn't even begin to cover it." I tilt my head toward my daughter.

My sister scoots a little closer and rests her arm behind me on the back of the couch. "Why don't you start by telling me why you're so flustered?"

Where to start? Or … where to end?

"Well … there was a walk."

Her eyes widen. "Oh, there was a walk?"

"There was a walk," I confirm dreamily.

"Must have been some walk." She smirks.

"It was." I lay my head back and close my eyes. "There was a kiss."

"I knew it!" she whisper-shouts. "Did you kiss him back?"

"I shouldn't be held accountable for my actions. He kissed *me*. And it wasn't just any kiss," I admit. "It was the kind of kiss that made me want to do … more."

"A little out of hand, maybe?"

I take a deep breath, shaking my head. "Not out of hand really, since we were in the middle of the sidewalk, but enough to make me consider—for a split second—going home with him."

"Did he ask you to go home with him?"

"No." I shake my head.

"Did you want him to ask you?"

I pause before saying, "Yes."

She audibly gasps. "Alie! Scandalous!"

I groan, "I know. But I can't."

"Because of Sera?"

"Because of everything," I say.

She watches me carefully, then asks the question I've been purposefully avoiding since I got home. "What did he say when you asked him why he didn't want to be a part of her life?"

My stomach twists. "I didn't."

"Alie!" She looks at me pointedly. "That was the whole point of going to dinner with him. When are you planning on having this talk then?"

I stare down at my daughter, touching her soft cheek, tracing her face with my finger.

"I don't know. Not yet."

"Why not?"

"I just … can't." The words feel heavy, yet fragile at the same time. I run my hand through my hair and look up at the ceiling. "I don't know why, but I thought I would know how I'd react with him. In the end, I couldn't risk asking and having him say all the things I feared I'd hear. Maybe because I don't want to know the answer."

"Alie," she sighs.

"I know, okay? I know I need to." My hand is now on my neck as I lower my gaze and stare back at her. "You know what he did say?" I ask her.

"What?"

"He told me that he'd looked for me. And that he texted and called Aaron and that Aaron never responded to him."

Presley's mouth drops. "What are you saying?"

"I don't know, but I definitely need to ask Aaron about it. It doesn't make sense with what he told me, so it makes the whole situation even more confusing."

"Well, someone is lying. And you know I'm not Aaron's number one fan, but he was there for you throughout your entire pregnancy. Hell, if you asked him to be her father, he would. The man has been your friend forever and nothing but good to Sera."

"I know. I know. This is crazy. Maybe Liam is lying to make himself look good." I drop my hand from my neck and look at her, confused. "Right?"

She gnaws on her lip. "Shit, Alie. I don't know. Liam could be lying to get on your good side, but … " There's something in her face that morphs, as if a thought just came to her. "Alie, have you and Liam even talked about Sera?"

"No. I told you, I can't ask him–"

"I mean, have you spoken about Sera at all?"

I shake my head. "No. What are you getting at?"

Her mouth opens and then closes, as if she's considering the thoughts about to leave her mouth. Then she shakes off her thoughts, as if they're insane for her to speak.

After a pause, she says, "Alie, have you considered that Liam might be telling you the truth about Aaron?"

"I think … " I swallow. "I need to spend a little more time with him before I ask him about why he gave up on Sera, before I introduce him to her."

She immediately shakes her head. "Bad idea. Really bad idea."

"Why? I just want to protect her. And myself."

"No, listen," she says softly, but firmly. "Liam Pitz is not a bad man. And from everything you've said, and everything I've seen about him, he's a good guy."

"I think he is, but do I really know him?" I argue.

She waves me off. "So I don't understand why you feel like you need to wait or prolong asking him. I think this has the potential to blow back —badly—if you don't handle this quickly."

"I just don't understand," I whisper. "I don't understand why he didn't want to have anything to do with her, yet he's asking me out to dinner and kissing me senseless. He knows she exists, so why isn't he asking about her?"

Presley goes still.

"It just doesn't make sense. His behavior isn't making sense, no matter how irresistible I think he is."

Sera lets out a little snore, and I kiss the top of her silky hair.

"I want to protect her." I kiss my daughter again. "And myself."

Presley's eyes soften, but she also looks like she's trying to figure something out.

"If he asks me to spend more time with him, and I agree, it will only be me and him." I pause. "I just can't trust him with my heart yet, let alone hers."

Silence settles between us.

Then she nudges my shoulder gently. "But you still want him."

"More than air." I sigh dramatically.

Presley pulls her knees up onto the couch. "Okay, one more question."

"What?"

"How did it feel, being with him?"

"Hmm ... safe," I admit. "Familiar. But also more intense than a few years ago."

She grins. "And the kissing?"

"Pres, you're relentless."

"What? Throw me a bone. It's been a while, and this is juicy. I'm completely invested in your love story."

"Love story?" I huff.

She pushes me. "The kiss?"

I groan. "Fine! Yes, it was amazing."

She flops backward onto the cushion. "This is better than reality TV."

"I'm happy to entertain you, Pres."

She giggles. "You're glowing, you know?"

I fall silent at that.

Because I don't think she's wrong. My heart hasn't felt this alive in a very long time. And that's what scares me.

Presley lowers her voice when Sera stirs. "So, what do you think will happen now then?"

"I think ... " I look at my daughter. "Everything's about to change for all of us."

I look at the window into the night, city lights twinkling in the sky.

"Alie, he could turn out to be the man you think he is," she says quietly.

"I hope so. For her sake, and mine." I brush a hand over my daughter's head. Emotions swelling.

Presley stands and stretches her arms. "I'd better get going before we make this a sleepover."

"You're not going back to your place, are you?"

"Not tonight. I'll just stay in my room at Mom and Dad's and ride in with you guys tomorrow since we have to be there early anyway."

"Hey." I stand. "Thanks for staying with her tonight."

"Of course. I love my little peanut." She touches Sera's back. Then she starts to speak, but stops. "Al—"

"What, Pres?"

She inhales. "Well, Mom and Dad still don't know who Seraphina's father is."

This time, I do glare at her.

She shrugs. "I'm just saying that some secrets can't be kept. Maybe they don't need to know yet, until you guys figure things out."

"You're such a brat."

"But I'm not wrong."

I sigh and shake my head.

She grabs her bag off the coat rack by the door.

"If he is truly the man he appears to be, don't push him away because you're afraid. Let him tell you his side of the story."

I swallow. "I'll try."

She smiles and squeezes my arm. "See you bright and early."

I close the door behind her, and the apartment falls silent, except for my daughter's sweet, sleepy sounds.

I carry her to her room, then lay her gently in her bed, watching her sleep. She's so perfect.

My heart feels like it's splitting in two. I need to know why he didn't want to be involved.

Can I do this? Can I let him into her life?

When I finally turn off the light and close the door, my thoughts still whirl. I don't know that I am ready for Liam.

But I'm still … curious.

As I walk toward my room, I remember to grab my phone so I can plug it in.

When I pull it out of my bag, it buzzes with an incoming text.

No one texts me this late at night, which means …

Liam.

When I look down at the screen, my stomach tightens.

I swipe my finger across the screen to open the message.

Liam: Did you make it home safely?

A small smile tugs at my lips, and I can't even stop it.

Alie: I did. Just getting ready for bed.

Three dots appear, then disappear just as quickly.

When they flicker again, my pulse spikes.

Liam: Good. I've been trying to be chill since I've been home, but it's not working.

Heat spreads through me.

Another message pops up.

Liam: I meant what I said tonight. I don't want to pressure you, but I want to see you again. And often.

My chest tightens. Good Lord, I feel like I'm reliving my first crush with the way he makes my stomach flutter with nerves.

Before I can reply, another one arrives.

Liam: Dinner again soon. No work talk. Just us.

I let out a soft laugh and bring my phone to my chest.

Bossy.

I look at my phone again and finally reply.

Alie: I'll think about it.

He replies instantly.

Liam: I'm not letting you disappear on me again. Sweet dreams, Alie.

I stare at the screen, sigh, then drop my hand to my side.

My world feels like it's tilting.

As I walk, I turn off the hallway light and whisper to myself, "What the fuck are you doing, Alie?"

But the truth follows me in the dark.

A truth, I already know. I'm definitely going to see him outside of work again.

CHAPTER EIGHTEEN

LIAM

The second I walk into the facility, I know that my focusing on my job will be difficult.

Not because of my schedule.

Because Alie is here.

Somewhere in this building—behind glass walls, closed doors, and professional boundaries—is the woman I've been thinking about, craving for two years.

Apparently, one kiss isn't gonna cut it for me. I want more.

I walk into the locker room, toss my bag down into my cubby, and try to focus on my routine. Tape, stretch, talk to my teammates as they arrive. It should feel normal. I've been doing this for years.

But nothing feels the same.

I'm a grown man. A professional athlete, for fuck's sake. I thrive under pressure. Two minutes on the clock, down a touchdown? I live for it. Media, contract negotiations? Bring it on.

But somehow, the idea of seeing Alie today—knowing I'll

likely see her in some of these meetings—has my mind spinning and my heart pumping like it's a playoff game.

I grab my phone, headphones, and a towel, then head into the gym and start my sets.

I last about forty minutes before I give up the pretense of patience.

"Where you going, Pitz?" one of my new teammates, Wyatt St. Clair, asks.

"Uh, I have a paperwork thing upstairs."

He nods like it makes sense and continues lifting weights.

It absolutely doesn't make sense. All my paperwork has been signed, sealed, and delivered.

"I'm heading out after I'm done, so I'll see you tomorrow," he calls after me as I pull the door open.

"Later, man," I say over my shoulder.

I take the fastest shower of my life, toss my bag over my shoulder, and make my way up to the administrative floor.

It's quieter up here. A more controlled environment—carpet instead of turf, coffee instead of sweat.

When I find her door, it's closed. I look up and down the hallway to see if anyone else is around, and then I knock lightly.

I can hear movement and a muffled sound that definitely isn't Alie's voice.

I knock again.

"Just a second." Alie's voice carries.

The door opens then, and the moment I see her, everything else just fades away.

Her hair is tied back today, and she's got glasses on. She looks beautiful in a way that hits hard.

"Liam," she says, startled. "Hey." She moves into the doorway and closes her door slightly.

"Hi," I reply slowly. "You got a minute?"

She hesitates. Just for a moment.

Then I hear it.

A tiny laugh.

It takes my brain a second to process what I'm hearing.

When I look over Alie's head, I see her.

A little girl sits on the floor in front of Alie's desk, surrounded by crayons, paper, and coloring books. Dark wavy hair. Big brown eyes. Tiny sneakers on her little feet, tapping on the floor as she looks up at me curiously.

Everything inside me freezes.

"Can I come in?" I ask, my voice coming out a little rougher than I intended.

Alie moves back and pushes the door open. "Uh … " she looks over at the little girl. "Yeah, come in."

She closes the door behind me.

"What … " I look from the girl to Alie. I can't seem to form words.

Alie clears her throat.

"This is Seraphina," she says softly with a smile. "Sera."

I can't stop looking between them, trying to put the pieces together.

The little girl grins. "Hi!" With her chubby fists in the air, she looks at Alie and asks, "Who dis, Mommy?"

Mommy?

I stare at Sera because something about her hits me like a punch in the chest. Not because she's here. Not just that she's adorable. It's the way her eyes look … familiar.

My stomach drops, and I turn to look at Alie.

She won't meet my eyes.

Suddenly, the air in the room shifts, and I think I might just pass out.

"How old is she?" I ask slowly, my voice gravelly.

Alie scrunches her brows and looks at me like I've done something wrong by asking.

"She'll be two in September." She crosses her arms and glares at me.

Two. My brain does the math before I'm ready. Then the room tilts.

I can't stop the sharp, disbelieving laugh that slips out. "Alie."

She closes her eyes briefly, like she's trying to school her emotions. Then she takes a deep breath.

"Liam, before you say anything else, we need to talk privately. Not in front of her."

My heart is pounding in my ears.

"Is she ... " I swallow, forcing out the words. "Is she mine?"

Alie's silence is answer enough, and she still looks ... angry.

Everything inside me detonates, and I drop my bag and have to take a step back, bracing myself against the wall.

I look at Alie. "You—" I run my hand through my hair, trying to catch my breath, trying to think. "You didn't tell me."

Sera looks between Alie and me, sensing the shift in the room. "Mommy?"

Alie immediately moves to comfort her, running her hand over her wavy brown hair. "Hey, baby. Why don't we take your coloring books into Poppy's office for a while, and you can color with him?"

Sera nods happily. "Yes, Poppy color too."

Alie glances at me as she opens the door. "I'll be right back."

Silence crashes down on me, and my gaze hasn't left the door.

She comes back into the room only seconds later, closing the door behind her.

"You didn't tell me." My voice is quiet, but no doubt she can tell that I'm upset.

"Excuse me?" She crosses her arms defensively. "I tried—"

"When?" I interrupt. "When did you try to tell me, Alie? Because I sure as shit don't remember being told that I have a daughter!"

Her face falls, and she looks like she's going to be sick. "I found out a month after our night together."

I laugh, harshly. "And you couldn't pick up a phone? What exactly stopped you?"

"Liam," she starts.

"So … you just what? Decided for me?" I pace around the room. "You decided I didn't get to know?"

Tears well in her eyes. "I don't … I don't understand what's happening here. *You* decided you didn't want her. You did, Liam. Not me." She points at me.

"What the fuck are you talking about? How could I decide anything when I didn't know?!" I raise my arms in frustration and anger.

"I didn't have your number, so Aaron said he would take care of it and contact you. I told him to give you my number so we could talk. He said that his texts came back undelivered. Then he told me you'd changed your number, and when he finally got a hold of you and told you about the pregnancy, you said you wanted nothing to do with the baby or me." She wipes the tears from her face. "He said you told him that football was your priority."

My chest tightens, and rage consumes me.

"Aaron Muldoon told you I didn't want my child? And you believed him?" I point to my chest. "You really think that *I'm* that kind of man?"

"Liam—" she starts, but I don't let her finish.

"You erased me, Alie," I say hoarsely.

"That's not fair. He's one of my oldest friends. My best friend. I believed him when he said you didn't want anything to do with us." She begins to cry again.

"Two years, Alie." I'm so bitter, but it's also hurting me to see her cry.

"And now?" I run my hands through my hair. "Fuck. Your family knows I'm the father?"

She shakes her head. "I never told them who the father was. Presley knows though."

I laugh humorlessly. "Of course not. There's no way a trade would've been made if they'd thought I didn't want my own kid. And that explains why Presley's been less than friendly with me."

"Liam, I understand that you're upset, but I am too. All this time, I believed you didn't want to be involved in her life." She sniffs. "Knowing you were coming here, as I made that decision with our team to bring you here—it was one of the hardest business decisions I've ever had to make. And I had no one to talk to about it!" She raises her hands. "Then when I saw you again—"

"What? You decided to test me? Is this some kind of game to you?"

"I was confused. You didn't say anything about it. I guess I was trying to figure out your angle."

"My angle? I don't play games with people, Alie."

"We spent one night together! I hardly know you!"

"So then, why did you agree to go to dinner with me? If I'm some stranger?"

"Like I said, I was trying to figure you out." She covers her face with her hands.

"And have you?" I pause. "Figured me out?"

She drops her hands and looks at me. "It's my job to protect my daughter. I needed to understand why you wanted to see me—outside of work—after all this time."

"Right." I huff a laugh. "And you think you needed to protect her from me."

"If I needed to, yes." She stands taller.

"Unbelievable." I shake my head.

We stand in silence as I try to wrap my head around this.

Then I walk around the room, my adrenaline in high gear.

I think about that little girl— *my daughter*—sitting on the floor, laughing and coloring.

All the time with her I missed.

Ultrasounds.

Doctor appointments.

Her first birthday.

Bedtime stories.

"You took that time from me," I say quietly.

She sobs softly. "I wouldn't have if I had known—"

"But you did," I whisper.

I feel like I'm getting smothered by my emotions right now, and I can hardly breathe.

"I need—" I stop, breathing deeply. "I need to get some air."

"Liam, please," she says, reaching out for me.

I hold out my arm. "I can't do this right now."

"You're just going to walk out then?"

"I don't walk out on people, Alie. You do."

I know it's a low blow, but I've never been angrier than I am right now.

"And I'm not walking out on her—I would never. I'm walking out before I say something I can't take back."

She takes a step toward me. "Can't we just—"

I pick up my bag, and my hand pauses on the handle.

"Not right now," I say, firmly.

"She has your smile, you know?" she says softly.

That nearly does me in. I close my eyes, jaw clenching, fighting off the tears threatening to fall.

Then I open the door and walk out.

Presley is in the hallway with Sera in her arms, smiling, but it drops the second she sees me.

I turn away quickly because if I don't, I won't leave.

So, I keep walking. Past the offices, past people milling around in the lobby, and out the main door.

The air outside hits my lungs like a shock.

I don't remember calling for a car.

I just know that I'm sitting in the back, squeezing my hands so tight that my knuckles are starting to ache.

I have a daughter. Who is almost two years old.

Resentment churns in my gut. I'm stunned, and I feel like I'm grieving all that time I lost. But I also feel this overwhelming feeling of love. The need to protect her. The need to know her. And for her to know me.

I lean forward and rest my elbows on my knees, and cover my face with my hands.

"Fuck," I whisper.

My phone buzzes in my pocket, so I take it out.

Alie.

I don't answer. Not yet.

Because I don't trust myself right now. Because this … is a game changer.

CHAPTER NINETEEN

ALIE

The moment Liam walks out of my office, I feel like something inside me has split in two.

I stand there staring at the door, maybe hoping that if I don't move, he'll come back.

He doesn't.

I feel like my knees might just give out, so I make my way to my chair and sit. My hands are shaking so badly that I try to grab onto the edge of my desk to steady myself, but I can barely hold on.

"Oh God," I whisper to myself.

Everything that I thought I knew was wrong. It feels like all the air in the room has been sucked out, and my heart is beating outside my chest.

I should have been the one to tell him.

With something this important, I should have found a way to get a hold of him.

I should have asked him about it at dinner the other night. I should have been more direct.

But I wasn't. Now I have to face the fallout of my mistake. And the fact that my daughter hasn't had her father. I might be sick.

I lay my head down on my desk and fight back my tears. I need to get it together.

A knock on the doorframe makes me practically jump out of my seat.

Presley pops her head in first, then slips inside with Sera on her hip.

"Hey," she says gently. "He just left."

I nod, my throat too tight to speak yet.

"He saw her?"

I nod again.

Sera reaches for me. "Mommy."

I stand quickly and take her from my sister. Holding her close, I press my face into her hair and breathe her in like she's the only thing solid in my world.

"Mommy sad?" she asks, patting my back with her little hands.

"I'm okay, baby." I sniff.

Presley's voice softens. "Do you want to get out of here?"

I look up at her, eyes watering. "Yeah."

"I'll be right back," she says as she walks out the door.

"You ready to go home?" I set Sera down on the floor so I can start to pack up for the day.

"Ready." She gives me a wide smile.

Presley walks back in seconds later. "A car will be here any minute."

"Thanks," I reply.

"I'll be right back. I need to go get my bag from my office." She walks out the door again.

Once I have my bag and my daughter's backpack, we make our way to the lobby to wait for my sister.

Thankfully, I don't see my dad when I leave because I have

no doubt I look like a wreck. Then he'd have questions that I don't want to answer yet.

Presley joins us, and we walk out just as the driver is pulling up.

"We could go stay at the house tonight instead of going to the city," she suggests.

My parents have a home in Alpine, New Jersey, that we stay at sometimes too.

"Nah, I just want to go home."

"Okay," she says as she holds my bag while I get Sera into the car.

Once she's locked in her car seat, I stand and take the bag from my sister.

"Do you need a hug?" She holds her arms out to me.

"No, not yet. I don't want her to see me crying." I touch her arm though before I get into the car.

Presley gets into the car on the other side, and as soon as we start to drive away from the complex, she looks over Sera at me.

What happened? she mouths.

I shake my head and mouth back, *Not now.*

"Mommy songs?" Sera grabs my hand.

"Sure, we can play some music." I reach in front of me and turn on the music player, letting the *Frozen* soundtrack fill the silence.

I stare out the window the rest of the way home, lost in thought and regret.

. . .

It's been a long day, and Sera was definitely feeling my emotional upheaval because she didn't want to go to bed tonight.

When I make my way to the family room, my sister is sitting on the couch, waiting for me, scrolling on her phone, wineglass in hand.

She sees me and sets her phone down on the cushion beside her. "I got you a glass too," she says, pointing to the glass on the coffee table.

"Thanks. I think I need about five of these tonight." I pick up the glass and take a sip.

"So, tell me."

I turn my body and fold my knees so I'm curled on the couch, facing her. "He saw her."

"Obviously." She rolls her eyes. "I saw him walk out. What did he say?"

It's not what he said that has my mind reeling. It's how he looked.

It was easier to picture Liam choosing football over us than to picture him looking at me in disgust. I could see it on his face, the moment it clicked for him. It was in the way his jaw locked, the way his hands dragged through his hair. It wasn't indifference. It was loss. Two years of it.

"Well … he was genuinely shocked." I rub my thumb along the rim of the glass. "I've replayed that conversation a hundred times in my head, and it was genuine hurt. And he looked … " I hesitate, searching for the right word. "He looked like someone had just told him he'd missed the most important game of his life. He got really angry when I told him that Aaron had told me he wanted nothing to do with the baby or me, and that football was more important."

"I knew it … " she mumbles.

"What did you know?"

She shakes her head. "I just had a gut feeling that Aaron wasn't being completely honest with you about reaching Liam."

"Why didn't you say anything?"

"Alie, you didn't want to hear it, and I get it. At the time, you were totally overwhelmed by the idea of having a baby, and I think it was easier for you to think Liam was the bad guy rather than considering the possibility that Aaron wasn't telling you the truth."

She's not wrong. I was on a roller coaster of highs and lows in the beginning of my pregnancy. Aaron was my ally and best friend. I wouldn't have thought—and still can't imagine why—he would lie to me about this.

But I think … he actually might have.

"Well, now I feel horrible. Like I want to crawl into a hole. I feel confused. I feel nervous about what this means for Seraphina."

She nods. "Understandable. This is a lot."

"You should have seen him when he asked me if she was his." I put my hand on my heart. "I think it broke something in me. He looked shattered. And that's why I think he's telling me the truth. You can't fake raw emotion like that."

"Not unless you're an amazing actor, which he isn't. He can't even look at you across the room without it being obvious he wants you."

"I don't think he'll want anything to do with *me* after today. And I have no idea what he wants with Sera."

I start to cry again—exhausted tears like they've been waiting years to fall.

Presley scoots closer to me and takes my glass from my hand and sets it on the table, then wraps me in a hug.

"You should have been the one to tell him," she whispers.

"I know."

"I understand why you didn't at the time. You were fresh out of college, scared, and you thought he was a player with another baby on the way with another woman. You were an emotional wreck, who was also worried about what your parents would say and if the media would find out and make a big deal about the Grants' daughter having a love child. It was a rough pregnancy for you. You trusted your best friend when he said he would have your back. He promised to take care of the hard part for you, but the responsibility fell on you." She lets me go, but stays close, resting her hand on my leg.

"Don't you think I know that? God, Pres, you're making me feel even worse."

"You're upset because I'm right. And I know you, and I know you'll beat yourself up over this for a long time."

I press the heel of my hand to my sternum, like I can physically hold the ache in place. "I'm scared that this can't be fixed."

"What can't be fixed?"

"My mistake. I took away time with his daughter. She lost time with her father. He'll never trust me, and it will affect his relationship with Seraphina. How does he get over this? He's missed so much."

"Is it just Seraphina you're worried about?"

"Of course it is. I have to coparent with him. And I don't want him to treat her differently because he resents me."

My sister looks at me knowingly. "And?"

I drop my head back and sigh. "Okay, fine." I look at her, my eyes starting to water. "How could he trust me now? I thought I'd gotten over him. But after seeing him and spending time with him, clearly, I haven't. And now, whatever it is that we've started, it could already be over."

"You don't know that."

"I think I just all but guaranteed that it is."

"Alie, I don't know the guy well, but based on the look on his face when he walked out of your office today, I don't think it is."

"I can't stop thinking about the way he looked at me before he left. Like I'd broken something that he couldn't fix."

She doesn't say anything—because what can you say to that?

"What am I going to do? I've ruined this. And any feelings he might have had for me … oh God, our kiss. He must think I'm awful."

She takes my hand and squeezes it. "Or maybe this is just the hard part before it gets better."

I wish I believed her.

CHAPTER TWENTY

ALIE

It's been seventy-two hours since I've seen or heard from Liam. And today is my birthday, which I pretty much forgot, which says a lot about my mental state.

But my sister and parents didn't forget. They brought in lunch for me today, and we had a small cake in one of the conference rooms, just the five of us.

When I get back to my office from taking Sera to the nursery, my sister is waiting on the couch.

"What are you still doing up here?"

"We're going out tonight," she declares. "I'm not letting you sit on your couch, alone, on your birthday."

I shake my head. "Nope. No, I'm not at all in the mood for going, Pres."

"Too bad," she cuts in. "You need a night out so you're not overthinking every life choice you've ever made."

"I have a toddler."

"Already taken care of. Mom and Dad are going to watch her so we can go out."

I drop my head back and groan, "I can't believe you basically kidnapped my child."

"Pfft. Kidnapped? She's thrilled to spend the night at Mom and Dad's. They spoil her rotten."

It's true, but still.

"Come on. Finish up your day, and let's get out of here." She stands and claps twice.

"You know, you're really annoying sometimes."

"Oh, and wear that little plum-colored slip dress tonight."

"And you're telling me how to dress?"

She waves as she walks out, so I give her the finger, and her laugh rings out all the way down the hall.

By the time we reach the bar downtown, the music is loud, the lights are warm, and the atmosphere is a pleasant surprise.

Presley invited a few of our friends to come with us tonight. Blair and Willow grew up with us, and they are also sisters. They're fun to hang out with from time to time, but they can be a lot.

My sister tells us a story about catching two of the equipment managers going at it in a storage room, and I can't help but laugh.

Drinks flow, and Presley orders another round of shots. One of them has a birthday candle sitting in whipped cream, and everyone around sings "Happy Birthday." I'm mildly embarrassed, but I'll admit that I'm having a good time.

And slowly … I feel like I can release the breath I think I've been holding since Liam got to New York.

I laugh and dance with my sister and our friends. I let myself exist for a moment outside the bubble of being a mom, and all the weight of Liam and the what-ifs.

By drink number three, I'm not exactly drunk. But definitely tipsy enough that my emotions are sitting a little too close to the surface.

Presley leans in when we get back to the table from the bar. "Have you talked to him?"

"Who?"

"Liam, dummy."

I shake my head. "No. And I also texted Aaron and told him about Liam's reaction, and he's not responding. I thought about calling him, but honestly, I just don't know if I can hear his explanation right now."

"Ugh." She rolls her eyes. "I can't even tell you how pissed off I am at Aaron. Do you want to know what I think?"

I raise my eyebrow. "I don't know, do I?"

"Of course you do." She brushes her long hair over her shoulder. "I think Aaron's in love with you. And I think he thought he'd just … get Liam out of the way and pretend to be the hero."

I shake my head. "No, he's not in love with me. We're just friends."

At least that's what I'm telling myself because if I even consider what she's saying to be true, I've been betrayed by my best friend in the worst possible way.

"I'm right, Al." She nods. "But I think you should talk to Liam."

"I texted him, and he didn't reply."

"When?"

"The day it happened." I lift a shoulder.

"Aliette Grant. Once?"

"Yeah. And he's definitely avoiding me at the complex. I know he's been there, but it's like he slips in and out before anyone can see him."

"I've seen him." She smirks.

"Well then, maybe you should talk to him."

She just laughs at the edge in my tone.

"Seriously though, do you want to talk to him?" She watches me carefully.

I stare at my glass.

"Yes … " I answer before I can even stop myself.

Because the truth is, I don't want things to end like this. With him walking out of my office, angry.

I don't want a bitter, contentious relationship with him. It wouldn't be good for Sera, and it wouldn't be good for the team.

I want to know that I tried. And I don't want Sera's father to be someone I never fought for. At least to see if we could make something work. Even if it's just between them.

I set my glass down and take a deep breath.

"I think … I need some air." I slide out of the booth.

"Alie … " Presley eyes me.

"I'm fine," I assure her. "I just need some air. Go dance with the girls. I'll come find you when I come back inside."

I give her a faint smile, then turn and walk away. I can feel her eyes on me as I go.

And the minute I step outside, I already know where I'm going.

• • •

The ride to his apartment is a blur, and before I know it, I'm standing in front of his building.

When I walk in, there's a doorman sitting at a desk.

"Hi." I clear my throat. "I'm here to see Liam Pitz."

"Your name?"

"Alie Grant."

He picks up the phone and dials.

"Mr. Pitz, there's an Alie Grant here to see you." He pauses. "Yes, sir, I'll send her up."

"Thank you." I nod when he gestures toward the elevator.

On my way up to his floor, I think about what I'm going to say to him, and before I can put any thoughts together, I'm standing in front of his door.

My heart is hammering, my nerves buzzing from the alcohol and all the angst from the last few days.

Then the elevator door opens, and Liam is standing in his doorway, wearing gym shorts low on his hips, no shirt, and bare feet. His hair is slightly messy, like he's been running his hands through it.

Christ on a cracker. He is gorgeous. Without even freaking trying. His brows lift high on his forehead, then draw together, confusion chasing the shock. His chest stills mid-breath.

Like he forgot how to inhale.

"Alie?"

"Hi," I say, a little breathless.

"You're … here."

He studies me carefully, eyes squinting as they roam over my body.

I step out of the elevator.

"Have you been drinking?"

"Just a little."

I shift on my feet, starting to feel uncomfortable under his stare.

"Sorry, I shouldn't have come," I say and start to turn.

"Alie." He grabs my arm to stop me.

When I look at him, his jaw tightens.

"I'm sorry," I blurt out. "A few days ago, I thought you were the bad guy. I'm not entirely sure how it all happened the way it did, but I know from the sheer look on your face that I was wrong. I know I hurt you. I hate that I let my fears dictate what I thought about you that morning I left. I hate that I didn't have the courage to tell you about the pregnancy myself. I hate that I trusted Aaron with the most important phone call of my life. I hate that I didn't give us a chance. But mostly, I really hate that the first moment you saw her was like … that."

His expression shifts; anger still lingers, but there's something softer underneath.

"I didn't come here to fight." I hang my head. "You didn't answer my text, and I just needed to see you. I …" I swallow, knowing that I've had too much to drink and I'm laying myself bare, but I don't care. "I needed to be with you."

I hear him exhale slowly, long and controlled, like he's forcing the air out of his lungs. His shoulders rise and fall with it, and his jaw shifts to the side, muscle ticcing, but his eyes never leave mine.

Like everything, he's thinking is pressing against the inside of his ribs, and he's determined not to let it spill out too fast.

"You showing up here tipsy and in this tiny dress isn't exactly helping."

I blink up at him. "You like my dress?" My teeth skim my bottom lip as I look up at him. "That's good to know because it's my birthday, and I'm pretty sure bad decisions are allowed."

"It's your birthday?" he asks, surprised.

I look up at him and nod.

He looks away from me, dragging in a deep breath through his nose. When he finally looks back at me, his eyes are darker. Focused. No longer surprised—just intensely aware.

"Come inside," he says quietly.

I walk in and look around. I'm not sure what I was expecting, but it's clean and simple. And then I see them on the counter. The ornaments we got from the street vendor from our night together.

I pick up the apple ornament, letting it spin on the string.

"You kept these?"

He doesn't answer right away, so I look up at him, still holding the ornament like it's a prize. His hands are on his hips, and his head is down.

"You had a souvenir from that night. These are mine."

He walks past me toward the couch and sits down heavily.

I stay where I am, not really sure where to go.

"A few days ago, you might have thought I was the bad guy, but a few days ago, I was still reeling from losing the woman of my dreams. I'd been thinking about you, wondering where you'd been. The last thing I'd have ever believed was that you had my baby. So, although you showed up here, looking like sin in a dress … I can't stop thinking about what I missed. Two years, Alie." He leans forward and props his elbows on his knees. "I missed two years."

My chest tightens. "I know."

"I should have been there."

I set the ornament down and take a step toward him. "I know."

"I don't even know what her favorite food is. Or her favorite color. What makes her happy … "

My throat tightens, thick and sudden. "Strawberries and dinosaur mac n' cheese. Her favorite color is blue, but she always asks for things that are pink."

He lets out a shaky breath. "I'm so fucking angry with you, Alie."

"I know."

"But I'm also"—he pauses—"fucking terrified."

"Of what?"

"How much I already care for a little girl I don't even know."

That hits me straight in the heart.

"If I could do this differently, I would. But I can't, and I have to live with that." I sniff, pressing my fingers to the corner of my eye before anything spills over.

"Knowing I hurt you this way ..." My voice falters. "And knowing I took something from her ..." I swallow hard because that's the part that sits like a stone in my chest.

"She deserved those first two years with her dad. The midnight feedings. The first steps. The first time she said a word that sounded like anything close to Daddy." My throat tightens around it. "And I'd made a decision that erased that."

The guilt is constant. Quiet some days. Crushing on others.

"I told myself I was protecting her," I whisper. "Protecting us."

I look at him then, forcing myself not to look away.

"I can live with you being angry with me," I say softly. "I don't know how to live with the idea that I stole time from my own child."

The silence between us is heavy.

"Well, you're here now."

"Yes," I say quietly.

"And you're looking at me like you just expect me to what, forgive you?"

"I don't expect anything." I spread my arms. "I just wanted to see you. I *needed* to see you. To explain."

Our eyes lock, and all the anger, hurt ... and attraction, still burns.

He stands and steps closer to me.

"Do you have any idea how hard it's been to keep myself from seeing you?" his voice rumbles.

I suck in a breath. "Probably as hard as it's been for me to not come down to the locker room to see you."

We're inches apart now.

"Liam ... " I pause. "Maybe this was a bad idea, me coming here tonight."

"Probably."

"You're still mad at me."

"Very."

I still. "Right. Okay."

But neither of us moves away. Instead, his hand slides to my jaw, fingers warm on my cheek.

"You drive me insane," he says.

"But I showed up at your door to figure this out," I counter softly.

"Yeah," he admits, "you did."

And then he kisses me.

This kiss isn't soft. It's frustrated and a bit desperate. And full of everything that still needs to be said.

My hands grip his shirt like I'm afraid he'll disappear if I let go.

His arms wrap around my waist, and he pulls me in closer.

"You hurt me. Not once, but twice," he says against my lips.

"I'm sorry," I whisper.

"Don't disappear again, Alie. No matter what."

"I won't." And I mean it.

No matter what happens between the two of us, I won't because of Seraphina.

The next kiss is deeper. Hotter, messier. And neither of us stops it.

The distance to the bedroom disappears in a blur of hands and unfinished sentences, the tension between us finally snapping under the weight of everything we've been holding back.

When we get into the room, he turns me and presses the front of his body against my back, his hands at my waist. His grip is firm, and he tugs me back into him so I can feel his erection.

"I'm not fucking you tonight."

I lean my head back against his shoulder, raising my arms and winding them around his neck.

"Okay," I whisper. "Yeah, we probably shouldn't."

He brings his mouth to my neck, trailing kisses from my ear

to my jaw. I turn my head, and he traces my lips with the tip of his tongue. I open with a moan, and our tongues tangle. His hands slide up my slides and he cups my breasts over my thin dress. Then he pinches my nipples, which makes me break the kiss with a gasp.

"I'm not fucking you, but I am going to make you come." He rolls my nub between his fingers. "Happy birthday."

"Liam … " I moan when he pulls on my nipple and runs his tongue from my neck to my mouth.

His hands move from my chest to my stomach. "If you don't want this, just say the word, and I'll stop right now."

I shake my head. "Don't you dare stop."

He kisses me again, deeper this time, and as he does, I glide my fingers up the back of his head, through his hair, holding him to me. His hands move to the bottom of my short dress, and his fingers skim along the inside of my thighs.

When he reaches my center, he moves the thin strap of my lacy thong to the side.

"Is this all for me?" He slides his middle finger up and down my center.

I haven't been touched like this since our night together. The sensation is overwhelming, and I can't find words, so I just nod.

"Fuck. You're so wet."

I should be embarrassed by the obvious sound of my arousal, but I'm not.

Instead, my body feels like it's on fire. And I don't want this feeling to end.

Liam's hand falls. "Turn around."

So, I do.

He takes hold of the hem of my dress and fists it in his hands. Almost like he's going to rip it right off of me, but he doesn't take it off.

My palms smooth over the muscles on his warm chest. Then I make my way to the edge of the waistband of his shorts, noticing he's not wearing any boxers. Slowly, I reach inside and take hold of his erection.

All rational thought flees my mind as I stroke him.

He swallows and closes his eyes for a minute.

I pull my hand out long enough to take the sides of his shorts and pull them down his legs. I kneel in front of him. His cock is thick and hard and right in front of my face. I have to get my mouth on him. I slide my hands up his legs and wrap one around his thigh before moving it up to his ass and the other around his cock.

I lick the crown first, tasting him. He groans as I wrap my mouth around the head, then take him deep to the back of my throat. I gag, so I pull back, but keep his cock in my mouth.

"Alie, fuck."

I look up through watery eyes and see him looking down at me. I see heat, desire, and something else I can't name right now. He sweeps my hair into his hand, tugging, then starts rocking his hips with the rhythm of my mouth.

I'm so turned on by him, by this, that I can feel my slickness along the inside of my thighs.

Pausing, I look up at him and hold my hand out. "Spit."

"Jesus, Alie. You're gonna kill me."

He spits into my palm, and then I wrap it around his shaft, coating him as I run my hand up and down. Then I lick up his length to the tip, then wrap my lips around the crown and suck.

"Come here." He releases my hair, then reaches under my arms and pulls me up.

Then he sits on the edge of the bed, and he slowly pulls the ties on the straps of the dress, making it fall and pool at my feet. "You're so beautiful. Just like I remember. And I fucking love that you're not wearing a bra."

"Doesn't work with this dress," I pant.

He kisses across my stomach, then up to my breasts, twirling his tongue around my nipple, making it pebble even more than it already was.

Then he releases me and scoots back to the middle of the bed.

He holds his hand out to me, so I climb on and straddle him.

His hands grasp my waist. "Come sit on my face. I need to taste you."

"Okay," I say, voice husky to my own ears.

I reposition myself so my knees are on either side of his head.

He grabs my waist and pulls me to his mouth. Then he leans in and swipes his tongue through my center, oh so slowly. "I love the way you taste. I've never forgotten." He flicks my clit with the tip of his tongue and slides a finger into me.

"Wait, I want to make you feel good too."

I move to his side and turn my body, repositioning myself over his head. Taking hold of his dick with one hand, I spit on his cock, then slide my hand up and down his shaft.

"I love the way you feel in my mouth," I say, then wrap my lips around the head and suck, making his hips buck.

He pulls my hips back down to his mouth, and he circles my clit with his tongue as two fingers slip inside my pussy.

We find a rhythm together, and it's not going to take long for me to erupt. My body feels hot all over, my heartbeat pounding in my chest. The feel of his tongue and fingers inside me and tasting his salty pre-cum in my mouth ... it's almost too much. A tingling sensation spreads through me, and my pussy starts to contract around his fingers. I release his dick with a pop, but I don't stop stroking him.

When I moan, he pumps his fingers in and out of me, and then he sucks hard on my clit, making me come. Then, before I can catch my breath, ropes of cum hit me on my chin and chest. It's so fucking hot that another orgasm rushes through me.

His hands move to my thighs, and he holds me gently. "You, okay?"

I nod, trying to speak. "I'm more than okay."

But I'm also a mess now, and I need to go clean up. So, I lift off of him and shift to the side.

"I just need to go clean up a little." I turn to look at him and smile.

"Come here first." He pats the bed next to him.

I lean toward him, and he runs a finger through his cum—from my chest to my chin, then into my mouth.

I take hold of his hand and suck on the finger in my mouth, looking him in the eye while I do it.

"Fuck," he whispers. "You're so fucking sexy."

I twirl my tongue around his finger and slowly pull it out of my mouth.

"Be right back." I get off the bed, then go clean up in the bathroom.

When I get back to the bed, I lie beside him, my heart still racing, now for a different reason. I'm not sure what to say or do now. So, I just rest my head next to his, curling into his side. I absent-mindedly start tracing patterns across his chest.

He's quiet, but not distant. More like he's lost in thought.

"What do we do now?" I whisper.

He exhales slowly. "Now," he says, voice rough but steady. "I meet my daughter the right way."

Tears fill my eyes. "Okay."

He tips my chin, forcing me to look at him. "What we just did doesn't erase the anger or hurt. It's going to take me some time. But, we'll figure this out."

It's a promise, but I know we haven't reached forgiveness yet. I see it in his eyes.

But it does feel like something real. And for the first time since he walked out of my office, I feel like everything might just be okay.

CHAPTER TWENTY-ONE

LIAM

As much as I wanted her to spend the night, I thought we both needed some time to process what to do next. And she wanted to get home so she could get Seraphina early in the morning.

But I haven't been able to sleep at all since she left.

Not because of what happened between us, but because of what comes next.

Meeting her. Seraphina. My daughter.

The word still feels unreal in my head. Like something I'm afraid to touch, in fear that it will disappear.

I stare at the ceiling, thinking of her sitting on Alie's office floor—tiny sneakers, crayons, a smile that could light up a room.

Two years.

A little life I didn't know existed.

As the sun comes up through my window, I know today is the day. I need to meet her today. I'm not waiting any longer to meet my little girl.

I pick up my phone what feels like every ten minutes. Just waiting for a decent time to text Alie.

By eight, I can't wait anymore. I feel like I'm crawling out of my skin as I pace around my kitchen.

Liam: Hey. Are you free today?

The reply comes a few minutes later.

Alie: Yes. You want to meet her today?

Liam: I do.

Three dots appear.
Then disappear.
Then return.

Alie: Okay, we can do that. Can you come by around noon?

My heart kicks up instantly.

Liam: Your place?

Alie: Yes, I think that would be best.

Liam: I'll be there.

Alie: I'll send a car for you.

Liam: I can get my own ride.

Alie: No, it's okay. I promise it's not a problem.

Liam: Okay, I'll see you then.

I set my phone on the counter and take a deep breath. I've never been more nervous in my life.

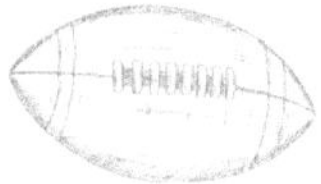

By the time the driver pulls up to one of the fanciest buildings I've ever seen, my hands are aching from clenching them so hard.

I've played championships in front of eighty thousand people. I've handled critics and press conferences after tough losses. I've signed life-changing contracts.

But none of that compares to this.

I sit in the car for a minute and stare at the building.

"Sir." The driver holding the door for me prompts.

"Right, sorry." I climb out and straighten my shorts and shirt.

When I walk in, I take in the ambiance. I imagine what my little girl sees when she walks through here every day. But I guess this is all she's known, so to her, it's just home.

The doorman guides me to where I'm supposed to go, and then I'm on my way up to Alie and Sera.

I inhale a deep breath in the elevator. *You can do this.*

As I exit, I see Alie standing against the wall in shorts and a short-sleeved sweater. She looks as nervous as I feel when her eyes meet mine.

"Hi. Reggie, my doorman, called and told me you were here." She smiles softly.

"Ah, okay." I nod.

"Come on." She holds her hand out to me.

I take hers in mine, and we walk down the short hallway.

The door is cracked open, and when we walk in, Alie drops my hand.

I look around, noticing the cozy feel of their home. It smells like clean laundry and cookies.

Then I hear a tiny voice say, "Mommy?"

My chest tightens.

"I'm right here, baby," Alie says.

Small footsteps sound, and then she appears.

She's holding a stuffed football, her hair is slightly messy, and she's wearing leggings and a T-shirt that has some Disney princess on it.

When she sees me, she stops in her tracks. Her eyes are wide, but not like she's scared. More like curious and assessing.

"Sera, this is my friend, Liam," Alie says, gently.

She tilts her head. "Hi."

My throat goes dry.

"Hi," I manage to squeak out.

She's real and mine. And I have no idea what to do. I always thought I was good with kids. I can handle Archie and Emma's like a champ, but I'm completely lost right now.

Sera walks closer to me, slow but confident. Not afraid. More like she's trying to decide if I'm interesting enough.

"You tall." She points at me.

Alie laughs. "He is tall, yes."

I crouch down instinctively so I'm closer to her level.

"Yeah," I say. "I guess I am pretty tall."

She studies my face.

"You play football?" she asks.

My chest pinches.

"I do." Christ, why can't I say more than two words at a time?

"I wuv football. I watch Twitans," she says proudly.

"Titans, baby," Alie corrects.

"Poppy's team." She smiles.

"That's right; it is." I nod.

Sera looks at my hands, my shoes, then back at my face.

"You pway with us?"

The innocence of her questions hits like a punch.

I glance at Alie. She just smiles.

"I do. I'm the quarterback for the Titans now," I explain.

She seems satisfied with my answer.

"See my room?"

I laugh shakily. "Yeah, I'd love to."

She holds out her little hand to me, and it nearly does me in. I look at Alie, and she nods, encouraging me.

We walk hand in hand to her room, and it's the biggest kids' room I've ever seen. Chaotic in the best way, with stuffed animals, crayons, books, and dolls. And very pink.

Sera sits on the floor and starts talking a mile a minute.

"This bunny Luna. This my book. This my horse," she says, holding up a drawing of what looks like a possible horse.

I sit cross-legged on the floor, listening like each word matters more than anything else in the world. And it does because I missed all these little moments. But I'm here now, and that realization hits me hard enough that I have to take a breath to steady myself.

Suddenly, Sera crawls into my lap, like she's done it a hundred times.

"Read," she says, holding out a book to me.

I look over at Alie, who just smiles a little tearfully.

"She loves that one."

So, I read. And my voice shakes a little at first, but Sera doesn't notice. She just leans back against me, completely comfortable, flipping pages and pointing at pictures. Like I've always been here.

A while later, Sera's in the living room watching a cartoon, and Alie takes me into the kitchen.

We stand there quietly for a second, watching Seraphina.

"Well?" she asks. "How are you doing with this?"

I exhale slowly. "She's … incredible."

Alie smiles through watery eyes. "Yeah, she is."

I shake my head slightly, overwhelmed. "I don't know how I missed two years of that."

Guilt flickers across her face. "Liam—"

"I'm not here to fight today," I say gently. "I just … want to figure out how to be here now."

Relief floods her expression. "I want that too," she whispers.

I glance back toward the living room, where Sera's laugh bubbles at something on the screen.

"She hugged me," I say quietly.

"I would say she likes you." Alie sets a hand on my arm.

"Thanks for letting me come over today." I cover her hand with mine.

"Of course."

I drop my hand, but wrap my arms around her waist, burying my head in her neck.

"I just can't even tell you how I'm feeling right now."

"I know," she says, sounding a little choked up too. "It's the same for me, but in a different way. I've been doing this on my own, and now you're here."

I pull away and look at her face. "I'm not going anywhere, just so we're clear."

"Okay." She nods.

"We'll figure out what works for her in terms of getting to know me. I'll let you set the pace, but I want her to know I'm her dad. Soon, Alie."

She nods and swallows. "Okay, I agree. She needs to know you're her dad."

"And I want to see her as much as I can."

"I understand. I will need to tell my parents, too, so we'll need to decide how to handle that."

"Do you want me to do it with you? I would like to be there. I don't want them to think I abandoned her."

"Let me think about it. It might be best for me to handle that alone first."

"Alie," I start to argue.

"Let's enjoy our day, and I'll come up with a plan and let you know."

I look at her for a minute, assessing. "Okay, but that's a conversation that needs to happen immediately."

"You're right, and I will."

"Mommy," Sera calls from the other room. "Lunchtime?"

"I'm working on it now," Alie answers.

"I want nugs."

"Dinosaur nuggets?" I ask Alie.

"Yep. We'll eat something else; don't worry. I had some sandwiches delivered before you came."

"Thanks." I turn, looking at my daughter.

She takes a drink from her sippy cup, then looks over her shoulder and sees me. Her little hand lifts, and she waves with a toothy smile.

And when our eyes lock, I feel like time stops. She has my eyes. They're brown, and her lashes are long. Same sharp assessment in the way she looks at people, like she's trying to figure out who they are.

I feel like I'm looking in a mirror.

"Time for lunch," Alie calls from behind me.

Sera hops up and rushes over to us. Alie lifts her and puts her into a booster chair at the table, and I see her kicking her little feet back and forth, like she's got nowhere else she'd rather be.

I take a seat across from her, and I'm captivated by this little ball of energy.

She talks in determined toddler half words as she picks up a nugget, dipping it in some kind of yellow sauce.

When she finishes eating one whole nugget, she lifts up her little arms above her head and claps.

"Bite one down. See?"

"I see," I say, leaning forward in my seat like this is the most important play of my career.

She beams, and in that moment, something in my chest caves in. Because that smile was for me. And I know without a doubt that I would burn the world down for her.

"Good job, Sera. Now eat the other ones on your plate," Alie instructs.

I look between them. The love clear on their faces. And instead of jealousy for missing out on all these moments, I feel … content, peaceful. Because I know that even though I wasn't here, this little girl of mine has been loved and cherished.

She dips another nugget into the sauce, and some of it drips on to her shirt while she lifts it to her mouth.

"Uh-oh, Mommy."

Alie reaches for a napkin at the same time I do, and our fingers touch. She looks at me and smiles in offering, but I pull my hand back. I'm not sure if Sera would want me to help yet.

So, I watch as she tries to help her mom clean her shirt, only to make a much bigger mess, making me laugh before I can stop it.

She freezes and looks at me. Then she starts laughing, too, and I'm done for.

After she's cleaned up—the best Alie can get her anyway—we finish our lunch, listening to Sera tell me about her favorite color, her school, and her eyes light up when she asks me about football.

So, I talk to her about throwing the ball to different players in the easiest way I can explain my job. And she just stares at me the whole time, like what I'm saying is the best thing ever.

Once she finishes her last nugget, she starts to rub her eyes.

"I think someone is ready for a rest." Alie stands and starts to clear the table.

"No nap, Mommy." She pouts.

"Yes, you need to rest just for a little bit because we have to go to Mimi and Poppy's later for dinner."

"Oh, cake!"

"Yes, we'll have cake for my birthday."

Taking this as my cue to leave, I stand and join Alie in the kitchen to help clean up.

"I got this," she says, trying to wave me off.

"I like helping." I look down at her and smile. "Thanks for lunch."

"Of course."

"Mommy, down."

I look over at Seraphina, and she's wiggling in her seat.

"Go ahead. I'll finish cleaning this up," I say, nodding toward Sera.

"Thanks," she says, smiling.

I take care of the dishes and trash, then meet them in the family room.

As much as I would love to stay and just be near her—and if I'm honest, Alie too—I think it's time for me to go.

Sera wiggles out of Alie's arms and over to me.

"You come back?" She looks up at me with her big brown eyes.

"Yeah," I say. "If that's okay with you."

She nods enthusiastically. "Yes, we play football."

I can't help but laugh, and I look over at Alie, who's watching us, eyes a little watery.

"We can absolutely do that the next time I see you."

"Sera, you'll get to see Liam on the field at practice on Monday."

Sera claps her hands. "Yay!"

I look at Alie. "She will?"

"Yeah, she'll be with me while I'm working. She likes all the pictures and drones and the snacks that all the players sneak to her." She winks at Sera, who giggles.

I nod. "Good. Then I'll see you both then."

Sera walks over to me and wraps her arms around my leg, like it's the most normal thing in the world.

Shocked, I look at Alie for guidance, and she nods with a smile.

I squat down, breaking her hold on me, but before she can move away, I open my arms in invitation. She dives into me, almost knocking me off-balance.

"Oof, you're strong," I tease.

She giggles the sweetest sound. "Bye," she says, then releases her hold around me.

I swallow hard.

"Bye, Seraphina," I say as she skips away to the couch.

Alie walks me to the door, and we stand there quietly, just looking at one another.

"You were really great with her," she says softly.

I shake my head. "I feel like I have no idea what I'm doing."

"None of us do." She shrugs. "We just figure it out."

"Right." I nod.

"I'll talk to you later?"

"Yeah, that would be nice." I lean down and kiss her cheek.

Then, with one last look over Alie's shoulder, I see Sera watching us carefully, a stuffed football in her hands.

I wave at her, and she waves back with a smile.

Something settles deep in me. It's not fear, or anger, but something … steadier and protective. And I can't wait to see them both again.

CHAPTER TWENTY-TWO

LIAM

Monday rolls around, and it's media day. The facility feels louder. Even from the outside.

More … alive. Almost like game days.

The buzz in the air hits me the second I walk through the doors. Cameras. Staff running around. Equipment carts loaded with jerseys and banners.

It's a controlled type of chaos that I typically thrive in.

I nod to people as I make my way through the traffic and head down to the locker room. Before I even open the door, I can hear Aston Griffith.

"They seriously can't expect me to smile for a hundred photos without being properly caffeinated," he says loudly in his thick Texas accent.

I can't help but smile as I walk into the room.

Aston is leaning against his station like the room exists solely for his commentary. He might be a rookie, but he'll be one of our starting defensive players this year. He's a walking highlight reel. Equal parts talent, ego, and charm.

When he spots me, a huge grin spreads across his face. "There he is. Mr. Prime Time."

"Don't start." I laugh, shaking my head.

"Too late. What's got you all smiley this morning?" He walks to me and gives me a hug.

"I'm not extra smiley. Same as always."

"Uh, you sure it doesn't have something to do with a particular lady?"

I lean in, whispering, "What are you talking about?"

"I mean"—he lowers his voice—"I think there's something you need to tell me."

Shit. What did Archie tell him?

I called Archie last night to tell him about Seraphina. He was shocked and angry on my behalf for the time I missed, but he's really happy for me, and he wants to come meet them both soon.

And because the Griffiths all talk on a daily basis, I have to assume Archie told them all the news. And I don't mind; everyone will know soon enough. I just … need to do this the right way.

"I don't have anything to tell you." I shrug.

He smirks. "Okay, sure."

Before I can respond, our defensive captain, Wyatt St. Clair—otherwise known as Saint—tosses a towel at Aston's head.

"Save the gossip for after practice, Griffith," he says. "We need to be on the field in ten."

Saint is a steady kind of guy and built like a brick wall. A true leader on and off the field. He's the perfect balance for Aston's personality.

"Pitz," he says, holding his hand out to me, smirking. "Glad you could make it, man."

"Thanks." I shake his hand, smiling. "Don't think I had the option to miss it."

Behind him, one of our tight ends, Brody Vaughn, jogs over, and we also shake hands.

"Media team is already out there," he says. "They have the drones flying."

"Gotta love the aerial shots." I smirk.

"I do. Any angle of me, though, is prime," Aston chimes in.

We all laugh, and I shake my head. It's going to be fun playing with him this year. But it does make me miss Archie more than ever.

A few minutes later, I make my way onto the practice field.

Staffers move between camera set ups. Media directs us where to go. Sponsor reps hover like nervous parents at the first game of the season.

And over near the sideline …

Alie and Seraphina.

She's standing with a clipboard in her hand, talking to Presley and someone wearing a headset, completely in command, while Sera tosses a football into the air, letting it drop, only to pick it up again.

My chest tightens, and I have to fight the urge to run over to her and pick her up, then kiss her mom.

Aston walks over to me and follows my gaze. "Is that her?"

"Aston, not now."

"She's why you're all smiley, isn't she?" he chides.

"I'm not smiley."

"Yeah, you are." He bumps my shoulder with his.

"Shut up." I bite back a smile.

He grins. "I'm just fucking with you."

A whistle blows, and we're directed to an area where some of our coaches are standing.

"All right, listen up!" Coach shouts. "Quick run-through for the media scrimmage. Nothing fancy. Keep it clean. Show some energy. And for the love of football, no one say anything dumb on camera."

"Define *dumb,*" someone says.

"Anything you say without thinking."

"So, I guess I should keep my mouth shut then." Aston snickers.

Laughter ripples around us.

Even Coach fights a smile.

The scrimmage is light, mostly for show and photos. Once the ball is in play though, my instincts kick in, and it's hard to keep it casual.

Noise hums around us, and cameras flash.

At the first snap, I see Saint across from me, calling the defense, following my moves.

I take the handoff and fake right, roll left, then scan the field.

Brody's running down the field, double coverage trailing him, like they already know he's gonna be trouble.

I launch the ball into the air, creating the perfect arc.

He jumps, snags it in a one-handed catch, and lands on his feet like he planned the play just like this.

Brody makes a show of spinning the ball on the turf and walks over to one of the cameramen. "That's how you do it, boys."

I shake my head and laugh.

When I look over toward the sideline, I see Alie standing there smiling. Not a professional, work-mode smile. A real one.

And, yeah, that's enough to throw my concentration for the next play.

Thirty minutes later, we wrap up on the field and start to rotate through interviews.

When I finish mine, I walk over to the hydration station and grab a bottle of electrolytes.

I look to my left and see Presley reprimanding—politely but firmly—one of the rookie players who got a little rowdy on the field.

Presley seems to be really good at her job. She's smart and organized, and she isn't intimidated in the least by anyone, let alone the players. But more than that ... she really seems to care about our well-being.

I notice Saint walk up behind her, listening in on her conversation with the rookie.

He's calm while she talks, his arms folded over his chest. Watching her with a quiet amusement that suggests he's enjoying this more than he should be.

She finishes her point, turns, and nearly runs right into Saint.

"Oh, sorry." She places her hands on his chest.

"You're good," he says, voice low and steady.

"Did you need something?" She steps back.

"Nope. Just making sure no one steamrolls our schedule today."

"Uh-huh." Presley looks at him skeptically. "Right, well, stay hydrated."

"Will do, Doc," he says, smiling.

The way he says it makes her pause, but she doesn't turn around.

Aston walks up and leans in. "Well, well, well."

"You see that too?" I murmur.

"Oh, I absolutely saw it." He laughs and rubs his hands together.

"She looked a little flustered when she walked away, yeah?"

"That she did, Pitzy."

I smack his chest. "Okay, show's over. Let's head inside."

When we get back into the building, I immediately see Alie. She's bent down in front of Sera, wiping something off her face.

When her eyes meet mine, a spark flashes. Then she stands and clears her throat.

"Liam," she says evenly. "You're up for sponsorship photos in five."

I smile and nod.

"Hi, Liam." Sera jumps up and down.

I bend down. "Hi, sweetheart. You having fun today?"

"Oh, yes. Football all day."

"I saw you with that ball earlier. I'd better watch out, or you'll take my job." I tip my head to her and smile.

She giggles and covers her mouth with her small hand.

Next to me, Aston nearly chokes, trying not to snicker.

Alie clears her throat and glances at him. "You too, Griffith."

He straightens. "Yes, ma'am."

"I'll see you later?" I stand and look at Alie.

She gives me a subtle nod, and as we pass by her, her fingers brush mine for a half second.

No one would notice if they weren't watching us closely.

But it's enough to send a rush right through me because even though we have a lot to work out, I still want her.

Jesus, I feel like a hormonal teenager who can't control himself. I need to get ahold of this. I can't be walking around her all the time, half-cocked and confused. And definitely not in front of our daughter.

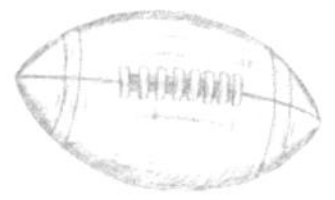

After photos and more interviews, I head back to the locker room.

Most of the guys are in there already, changing or packing up.

I see Saint sitting at his station with an ice pack wrapped around his knee.

"You good?" I point at the ice.

"Oh, yeah. Doc just wants me to ice it after workouts. I had that surgery on my ACL at the end of last season."

"That's right. How's the recovery going?"

"Right as rain." He smiles.

"Glad to hear it. We need you out there healthy."

"I'm primed and ready."

Next to me, Brody texts with someone.

Then our veteran kicker, Caleb Brooks, walks in like he owns the place.

"You boys looked quite photogenic out there today," Caleb says.

"Because we *are* photogenic," Aston replies.

Saint shakes his head. "One day, that ego of yours is gonna need its own locker."

"Already does. The one next to you taken?" Aston jokes.

Brody looks between us. "He always like this?"

"Pretty much. But you should see his twin," I say, laughing.

"Right. I forgot Ace Griffith was his twin."

"Yep. The whole family is like that though." I smile. "But I love 'em all."

"You played with Archie, right?" Saint asks.

"I did. He's my best friend."

"Solid." He nods and starts taking his ice off.

I glance around at my new team. This group … it feels like something that could be special. Makes me anxious to get the season started.

But for now, we prep.

I finish packing up the few things I brought in with me today and say my goodbyes.

As I walk through the building, I catch another glimpse of Alie, but no sign of Sera.

She's laughing at something Presley said, seeming much more casual than she was earlier.

I notice Saint walk toward her, but he stops and talks to one of the trainers. I don't miss his eyes flicking over to Presley.

Very interesting. Looks like Presley might have a little secret.

Aston slings his bag over his shoulder as he comes up behind me, wearing a cowboy hat.

"You heading out?" he asks.

"Yeah. You?"

He nods. "You got any dinner plans?"

I pause and look over at Alie. "Not tonight, no."

Aston smirks. "Okay, buddy. Come by, and I'll show you my place before we eat."

"You here in Jersey or the city?"

"Here. You know I'm not a city boy. I need to have space." He tips his hat and winks.

"Right. I'll text you later when I'm on my way."

He walks away and holds his hand in the air in goodbye.

With one last look at Alie, I walk out of the building into the late afternoon sun.

As I make my way over to the car, where Joey is waiting for me, one thing is clear to me: this season isn't just about football anymore.

CHAPTER TWENTY-THREE

ALIE

The week went by in a blur, but I talked to Liam every day, and he ate lunch with Sera and me on the days he was at the facility.

My parents had to take a quick trip to Florida, so it's been easier to quietly navigate this situation without feeling like we're under a microscope. But I'll need to tell them when they get back. Liam wants them to know, and I know it's time.

Yesterday, Liam asked if we could do something as a family so he could spend some more time with her—or I guess … us. So, we planned to go to Central Park today.

I overthink every little thing while we wait for him to come get us.

What should Sera wear?

What if a sudden cold snap comes through?

How many snacks should I bring?

Is this too soon?

Is this too much?

Is this the moment that makes everything work or crack?

By the time Liam knocks on my door, I've rearranged Sera's backpack three times and changed my own outfit twice.

Sera beats me to the door, her tiny sneakers tapping excitedly on the floor. "Liam here?" She asks.

My heart does this strange, fragile twist that's one part hope and the other … fear.

"Let's see," I say, opening the door.

Liam stands there, looking confident and sure. And holding a small stuffed horse.

"For Sera," he says, bending down to present it to her.

"I wuv howses!" She snatches it out of his hand.

"Sera, what do you say?"

"Thank you, Liam." She beams up at him.

"That's a special horse for a special girl. It came from Oklahoma, from where I used to play football. It's a Walker Stallion."

"I wuv it!" She bounces.

"You'll give it lots of hugs?" he asks her.

"Lots." She squeezes it to her.

Warmth fills me, and all the nerves I was feeling fade away when I watch them together.

"Ready for the park?" he asks her, then looks at me.

She nods excitedly. "Park! Slides! Ducks!"

I grab her backpack and take one last look inside, making sure I have everything we might need.

"Let's leave your horse here so it doesn't get lost at the park." I take it from her and set it on the table near the door.

"You sure Central Park isn't too crowded today?" he asks, unsure.

I shrug. "It's New York. Everywhere is crowded outside, especially when the weather is nice like this."

"Okay then."

"We'll stick to the quieter side if we can."

"Sounds good to me." He reaches for the backpack. "Let me take this."

I'm not gonna argue, so I hand it over to him. "Thanks."

We walk out, and I lock the door.

When we get into the elevator, Sera stands between us and takes both of our hands. I look over at Liam, and from the way he's smiling, you would think Sera just hung the moon.

This all feels too easy. Too comfortable.

Like this is how it always should have been.

And a rush of regret hits me because I wish more than anything that it had been this way from the beginning.

Central Park is indeed alive today. Kids laughing and running around. Dogs barking. Musicians playing. The smell of pretzels and nuts drift in the air.

Sera's eyes go wide the second we step on the path leading to the playground.

Liam crouches beside her. "You want to race to the swings?"

"Yes!"

"Should we let Mommy get a head start?"

"Hey." I put my hands on my hips.

Sera giggles, and Liam winks.

"Ready … set … go!" he yells.

She toddles forward, determined, and he jogs beside her, cheering like she's winning an actual race.

I follow behind them, watching the way he adjusts his stride to hers. Then the way he claps when we reach the playground. And the way he looks at her like she's the most important thing in the world.

Sera makes a beeline for the slide.

"Up!" She points to the stairs.

Liam looks at me. "You good with this?"

I laugh softly. "I think she's safe."

"Okay," he says, lifting her and setting her on his shoulder. "Let's do this."

He climbs up the stairs with her, then sets her at the top of the slide.

"You good?" he asks her.

She looks back at him, huge smile on her face. "Watch me go!"

"I'm watching," he says, smiling.

She slides down, squealing.

I'm waiting at the bottom to catch her. Again. And again.

By the fourth time, he's laughing. Then by the sixth time, he's completely wrapped around her finger. And by the eighth time, I realize I'm smiling so much that my cheeks hurt.

Eventually, we make our way to the pond, and Sera runs off to terrorize some ducks.

Liam and I sit on a nearby bench, close enough to watch her, but far enough that she can't hear our words.

"She's fearless," he says with pride.

"That she is."

"I think she gets that from me." He winks at me.

"Oh, yeah?" I smile.

"Definitely." He nods.

We watch Sera chase ducks, giggling when they waddle close to her.

"She's pretty amazing," Liam admits quietly.

"Yeah, she is."

"I hate that I missed so much."

"I really am sorry," I whisper.

He shakes his head. "I'm not saying that to make you feel bad. It is what it is, but I don't want to miss anything else, you know?"

Emotions swell in my chest. "You won't. If you want to be here, you can be."

"I do want to be here." He looks at me, gaze firm and steady. "For her and also for us."

His words hang between us. And of course, I want this too.

I reach over and take his hand. "Me too."

Seraphina runs back over to us, her cheeks pink, her smile wide. "Mommy! Liam! Ducks funny!"

"They are funny," Liam agrees.

She climbs right onto his lap like it's the most natural thing.

He looks at me, surprised, but also completely at ease.

"Snack time?" she asks.

Liam rubs his belly. "I could use a snack too." He looks at me. "Whatcha got in there?" He nods to the backpack.

I unzip it and pull a few things out. "We have some apples, pretzels, and some juice. What do you want, Sera?"

"Pwetzels and juice." She holds out her little hand, then leans against Liam while she eats.

I'm trying not to react in a way that would alarm her, but it's hard not to fight back a few tears as I watch them together. And good Lord, do they look alike.

This outing today makes me feel like we could be … that we are … a real family. And when Liam meets my gaze, I think he feels it too.

As soon as she's done with her snack and juice, she's ready to move again. So, we make our way down the path again. She's holding both of our hands again, swinging them as we walk.

She trips slightly, and both of us react instantly to steady her. Our hands brush when we do, and we freeze for a half second, the moment lingering. Liam's fingers close gently around mine instead of pulling away, and I let him.

We walk together like that for a few minutes, until Sera reaches for our hands again. Then she spots an ice cream vendor.

"Ice cream!" She points dramatically.

"You want some ice cream, Sera?" Liam asks.

I'm sure he'll never deny her anything. Even if that means she's bouncing up and down with a sugar high.

She nods. "Yes!"

"What do you think, Alie? Want some?" He gives me a sexy little smirk.

I clear my throat. "Um, yes. That's fine. Ice cream."

Liam lets her order, and she gets a vanilla cone with colorful sprinkles. Then she proceeds to smear some all over Liam's shirt.

"Oh no," I say, smothering a laugh.

He looks down at the glob of ice cream on his shirt.

"Eh, worth it." He tickles her, making her laugh.

I take her hands and wipe them with a napkin, then hand him one to clean up with.

"I think we should take a selfie, don't you, Sera?" I pull out my phone.

"Yes!" she claps.

I look at Liam and he smiles softly, pulling her in a little tighter, despite the ice cream that's still dripping all over both of them now. Then I lean in, hold my arm up, and capture our first family picture.

Sera doesn't know it, but we do. And when I lower my phone, he leans in and kisses my cheek.

"Thank you," he whispers in my ear.

"The first of many." I nudge his shoulder.

By the time she's done with her ice cream, the sun starts to dip lower in the sky, and the park grows quieter.

She's starts to get tired, so Liam carries her, like it's second nature, back toward the park's exit. Her head is resting on his shoulder, and by the time we exit, she's asleep.

"She's out," I whisper.

He nods, careful not to wake her.

"She feels comfortable with you." I stroke my finger down her cheek.

"I hope so. I want her to know, without a doubt, that I will also protect her and be here for her." He places a soft kiss on her head. "I'll spend my whole life trying to be worthy of her."

Tears prick my eyes.

"And you too, Alie."

My breath hitches. And if he wasn't holding our daughter right now, I'd show him just how much I want him too.

When we get back to my place, he's still carrying her, and she's still sleeping. So, I lead him to her room, where I take off her shoes and he lays her in her bed. He brushes her wavy hair off her face and leans down to kiss her gently on the cheek.

Is there anything sexier than a dad with his daughter? Seriously. Liam is a very gorgeous man, but he's never looked more irresistible to me than he does right now.

"Today was good," he says when we walk out of the room.

"It was," I agree.

I follow him to the door, not quite ready for him to leave.

We stand there for a moment, something unspoken settling between us.

He reaches for my hands and pulls me into him. "Can we do this again?"

"Yes." I smile.

"Can I kiss you?"

I lick my bottom lip, and I see his eyes move to watch it.

"Yeah, you can kiss me," I say as I edge closer to him.

He leans in slowly and kisses my cheek first, then places kisses in a path to my mouth. And these soft kisses feel meaningful.

When our lips finally meet, it's the kind of kiss that makes you forget your own name. I feel it from my mouth all the way through to my core.

This is a kiss filled with promise. Of building something. Moving forward together.

Our tongues swirl around each other. Neither of us tries to rush it. If anything, I want to drag him to my room and keep going.

His hands slide under the hem of my shirt, making me shiver, but he just runs his fingers up and down my spine reverently. Then deepens our kiss.

We stay like this, kissing, touching ... connecting, until he pulls back, resting his forehead against mine.

"I'd better go, before I can't."

"You don't have to go," I say, a little breathless.

He kisses me again. "I really do."

"Okay," I say, no doubt sounding disappointed.

"Can I call you later?"

"Yeah, you can call me." This time, I kiss him and let it linger for a minute before pulling away. "Bye, Liam. Thanks for today. She had a lot of fun. And you're ... a real natural with her."

"Thanks. I hope so." He pulls away and starts walking backward out the door. "Talk to you soon, Alie Grant."

"Bye," I say, smiling, "Liam Pitz."

And when I go to bed, after talking to him for an hour on the phone, I go to sleep, thinking of him.

CHAPTER TWENTY-FOUR

LIAM

Going to the park with Alie and Sera this weekend was incredible. I didn't see them yesterday, but Alie and I texted throughout the day. My anger toward Alie for not telling me about the baby is waning because I do want to have a relationship with my daughter, no matter what, but I also still want … Alie.

Aaron is an issue that needs to be addressed, but Alie told me yesterday that she would like to speak with him first. I will respect her wishes for now, but I really want to fucking know why he lied to us.

It's all I thought about during my workout today, making it hard for me to focus on what I needed to do. So after forty minutes, I gave up and showered. I have an afternoon meeting anyway, so I might as well stop by and see Alie before they start.

I make my way up to her floor, first taking a turn, and stroll by the nursery, but I don't go in. I look through the window and see Seraphina playing with a few other kids. She's laughing and happy, and when I see her sharing her toys, pride swells in my chest. She doesn't see me, and I don't want to disrupt her, so I head toward Alie's office.

It's wild when I think about how much has changed in such a short time. Less than a month ago, I was living in New Orleans, living a lonely bachelor life, where my sole focus was football. And now, I'm living in New York City, and I'm a dad.

As I reach her office, I'm not even sure what I want to say or my reasons for coming up here. I just know that I needed to. I'm drawn to her even more now than I was the December I met her. It's a pull, a connection that I can't explain, and I think she feels the same way. So, it's only fair to us and to Sera to see where this could go. We need time together as a family, but also just the two of us.

I knock on her door and lean in to see if I can hear her. The walls up here are glass, but they're sandblasted, so I can't really see inside to know if she's in there.

"Come in," she says, muffled.

I open the door and see her sitting at her desk. Her long, dark hair is draped over one shoulder. She's wearing glasses, a loose white silk shirt, and from what I can see under the desk, a short black skirt. There's a pair of black high heels with red bottoms lying next to her feet. She looks like a fantasy.

Shaking myself from my thoughts, I clear my throat. "Hey," I say gruffly.

"Hey," she answers, softer than professional, but also a bit guarded.

I lean against the doorframe, waiting to be invited in. "I wasn't sure if I would see you today in the sponsorship meetings or not, so I thought I'd come say hello."

"Uh, I'm buried in prep." She gestures to the organized chaos on her desk. "Contracts, donor briefing, event logistics, reviewing press packets …"

"Things always this intense in the mornings for you?"

She smiles tightly. "Pretty much daily. Unlike others who get to work out and eat all day."

"Are you suggesting that's all I do?" I chuckle.

"I don't know. Is it?" She cracks a smile.

"Hey, I resent the implication that I have nothing else to do with my days," I tease.

"Then prove that you do."

For a second, we just sit there, smiling at each other, but hers has an anxious edge to it. Like she's assessing my mood. I know things have been tense since I found out about Sera, but I can't help feeling the same pull I felt when I met her two years ago.

Then the air shifts.

She licks her bottom lip and tilts her head slightly as she looks at me. "Meeting starts in fifteen."

"Okay, I'll be there." My eyes are completely on her mouth.

"You should probably … go now." She gestures to the hall, smiling.

"I'll walk with you."

"Nope. Not a good idea." She leans back in her chair.

"Why not?"

She glares at me, and it's so fucking cute that I can't help but smile.

"This isn't funny, Liam. We're at work. We have to keep work life separate from …" She gestures between us.

"I'm not laughing, Alie. And I'm aware that we're at work, but I don't really care."

She laughs lightly, and it's the sweetest sound.

"Go. Conference room down the hall. And try to behave."

"No promises."

"I'm deadly serious, Pitz." She stands.

"See you in"—I look at my watch—"thirteen minutes."

I back out slowly, but I don't miss the pink in her cheeks and the small smile on her face before I turn to walk down the hall.

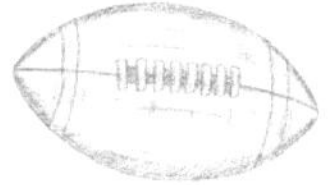

Slowest. Meeting. Of. My. Life.

It's packed with coaching staff, marketing, event coordinators, brand reps, and donors dialing in remotely.

Alie sits next to Presley, who's been looking back and forth between us, like she's in on a secret.

I ended up directly across from Alie. It's great, but also like torture.

Someone is droning on about sponsorship tiers and pointing to slides that are on a massive screen, and I'm not sure how this part applies to me, but I'm required to be here nonetheless.

I don't hear a word of what he's saying, and Alie keeps glancing at me, which is also distracting as fuck.

Every time I catch her, our eyes lock, and I can see the smile she's trying to hide.

Presley sees it though, and nudges Alie's arm.

Alie shoots her a warning look, and I have to bite back my grin.

Her gaze drops back to her notes in front of her, pretending to be invested in the presentation. She taps her pen, then stops. Looks up at me again. It's electric. This thing between us.

She knows it.

I know it.

And it's amplified even more for me, knowing that she's the mother of my child.

The meeting continues to drag on, and at one point, someone asks for my availability for some charity function next month. I answer automatically, having no idea what I'm saying because all I can think about is getting her alone.

By the time the meeting adjourns, I'm done waiting.

People stand, chairs bump the table, conversations start.

Across the table, I see Alie gather her notebooks quickly, like she's trying to slip out of the room unnoticed.

Not a chance, babe.

I don't even say goodbye to anyone. I just rush out the door after her.

"Alie."

She stops mid-step, her shoulders tightening before she turns.

"Liam, you can't just—" she starts.

"What? Talk to you?" I shrug. "Seems reasonable to me."

"And you need to talk to me right now?"

"I don't see the need to wait."

She glances around, giving a few nods and closed-mouth smiles as people pass us.

"Come on," she mutters.

She leads me down the corridor, past unused conference rooms and storage space. We reach a door, and she opens it, pulling me inside and shutting it behind us.

Silence falls instantly, and we're locked in a stare.

It feels close.

Dangerous.

Private.

"We can't be doing this. We *shouldn't* be doing this," she mutters. "Not until I have a chance to speak to my parents."

"You brought me in here." I smirk.

"That's not the point."

I step closer to her, crowding her space.

"Don't think I didn't notice that you couldn't stop looking at me in that meeting."

"You were looking at me too."

"I'm not denying that I was."

Her breath is shallow, and I can see a flush running up her neck. She's affected by me.

"This is risky. We could get caught."

"We haven't done anything wrong. We're just talking." I reach for her hands. "Tell me to leave then."

She doesn't.

"I … I can't stop thinking about our night together," she says, practically in a whisper. "Even with everything else going on with Sera."

My chest tightens.

"Yeah," I mutter. "Me neither."

"I keep replaying it in my head," she admits. "It's a total distraction."

"Funny. I'm having the same problem."

"Are you still mad at me?"

"Mad? No, but I think we still have a lot to talk about."

She nods. "Yeah, we do."

"That doesn't mean I'm not thinking about getting my mouth on your pussy again though." I smirk.

She laughs softly, a little nervous, and I can't hold back any longer.

I pull her in closer to me, slowly, giving her time to stop me.

Again … she doesn't.

I release one of her hands and bring it to her face, cupping her cheek. When my lips meet hers, it starts slow, testing.

But when she touches her tongue to my lips, all my restraint is pointless.

I deepen the kiss when she wraps her arms around my neck. My hand falls from her face, and I wind mine around her waist, bringing her close so our bodies are practically connected.

Goddamn.

Kissing her feels so familiar, yet new at the same time.

We break apart for a minute to catch our breath.

Her forehead rests against mine.

"This is such a bad idea, doing this here."

"I don't think so."

That makes her laugh.

"I think we should do this all the time." I smile against her lips.

She pulls back and looks at me like there's something she's trying to take hold of, something solid to grab on to.

"You're in my head. I can't stop it. No matter what I do or how hard I try."

"Good," I reply softly. "Because I don't want to stop it. And I think we should spend some time together. Alone."

"Alone?"

"Yeah. Of course I want to keep spending time together as a family, but I also think we owe it to ourselves to see what this is, what it could be."

"I … agree."

Silence buzzes around us.

Then she inhales deeply and closes her eyes. "Okay."

"Okay, what?" I bring my hands up to her face, stroking my thumbs on her cheeks.

"Let's spend time together alone."

Relief hits me like oxygen.

"Tonight?"

She hesitates.

"Come to my place," I suggest. "I'll cook for you."

"You cook?" she teases.

"You'd be surprised by how competent I am."

She studies me for a minute, smiling.

"Okay, I'll come to your place. Seven."

I smile. "Seven it is."

I kiss her one more time, not wanting to let her go, but knowing I should.

"You go first." I nod toward the door.

"Okay …" She looks at me curiously.

"I need to fix this." I point to my dick. "I can't walk through the halls with a hard-on."

"Oh God," she mumbles and covers her face with her hands.

"What? You did this," I tease.

"Bye, Liam," she says before pulling the door open.

"Bye, Alie. See you tonight at seven." I wink at her before she leaves the room.

CHAPTER TWENTY-FIVE

LIAM

By the time seven rolls around, my place smells like rosemary, garlic, and probably a little bit of nervous energy. I want tonight to be perfect.

I don't think I've ever cleaned my place so thoroughly either.

She texts me to let me know she's here and on her way up.

I open the door and wait.

In minutes, the elevator doors across the hall open, and I see her.

She's leaning against the wall, head down. She's wearing jeans and a T-shirt, her hair down, and she looks effortlessly beautiful. When she looks up, she smiles.

"Hi," she says.

"Hi," I answer, no doubt with a stupid smile on my face.

"Come in." I turn to the side so she can enter.

"Smells delicious in here." She walks in and looks around.

"Thank you. I hope you like Italian food."

"It's one of my favorites."

"Mine too." I brush her hand with mine as I walk by her toward the kitchen.

"Can I get you something to drink?"

"You have wine?" She sits on one of the stools at the high-top counter bar.

"I do. You ordered Pinot the other night. Does that work?"

She nods. "That's great. Thanks."

I pour us both some wine, and set her glass down in front of her. When she lifts it, I touch my glass with hers.

"Cheers," I say, smiling.

"Cheers," she replies.

We sip, and then I walk back to the stove to finish cooking our food.

"So, Aliette Grant, what do you and Sera do when you're not at work?" I glance at her over my shoulder.

Her spine straightens. "Uh … I don't know. Just the usual life stuff, I guess."

"Are you an outdoorsy type? I know you played hockey, and you like to ice skate, but what do Alie and Sera like to do in the spring and summer?"

"Hmm … we love anything on the water. My family has a sailboat, so we use it a lot in the summer. The beach is always fun. Sera loves making sandcastles and making a mess with the sand. She used to try to eat it, but has thankfully stopped that. Those diapers were no fun."

"Nice. I love being on the water too. Do you golf?"

"I mean, I can golf, but I'm not very good at it."

"Really? That surprises me since you played hockey. With the similar swinging and all."

She laughs. "Yeah, I'm not sure what it is, but I can't seem to master it."

"I'm a terrible golfer, but I love to play. Archie's wife was a golfer in college, and she's given me some lessons. Of course, she smokes me every time we play, but it's always a good time regardless."

"A humble loser, huh?"

"If I'm playing with her, yes." I chuckle.

"I think you told me about them a little bit when we met."

"Probably. I spend a lot of time with them in the offseason, usually, but not likely this summer with the move here and getting settled. They have a lot going on too. She's getting ready to have their third baby." I start to plate our food and look up at her and smile.

Her expression confuses me, and it almost seems like a wall is coming up.

Not gonna happen.

She clears her throat, seeming to shake off whatever was happening a few minutes ago.

"What's up? Where did you go?" I pause, looking at her.

"Huh? Oh, nothing. I'm fine, I promise." She feigns a smile.

"Alie, you can tell me," I say. "I don't want any more secrets between us. No matter what happens with us, we have a daughter to raise."

"Nothing is wrong. I was just thinking about the time we missed as a family. I'm feeling a lot of guilt about it, honestly. And I can't seem to get Aaron to answer my texts or my calls, so not having an explanation as to why he lied to not only me, but you is driving me mad."

"Well, you and me both. But he won't be able to avoid you forever. And as much as I want the same answers, I think we need to focus on … this." I point at her, then myself. "And, shit, I'm a new dad. It's a lot to be hit with out of the blue. We have time to deal with Aaron."

She nods and wrings her hands. "No, you're right. And I still need to talk to my parents."

"Let's try to get that part handled before the season starts, yeah?" I laugh.

"I will. I was thinking I would talk to them this weekend. They're likely to run into you at some point if you come over, so it's better if I do it sooner rather than later. Plus, I'm kind of surprised that Sera hasn't mentioned you to my dad at least." She grimaces.

"Right. Yeah, I don't want him to find out that way. What do you think your mom will say?"

"Mom is the easy one. Seraphina is the light of her life. If Sera's happy, she's happy," she says, smiling.

"That's good to hear. And I think your sister is warming up to me, so I assume you've told her everything?"

"I have. I hope you don't mind." She takes a drink of her wine.

"Not at all. I'm glad you have someone to talk to."

"Have you told anyone?" She tilts her head.

"I've told Archie, which, honestly, means Emma and the entire Griffith family know. And my friends from Walker. They're all excited to meet you both."

"So, Aston knows?"

"He does, but we had dinner together, and he knows not to say anything until we do."

"Okay, that's good." She takes another drink.

I'd better get her fed before the wine goes to her head.

"You hungry?" I tilt my head toward the dining room table off to the side.

"Yeah, sure." She stands and follows me to the table.

I set our plates down, then pull out her chair and push it in once she's seated.

Dinner is easy, comfortable. Wine loosens the edges as our conversation flows. We talk a little about work, traveling, what I'm looking forward to doing while living in New York, and her obsession with color-coded spreadsheets.

She seems more relaxed tonight. She's laughing more too.

After we clean up the kitchen, we end up sitting on the couch, closer than necessary, our knees touching.

"You really can cook," she says.

"I told you I could. I can make a mean dinosaur nugget too." I wink.

"Well, I'm impressed. And Sera will be too."

"Did you just pay me a compliment?"

She tilts her head, making her hair fall around her face as she laughs.

When she looks back up at me, the moment shifts.

The energy feels charged, and I can't stop myself from reaching out and brushing her jaw with my thumb.

She leans into it, and I can't hold back.

I'm not sure who moves first, but her hands are in my hair, and my arms are around her waist, lifting her onto my lap so she's straddling me.

We lean in at the same time, and our lips meet. It's fire, want, and need.

I push my tongue inside her mouth, tasting her. I have the overwhelming need to consume her completely.

She starts to grind her hips, and I can feel the heat of her pussy through her jeans.

These clothes need to come off.

My hands move to the button on her jeans, and I pop it open. I pull out the T-shirt she's tucked in, then run my hands up her sides, around to her back, and pull her in closer to me.

I can't get enough.

I can't get her close enough.

I unclasp her bra, then bring my hands to her breasts and move her bra out of the way. She's just as perfect now as she was then. Maybe even slightly fuller.

Fuck me.

She breaks the kiss and reaches for the hem of my shirt and pulls it off in one swift move.

In response, I lift her shirt over her head and toss it to the floor. Then I take her bra straps and slide them slowly down her arms.

My eyes haven't left hers, and I can see the fire in them. She wants this as badly as I do.

I cup her breasts and squeeze as she grinds her hips on my lap.

"Liam, I want you. I want this."

"Oh, it's happening, baby. But let me look at you. You're so goddamn beautiful."

Her fingers run through my hair, making me shiver.

I'm so charged right now; I don't think it would take much for me to come.

"I think we should go to your room." She leans in and kisses me, then sucks my bottom lip into her mouth.

That about shatters my desire to move slower, so I stand, holding her ass in my hands, and walk toward my bedroom, not breaking our kiss.

As soon as we walk through the door, I set her down and unzip her jeans while she does mine.

She pushes my jeans and boxers past my ass, and I use one hand to push them down enough to remove the rest with my foot and step out of them. Then I remove her jeans and black lacy thong and toss them somewhere into the room. Our mouths collide again, and I lead her toward the edge of my bed.

When the back of her legs hit the mattress, I lay her down without breaking our kiss. Then I push her legs open and run my index finger through her wetness.

I pull back and lift my wet finger. "This is all for me?"

Her breath hitches, and she nods.

The need to taste her makes me feel feral. I lean back and kneel on the floor, spreading her legs wide.

"I can smell your sweetness. And you're so pretty and pink and soaked for me. Aren't you, Alie?"

"Please," she begs.

I turn my head and kiss the inside of her thigh, trailing kisses to her center. Then I run my tongue from her clit to her opening. Aliette Grant has ruined me completely. No one will ever be as perfect as she is for me.

I suck, lick, swirl, and pump two fingers inside her tight heat.

She grips my hair tightly and grinds against my face. And I fucking love it.

I don't stop when I feel her orgasm around my fingers. I don't stop when she pulls my hair. I don't stop when I feel her body relax.

But when she reaches for my arms to pull me up to her … I relent.

I kiss my way up her body, tasting, savoring.

"That felt amazing." She takes my head in her hands and pulls me in for a kiss.

"You're amazing. And I can't wait to do *that* again."

I slide my tongue into her mouth, making her moan when mine touches hers, tasting herself.

"Are you going to fuck me, Liam?" Her hands wrap around my back to take hold of my ass.

"Do you want me to fuck you, Alie?" I glide my dick between her lips, the crown hitting her clit, making her gasp.

"I need it. I need you inside me."

"Let me get a condom."

I reach over and grab the unopened box from my nightstand and take a strip out, then toss the box to the floor.

"We need all of those?" she asks, smiling.

"I sure hope so." I smirk.

She shivers.

Ripping one off, I tear the packet open with my teeth and sit back on my knees, rolling it down my cock.

I settle back between her legs and push my dick slowly inside her, my mouth hovering over hers, swallowing her moan. I thrust in deeper to the hilt. "Holy fuck. You feel so good."

We move together slowly, at first, until the tension builds to the point of no return.

I lift up on my arms and take hold of her neck with one of my hands. "Look at me," I demand.

Her eyes meet mine, and I lose control. I grab one of her legs and bend it to her hip, making me go deeper inside of her.

She tries to turn her head, but I don't let her.

"No. Eyes on me."

Her lip trembles, so I place my thumb right in the center of her bottom lip.

"I got you, baby. Let go."

Her arms wrap around my neck, and she pulls me to her, and as she looks into my eyes, I see it.

Surrender.

I brace myself on my elbows, and I kiss her again, telling her without words that I'm right there with her.

My entire body starts to tingle, and I know I'm close. And I can feel her tightening around my cock.

"Come for me, Alie. I need you to get there."

Her legs wrap around my waist, and she meets me thrust for thrust.

"Yes," she pants. "Oh God, you feel so good."

I tilt my head and kiss her deeply, our tongues tangling. Heat rushes through me just as I feel her pulse around my dick. And I explode.

I tuck my head in her neck, breathing her in. We're both panting as we come down from our orgasms.

"Holy fuck, Alie."

"I know," she breathes.

I lift my head to look at her, and we both smile.

I kiss her softly, and then I hold the condom at the base and pull out slowly.

Grabbing a tissue off my nightstand, I tie up the condom and wrap it and throw it to the floor. Then I scoot up and lean against the headboard and pull her to me.

She seems to be as relaxed as I feel, and rests her head on my chest.

"Stay with me tonight?"

"I can't," she says with a whisper.

"Why?"

"Because, I'm … " she hesitates.

As much as I want to beg her, I won't. But someday soon, I'll want both of my girls under my roof. Or hers. Doesn't really matter to me as long as we're together.

"Okay, we'll get there."

She looks up at me and gives me a soft smile.

After a few minutes, she seems to relax, tracing lazy circles on my chest.

I haven't felt this … settled in a while.

"You good?" I ask her.

"Yeah, I'm just thinking."

"About?" I rub my hand gently up and down her back.

She hesitates. "I'm thinking that this could get complicated."

She's thinking it's complicated, and I'm feeling like everything finally makes sense.

"It doesn't have to be. Maybe we can just be honest."

She doesn't reply, but she doesn't move either.

We lie there, settling into a closeness that feels inevitable. And there's a slow unraveling of walls that she's built. It's in her laughter and kisses. This connection we have, it goes beyond the physical.

CHAPTER TWENTY-SIX

ALIE

Liam came upstairs to have lunch with me and Seraphina today. After, she insisted on showing him the tiny reading nook she loves. It has fairy lights and a giant beanbag chair. He listened to her like she was unveiling architectural blueprints for the next stadium.

He crouched down beside her to ask her questions. And when she pulled him down on the beanbag with her and let her read to him … I felt like my heart was going to explode.

We're still smiling when we walk out of the nursery.

"You know, I'm kind of surprised Miss Sandy hasn't asked about me coming in with you."

"Oh, I'm sure she's put two and two together. Anyone who sees you and Sera next to each other can see there's a resemblance."

In response, he takes my hand in his, twining our fingers, as if it's the most natural thing in the world, and smiles down at me.

"I've got film in twenty minutes," he says as he turns us toward the stairs leading down to the locker room.

"Right, okay."

He leans down and presses a soft kiss to my lips.

When he starts to pull away, I curl my fingers into his shirt, keeping his lips on mine.

And then a throat clears.

We both freeze.

When we look toward the noise, we see my father standing at the end of the hallway leading to the executive offices, his arms crossed over his chest. I can't really read his expression. It's not angry. More like surprised, questioning.

"Hi, Dad," I say, acting as if it were completely normal for me to be standing in the hall, kissing Liam.

"Alie," he says evenly.

"Hello, sir," Liam says, lifting a hand in a wave.

He looks from Liam to me. "I think you need to explain … this."

My stomach drops.

Liam stands straighter.

"Of course. Your office," I say in a much calmer voice than what I'm feeling.

Liam looks at me. "Can I come with you?"

I shake my head and glance at my father.

"No, it's fine. Let me talk to him first."

Liam studies my face.

"It'll be fine, I promise."

He nods, looking uncertain. "Okay, but if you need me there, just call me, and I'll come right up."

"Thank you."

He squeezes my hand, then drops a kiss on my cheek.

I look at my dad, and he's watching the whole thing.

"Sir." Liam nods to him, then walks down the stairs.

My father watches him go, then turns back to me.

"Well," he says calmly, "shall we?"

I nod and follow him down the hall in silence.

As soon as the door shuts behind me, the nerves kick in. I haven't felt like this since I was a teenager and got caught sneaking in after curfew.

The stakes are infinitely higher now.

My dad takes his seat behind his desk, but I remain standing.

"Sit, Aliette." He gestures to the seat across from him at the desk.

I sit.

"Would you like to start," he says evenly, "with why you were just kissing my quarterback—my new quarterback—in the hallway?"

I inhale slowly. "He's Seraphina's father."

The words land between us like something solid, but he doesn't react the way I thought he would. There's no explosion or outrage. Just a calm, assessing look.

"Hmm … I see."

"That's it?"

He shrugs. "Well, what can I say? The resemblance isn't subtle. I noticed the first time I met him in person. And by your demeanor when he came into that meeting, I suspected you knew him somehow."

I blink in surprise. "You never said anything to me."

"It wasn't my place to speculate."

That alone makes my chest tighten.

"Can I ask why you never told us?"

There it is. The question I've been avoiding for the last two years.

"It was a one-night stand," I say quietly. "I'll spare you all the details, but I convinced myself that's all it was. Then I found out I was pregnant, and he was already back in New Orleans. Aaron was there—"

My dad interrupts, frowning, "Aaron?"

"Yes, the day I found out."

"And?"

"He told me he would reach out to Liam for me and then told me later that Liam didn't want anything to do with the baby."

Dad goes still. "Why would you believe that without speaking to him directly?"

"Because, at the time," I say, my voice shaking slightly, "it made sense. I believed our night was just that—one night. And I thought he might be involved with someone else in New Orleans. Plus, Aaron said Liam wanted to focus on his career. So, I believed Aaron—you know, the guy who has been my best friend for most of my life."

His jaw tightens.

"Alie, I still can't believe you didn't speak to him yourself. Something this life-altering—"

"I was embarrassed. Humiliated and hurt," I admit. "I wasn't going to beg someone to be involved if they didn't want to be. It's not like I couldn't take care of the baby on my own."

"You being capable of caring for the baby on your own isn't the point, Aliette."

"Dad, didn't you always tell me not to trust football players? Not to get involved with them?"

"Alie, I think you had already made your bed, so to speak, by that point, no?"

I can't help but blush.

"Aaron's father and I are good friends, as you know."

"I know."

"And he told you this, with certainty?"

"Yes."

He sighs. "I'm just surprised."

"I was, too, but even more so now."

His eyes sharpen. "Now?"

"Liam had no idea about the baby."

He leans forward, elbows resting on the desk. "You're telling me that he found out he had a daughter two years later?"

My eyes water. "Yes."

"But you'd believed he didn't want her?"

I nod. "He says he tried to find me and even came here to New York and met with Aaron, who told him I wanted nothing to do with him."

"So, Aaron lied to you both, is what you're telling me?"

"It appears so."

He studies me.

"You brought him into this organization." He shifts his head back and forth. "We wanted him, sure, but you handled the trade."

My throat tightens, and I swallow. "It's what was best for the team."

"That's the only reason?"

I hesitate, and he sees it.

"Alie."

I shake my head. "I … don't know."

His brows lift.

"Okay, fine, if I'm being honest," I admit, "there's a part of me that wanted him close. To understand his reasons for why he hadn't wanted to be involved. Maybe to see if he'd change his mind."

He leans back in his chair again, slowly. "So, football wasn't the only reason."

"No," I whisper, "I guess not."

He studies me long and hard. "Well, by the looks of it, there's still some chemistry there." He chuckles lightly.

I grimace. "Right."

"And you feel it too?"

"Yes."

He closes his eyes, like he does when he's trying to put his thoughts together. "Does Sera know?"

"Not yet."

He raises an eyebrow. "Well, you came from the nursery, did you not? Who does she think he is to you?"

"A friend."

He shakes his head and sighs.

"She likes him."

My dad studies me. "And how do you feel about that? Her liking him?"

"It makes me happy that she likes him. And he lights up when he's with her. It's been really special to see."

"You need to tell her."

"We will."

He leans forward again. "Have you told your mother?"

"Not yet."

He reaches for the phone.

"Dad, wait."

He doesn't.

"Kate, darling, Alie has something she'd like to tell you."

I give him an exacerbated look. "Hi, Mom."

"What is it? What's wrong?" Her voice is anxious.

I feel sixteen again. Caught. Cornered. About to confess something I've rehearsed a thousand times and never actually said out loud. I suck in a deep breath. "Liam Pitz is Sera's father."

The words leave my mouth, and for a split second, the world goes unnaturally quiet. Like sound itself is waiting to see what happens next.

"I'm sorry," she says slowly, like she misheard. "What did you just say?"

"I said," I repeat, steadier now, "Liam is Sera's father."

Silence.

Then a little laugh.

"I knew it!"

I blink, looking at my dad. "Wait, what? You did?"

"Mmhmm. The first day I saw him in person. When he walked into the conference room, I could see it in the eyes, and that smile … matches hers. Then, with the way you were acting strange, I had my suspicions."

I glance at my dad, who's looking amused because he just said the same thing.

"So, what's happening then? Between the two of you?"

My dad laughs. "Well, I caught them kissing in the hall."

"Ohhh," she says, clearly entertained by all this.

I roll my eyes. "We're spending time together. He's been around Sera. And we're … taking things as they come."

"How is he with her?"

"It was," I say, my voice softening, "love at first sight, I think. After he got past the shock."

"Wait, what? He didn't know about her?"

"I'll tell you the story later, darling," my dad says.

"Does Sera like him?" she asks.

"She does." I think about them on the beanbag earlier and smile.

"Have you told her who he is?" she asks.

"Not yet."

"Alie, you have to tell her if he's going to be spending time with her."

"I know, Mom," I huff. "We'll handle it."

"No more secrets, Aliette Grant," she says firmly.

My dad nods in agreement.

"I agree. No more secrets."

"I have to run, but James, I expect a full report when you get home. Love you both," she says, but doesn't wait for us to reply before disconnecting.

"For the record"—my dad clears his throat—"I won't make this uncomfortable or awkward for him, but I do care that he's the father of my grandchild."

I nod.

"And there's more at stake here." He pauses. "We brought him here to win."

"You're right. I do think he needs to be the one to tell his teammates, if that's what you're thinking about."

He nods. "I agree. I think it would be best, coming from him, as their team leader."

Then he looks at me thoughtfully.

"You know what I can't get my head around?"

"I mean, the possibilities are endless." I laugh sarcastically.

He smiles, but it fades quickly.

"Aaron knew the whole time. And he's helped you with Sera quite a bit. Have you given any thought to why he would lie?"

"Yes." I nod. "Every day."

"Have you talked to him about it?"

"He won't answer my calls or texts."

His expression turns cold.

"Dad, please don't say anything to his father."

"I won't, but …" He pauses. "This kind of deception changes the dynamic of our relationship with him and his family. Despite all my years of friendship with his father."

"I understand."

"He knowingly kept my granddaughter from her father."

The weight of that, him saying it out loud, is heavy.

"Believe me, Dad, I'm thinking about it."

"All right, now get out of here, kid. I have work to do," he teases.

I laugh, stand, and make my way to the door. But before I leave, I turn around.

"Dad, thank you for always being so supportive. For everything you've done for Seraphina and me."

"My greatest pleasure in this life is my family, Alie. No matter what." He winks at me, then picks up his phone.

I walk out, feeling a little lighter and anxious to see Liam.

Making my way downstairs, I find him in the gym, talking to a few of the guys, towel around his neck. Sweaty.

How can he look so good when he's sweaty?

He sees me through the window and walks toward me, then out to the hallway.

"Hey, how did it go?"

"Well … he's not angry."

Relief flickers across his face. "Okay, good. And?"

I huff a laugh. "He had a suspicion. And so did my mom."

He smiles. "Oh, really?"

"Yeah, I guess the first time he met you, he could see similarities. Then, your first meeting here, they both saw it."

He laughs, shaking his head. "These Pitz genes are strong, I guess."

"We need to tell her, Liam."

"I agree." He nods without hesitation. "The sooner, the better. I want her to know I'm her dad."

"How about dinner? Tonight?" I suggest.

He doesn't even pause. "I'll be there."

Even though we're moving in the right direction, I worry that Liam hasn't completely gotten over the hurt of missing so much. We've been in a bubble of bliss, and soon, it may pop.

We're going to have to talk about it and really see if we can move forward. I hope we can. Because now that I have him and my daughter has her father, I don't want to let him go.

CHAPTER TWENTY-SEVEN

ALIE

Seraphina colors at the table while Liam and I cook. I decided on spaghetti because it's her favorite and it's easy. He stands beside me, bumping my hip with his lightly.

"You want to tell her during or after?" he asks.

"Um, I think when it feels right?" I suggest. Timing on something like this, I suppose, is instinctual.

"Can I be the one to tell her?" He looks at me hopefully.

I nod slowly. "Yeah, I think that makes sense."

"Hey, wook!" Sera shouts.

We both turn to see her holding up the picture she was coloring.

Liam wipes his hands and walks over to her. "That's beautiful," he says, taking it in his hands.

She beams. "Thank you."

He starts to come back to the stove, but I wave him off.

"I got this."

He nods, smiling.

I listen to them talk as I finish the meal. He's so sweet with her. And I can tell she feels a natural ease with him. If I had known him better before, I would have never believed anything Aaron said because this man that I see now … adores our little girl.

When we sit down to eat, there's a bit of nervous energy underneath the normalcy of the moment. We listen to Sera ramble on while we nod and smile.

Then, about halfway through dinner, Liam clears his throat.

"Hey, sweetheart."

She looks up at him.

"There's something we need to tell you."

"Okay." She looks at us curiously.

"You know how your mommy has a daddy?"

"Poppy?" She looks at me.

I nod. "Yes, baby. Poppy is my dad."

She looks back at Liam. "Yes, my Poppy."

"Right, exactly. Well, I'm *your* dad."

I look at his face, and I can see the emotion written all over it.

Sera looks from him to me. Blinks. Then back to him. "My daddy?"

He nods slowly. "Yes."

Then she looks at me, and I smile and nod.

"Okay," she says, shrugging.

Liam and I look at each other and laugh.

"Well, that was easier than I'd thought it would be." He reaches for her hand.

Her tiny hand rests in his large one, and I swear I feel like I'm on the verge of tears. But Sera … she has no idea what kind of emotional earthquake she just created. I look from their hands to Liam's face. I can't tell if he wants to cry or laugh at the simplicity of this moment for her.

"I call you Daddy?" She tilts her head.

Liam pulls in a deep breath and nods. "Yes, you call me Daddy."

She smiles, satisfied, then removes her hand from his and continues to make a thorough mess with her spaghetti.

"Who your daddy?" she asks him.

"My dad and my mom live in Kansas. They don't like to fly in airplanes, so I only get to see them when they can drive somewhere or I can go to them. But I told them all about you, and they're so excited to meet you."

"What's Kansas?" She asks, curiously.

"It's the place I grew up. I'll take you there to meet them someday."

"On an airplane?"

"Yeah, we'd take an airplane."

"I wike to fwy."

He takes a deep breath, like he's trying to get control of his emotions.

"Hey," I ask, touching his forearm. "You good?"

He looks at me and smiles. "I am."

"You stay for bath?" Sera asks him.

Liam looks at me, and I nod.

"Yes, I can stay for your bath."

"You read me story?"

"I would love to read you a story."

I watch my daughter and see that she really is content with this news. She's definitely not distressed. It's like it's the most obvious and natural thing in the world for her to have just found out who her dad is. I'm relieved that she knows now though. I can't imagine how this conversation would have gone had she been older. She might not even remember much about her life before Liam as she gets older.

We finish dinner, and as I clear the table, Liam cleans Sera's face and hands.

"I make mess," she tells him with the cutest smile.

"That's okay. We'll get you cleaned up. Sometimes, I make a mess when I eat too." He finishes wiping her, then tosses the paper towel in the trash.

"You do?" she asks him, eyes wide, like they share some secret.

"I do. Especially if I eat chicken wings or ribs."

"What's that?"

"Wings and ribs?" he clarifies.

She nods enthusiastically, like she can't wait for the answer.

"Wings come from a chicken." He imitates a chicken flapping its wings. "Bawk, bawk."

She giggles.

"And the other one can come from a cow or a pig." He pauses then. "Moooooo. Oink, oink."

Sera claps her hands and copies him. "Mooooo. Oink, oink."

He lifts her out of her booster seat, and she wraps her legs around him, and her arms hang over his shoulders.

He looks over at me with a smile full of love.

"We can finish this later?" Liam asks me, nodding to the dishes.

I turn off the water. "Yeah, we can finish after she goes to bed. Let's go get your bath done, baby."

We walk out of the kitchen and down the hall toward the bathroom.

Liam leans in and loudly sniffs Sera. "Smells like someone definitely needs a bath."

She laughs and tightens her hold around his neck. "Bubbles?" She looks at me hopefully from over his shoulder.

"Yes, you can have bubbles."

When we get to the bathroom, he sets her down.

"I'm going to let Mommy get you in the bath, and how about I go grab some pajamas for you?"

She looks up at him and nods. "My pink footballs."

He looks at me for confirmation and direction.

"The set should be together in the middle drawer of her dresser."

"Got it. I'll be right back." He ruffles her hair and walks out.

Just as I set her in the tub full of bubbles and kneel next to the tub, he walks back in with the pajamas.

"These the right ones?" He holds them up.

"Yes!" She claps.

"I wasn't sure about what she wears under." He looks at me and shrugs.

"We're starting potty training and she's doing really good, aren't you?" I brush her sudsy hair back.

"I go'd on potty."

"That's amazing!" He holds out a hand for a high five, and she smacks her hand against his.

"At night, she wears a diaper or Pull-Up. I'll go get one." I stand. "You good?"

"Yep, I got her."

When I get back, he's sitting on the floor next to the tub. It can't be very comfortable for him, given how tall he is, but it doesn't seem to bother him. He listens to everything she says and laughs when she's silly.

After, we go to her room and put the guardrails on the bed down and pull back the covers while she grabs a book off of her shelf.

"Oh shoot, I forgot her milk. I'll be right back."

"Okay," he says as I walk out.

Then I hear, "Daddy, you lay wif me?"

And I have to silence my gasp with my hand.

I wait for him to answer, and after a pause, he says gruffly, "Yeah, I can lie with you."

My heart.

I grab the milk, then quickly return. And the sight that meets me is just … everything. Liam's big body is sprawled across her full-size mattress, and Sera is in the middle of the bed with her head tucked into his shoulder.

She looks up at me when she notices me come in and pats the mattress on her other side. "Mommy lay too."

I press my hand to my mouth, then walk over, hand her the milk, and climb in.

Liam looks at me over her head, and I can see the emotion swimming in his eyes.

He reads her a story, and then she begs for another. And by the time he finishes, her eyes are heavy.

I kiss her on the head. "Night, my favorite girl in the world. I love you so so much."

"Night, Mommy. Wuv you." She yawns.

Liam kisses her on the head next.

"Night, Daddy. Wuv you," she whispers sleepily.

"Night, sweetheart. I love you too." He barely manages to say it back, voice thick.

My heart leaps and then falls down to my chest. As much as I love having Liam in our lives, I'm realizing my heart will break if our newfound family falls apart. Because I like this too much. No … I think I love this.

I love us.

And it scares me.

The house is quiet as we finish cleaning up the kitchen. Once he finishes wiping down the stove, he folds the towel and sets it aside.

I turn to face him and lean against the sink.

"That went better than I'd expected," I whisper.

He laughs softly. "Yeah, I guess I'm not really sure what to expect because my experience with almost two-year-olds is limited, but she handled it like I was telling her that the sky was blue."

We start to move closer to each other without really thinking about it.

"What does this look like, Alie?" he asks quietly.

"I'm not really sure. I think what we've been doing. Spend time together. Be consistent. Be present," I suggest.

"I can do that for her. I'll do whatever it takes."

"Good," I say, swallowing the lump in my throat.

It's been a really emotional night, and I feel like I can barely process one thing to another.

"And what about us?"

I hesitate. "What do you mean?"

"You know exactly what I mean."

He walks toward me and slips his arms around my waist.

"I think the same applies. We see what happens. I think … if you're still angry or harbor any resentment, it's hard to build a foundation on that, you know? And honestly, I'm still trying to wrap my head around Aaron's part in all of this too."

"I get it. And you're not wrong. I'm not angry in the way that I was when I first found out. I am mad at Aaron and think we need to confront him together. I need to understand what his motive was for lying to me, but also lying to you." He pauses. "And resentment? I'm not resentful necessarily, more like sad that I missed so much. But blaming each other for this isn't going to help Sera. We're going to have to be a team here. I'm not an expert by any means on relationships, but I do know, based on my parents' example, that we need to be good partners for our kid. That means assuming the best about each other. Not weaponizing every mistake. Talking things through instead of letting pride make decisions. And it seems that your parents have a good foundation with that as well. Patient. Consistent. You don't tear each other down in front of your kids. You don't keep score. You show up. And at the end of the day, it really is all about Seraphina. Me being angry and resentful won't move us forward. I want to do this with you."

He places his finger under my chin, tilting my face. His knuckle brushes the curve of my jaw, slow enough that my breath stutters.

"Okay, you're right. I think there are times that I look at you or look at you together, and I feel guilty for not reaching out to you directly. Like I not only kept you from her, but I failed her too."

"And I understand that, and I appreciate that you are also hurt by how this all happened. But it did happen, and we can move forward or lay blame with each other, but that's not what's best for Sera."

"You're right." I wrap my arms around his waist cautiously.

"I know I am."

Then he kisses me. It starts slow, then builds into something deeper, emotion heavy. Charged.

My fingers fist in the fabric of his shirt before I can stop myself.

His other hand finds my waist, pulling me closer—not rough, but certain. The kiss deepens. Opens. Emotion flooding through it. Regret. Want. Relief. Months—maybe years—of unsaid things pressing between us.

My heart pounds so hard that I can hear it.

He exhales against my mouth, and it almost sounds like my name.

I tilt into him without thinking, rising onto my toes, and that's when it changes—when slow turns into something electric. Urgent, but not frantic. Weighed by everything we almost lost. Everything we didn't know.

His thumb presses lightly into my hip. My pulse jumps.

When we finally break apart, we're both breathless.

"I need to go," he mumbles against my lips.

"Okay." I pause. "Wait, why?"

He rests his forehead against mine.

"Because tonight was big. And as much as I want to fuck you on every surface of this place, we should probably ease into overnights."

Seriously, you would think he was a veteran parent with all the sense he's making while I'm hormone-driven tonight.

I can't help it; I blame his kisses.

"You're right."

He kisses me softly.

"Alie, this isn't me running away."

I nod. "Oh, yeah, I know."

And I do.

"Walk me to the elevator?"

I back away from him and take his hand because if I stand here like this any longer, I might not let go.

"I'll see you tomorrow," he says with one last kiss.

"Bye." I lift my hand as the door closes, then touch my mouth.

This feels like the beginning of something real.

CHAPTER TWENTY-EIGHT

LIAM

I didn't think it was possible to feel so much in such a short period of time. But over the last few weeks, something shifted. It wasn't dramatic or even all at once. But it's becoming something … steady. Like puzzle pieces finally coming together that should have been there the whole time.

We're building our own routine. Pancake breakfasts. Midweek park visits. And bedtime stories when I can make it.

Alie and I are falling into an easy rhythm too. We see each other at the complex, eat lunch with Sera, and text when we're not together. And we linger long after Sera is sleeping. Being inside of Alie is becoming a favorite part of my day, but I haven't spent the night yet.

But then she invites me to go to her parents' house in the Hamptons, just the three of us. This means I get to stay with my girls overnight. For two whole nights.

The house is like something you see in a magazine. White siding, big wraparound porch, flowers everywhere, a pool, and tennis courts. And I can see the beach when we pull into the circular driveway. The ocean air blowing into the car windows is salty and a little cool in the summer heat.

Sera practically vibrates in her seat the minute she sees the water.

"Beach!" she shrieks.

I get out of the car first and open the back door, and Sera's little arms are up, waiting for me to get her out.

Alie laughs as I unbuckle her. "Be careful!"

I scoop Sera into my arms, and she points to the shoreline. "Go, Daddy!"

I can't help but laugh as I run toward the beach with my daughter in my arms, giggling.

Alie follows behind us, shaking her head but smiling.

The ocean is restless and loud, waves crashing against the shore in a steady rhythm.

Sera insists on being set down so she can run toward the water.

"Wait—" Alie starts.

But I've already got her hand.

"We'll stay in the shallow area," I promise.

Sera squeals when the cold water hits her toes.

"Cold!"

"Yeah." I laugh. "That's the Atlantic for you."

I take both of her hands and lift her when bigger waves reach us. She throws her head back and laughs every time I lift her.

Alie steps beside us, her hair whipping in the wind.

"You look like a natural with her," she says quietly.

Her words hit me more than she knows. It does feel natural, being with Sera. And I think she really likes spending time with me. At the very least, she thinks I'm fun to play with.

"Thanks." I lean down and kiss her cheek.

Her eyes twinkle in the sun, and her hand touches my back.

"I'll go get some towels. You good with her?"

"Yeah, I got her. I'd offer to get them, but I have no idea where they are. Do you want us to come with you?"

"No, I got it. I'll be right back."

"Okay, I'll get our bags later?"

"Yeah, that's fine, or I'll have the house manager get them. Sera won't want to leave the beach yet."

"House manager, huh? Fancy," I tease, making her roll her eyes as she walks away.

Sera tugs at my hand.

"Make a castle?"

"Well, we don't have any buckets, but I guess we can do a drip castle."

She points to a bin near the walkway leading to the house. "In there."

"Buckets?"

She nods. "Yes."

Guess we miss out on the oh-so fun trek to the beach with our arms full of sand toys and towels here.

"Okay, let's go get some buckets and see if there are any shovels in there too."

She skips along beside me through the sand.

We get a few buckets, shovels, and a small rake.

"Let's find a spot for our castle."

We walk back toward the water, but far enough that it won't get washed away by a wave.

By the time Alie gets back with towels and a blanket, we've made a very crooked sandcastle that Sera has named Princess Daddy Castle House.

I don't question it. I roll with it because my kid is freaking adorable.

Alie sits back on a blanket in her bikini, watching us for a while, snapping pictures on her phone with a look on her face that makes my chest tighten—soft, almost disbelieving.

When Sera loses interest in the moat we're working on and moves on to collect seashells, I wander over to Alie.

"I really like this little scrap of fabric you're wearing." I sit next to her and run my finger under the strap around her neck.

She grabs my finger and kisses it, then holds it in her hand, twining our fingers together.

"You okay?" I wrap an arm around her shoulders.

She nods. "I am. I just … I never thought this would happen."

"Never thought what would happen?" I suspect I know, but I want to hear her say it.

"This." She gestures to Sera then me. "You. Her. Together."

I glance over at my daughter, who's now filling a bucket with more sand than physics allows.

"I'm here now. And I'm not missing any more time," I say quietly, but firmly.

She studies me for a long minute. "I know. I believe you."

"You bringing me here this weekend? I can't tell you how much it means to me. Making memories with her … and with you."

A peace settles over us, and I take her hand in mine.

There's something special about being here. No cameras. No press. No pressure. No curious eyes on us. Just the wind and waves and the two people who matter most.

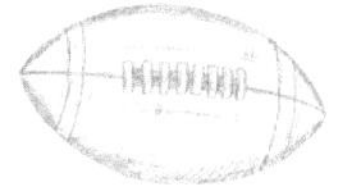

That night, Sera falls asleep quickly. Between the beach, then swimming in the pool, and too many cookies, she crashed hard.

Alie stands in the hallway outside her door for a second after we tuck her in. She's wearing a yellow sundress. Bare feet, no makeup, her hair swept back in a ponytail. Her skin is sun-kissed, and she looks relaxed and happy.

I reach for her hand. "What are you thinking about?"

She smiles softly. "I was just thinking that this is the first time we've all slept under the same roof."

The weight of her words settles in.

"I think it feels right."

"I think so too."

I lean down and kiss her, but stop it before we take it too far outside our daughter's bedroom.

"Should we go downstairs and have a glass of wine?" she asks.

I tilt my head to the side. "I need to start watching my alcohol intake as we get closer to camp, but I'll get you a glass, and we can take it outside to the porch."

"That sounds good. It's such a nice night."

We make our way down to the kitchen and get a glass while she picks the bottle she wants.

"Are we alone now, or is the house manager still here?" I ask, looking around.

"She leaves just after dinner unless we ask her to stay."

"Does she live on the property? I didn't realize how big it was when we drove up."

She nods. "Yes, she uses one of the smaller cottages on the south side of the property. You can't really see it from the main house."

I pour some wine into her glass, then grab a glass bottle of water from the fridge.

Alie grabs a baby monitor from the counter, and we go out to the porch.

The back porch opens to a view of the ocean, and the pool sits off to the left side, but it's connected. It's a large area, covered with couches, tables, lawn chairs, and one of those hanging beds I've seen in magazines. Everything is very classy, but not obnoxiously rich. Old-money type of fancy.

She sets the monitor down on one of the nearby tables and walks over to a low railing, leaning her hip against it as she looks out toward the water and sips her wine.

I watch her for a moment, and an overwhelming feeling of protectiveness and … love rushes through me. It doesn't scare me or even really surprise me. I was gone for this girl the first time we met. And spending time with her since I've been in New York has just made these feelings for her stronger. Add in the fact that she's the mother of my child … yeah … I'm falling.

I set my water bottle down next to the monitor and make my way over to her, standing behind her. My hands slide around her waist, and her head tilts to the side, giving me access to her neck, her ponytail falling over her other shoulder. I place featherlight kisses on her shoulder up to her neck.

"I'm really glad you came with us."

"Thank you for inviting me."

I continue kissing her, and when I suck on her neck, she moans and brings her hand up behind my head, running her fingers through my hair. I move my hands up to her breasts, skimming, teasing over the fabric of her dress. She loses her grip on her wineglass, and it falls over the railing and into the bushes.

"Oops," she whispers.

Then she turns her head and pulls my mouth to hers.

I slide my tongue into her mouth when she opens, tasting the sweet wine, and twirling my tongue with hers. My hands roam over her breasts, up to the straps of her dress, and I take them in my fingers and pull both straps over her shoulders, making the dress pool at her feet. She's not wearing a bra, so her bare back is pressed up against my chest. I can feel the heat of her skin through my shirt, but I want more. I break our kiss and pull my T-shirt over my head, tossing it somewhere behind me. Then I hook the thin straps of her thong with my thumbs and pull it down her legs.

"Let's not use a condom tonight," she says over her shoulder.

"Are you sure?"

"I'm sure. We're both clean, and I have an IUD. I want to feel you, be as close as I can to you."

"I want that too." I run my hands up her legs.

When I stand, I press my body against hers, keeping her in place. One of my hands skims her stomach, up to her breast, and I pinch her nipple between my fingers as I suck on her neck. My other hand slides from her hip to cup her pussy, and I slip my middle finger between her lips, her wetness coating it. I run it up and down and circle her clit.

Her hips start to move, making her ass grind against my dick. I move my hand from her breast to her face and turn it toward me.

"That feel good, baby? Grinding against my cock?"

Her tongue sneaks out, and she runs it across my bottom lip.

"Fuck, baby."

Her hand falls from my head, and she grabs the button of my shorts, trying to unbutton it with her hand behind her back, but I take over and quickly shred my shorts and boxers in one move.

"You want to touch me?"

"Yes," she pants.

She grips me and starts to pump, making my pre-cum leak from my tip. So, she runs her thumb over the head and smears it around the crown.

"Grab the railing and bend your hips."

I take hold of the back of her neck and push her body down.

"Spread your legs for me."

I step between her legs when she does and thrust my hips up, sliding between her ass cheeks.

She looks over her shoulder, her eyes heated, mouth slightly open. "Liam."

"Does that feel good?" I repeat the move, gripping her hip with my other hand.

"Yes." She nods.

"Rub your clit for me. I want to feel you dripping down your legs."

I keep my one hand on her neck, and the other moves from her hip to my dick. I rub the head from her ass to her opening and push the tip in, then take it out.

"Liam, don't tease me." She turns her head to the side.

"I got you, baby."

I push it in again, then pull out and slide through her center, my head hitting her clit, and it makes her moan.

I do it a few more times, until I can't take it anymore, and I push into her slowly, all the way to the hilt.

"Fuck, baby. You feel so good. So wet. So tight."

I pump into her, still at a slow pace. With the hold I have on the back of her neck, she can't really move, so she's at my mercy.

"Liam, fuck me harder," she begs.

"You want more?"

"Yes," she pants.

"Are you rubbing your clit for me?"

"Yes!"

I move my hand from the back of her neck to the front and pull her body up so her back is to my front as I pump into her. My fingers on my other hand dig into her hips, holding her in place as my thrusts become harder, deeper.

"It feels so good, Liam. Don't stop!"

"You love my dick inside you, Alie? Do I make you feel good?"

"Yes, so good," she moans.

I fuck her harder, making her body push forward, and my grip on her neck tightens. She leans her head back in invitation. And that just about makes me blow.

Both of her hands grip the railing now, and she pushes her

hips into mine, meeting me thrust for thrust, our skin slapping together. It's wet, and fast, and hard.

"You getting close?" I ask her.

"Don't stop, I'm almost there."

I pull her even closer to my body, and her head drops back to my shoulder.

"Come, baby," I demand.

"Fuck, Liam!"

Her arms wrap around the back of my neck, and her fingernails dig into my scalp. It stings in a good way.

When I feel her pussy tightening around me, I suck her neck hard just as I feel her strangle my cock.

As soon as her body relaxes, I release my hold on her neck and pull out.

"Grab the rail again, baby."

I jerk my cock, and within minutes, ropes of cum hit her back.

"Fuck yes." I milk every last drop on to her back, then rest my semi-hard dick on her. I run my fingers through it, then trace a path with it, skimming over her ass down to her pussy, then push my fingers inside her, mixing our cum together.

Goddamn. I need one more taste.

I drop to my knees and grab her hips, pulling them back. My hands move to her ass cheeks, and I spread them and then drive my tongue inside her pussy like it's my last meal.

She starts to squirm, like she wants to thrust her hips into my face. But I hold her still, fucking her with my tongue.

When I feel her trembling, I replace my tongue with my fingers, pumping into her until she's coming again. This time, she squirts, and I watch it drip down my fingers, then my hand in rapt fascination.

"Holy shit, baby," I pant. My cock is hard as a rock again.

I stand pulling my fingers out. Then I scoop some of my cum onto the tips of my index and middle finger.

She straightens when she feels my body flush against hers and turns slightly.

"Open," I say, sliding my fingers into her mouth.

She sucks and moans around my fingers.

"Alie … goddamn."

After she swirls her tongue around them, she takes my hand in hers and pulls out my fingers slowly, keeping my hand in hers.

"So good." She licks her bottom lip, then wipes it with her thumb. "We taste better together."

"My wicked little Vixen. Are you trying to kill me here?" I groan, then take her mouth with mine, thrusting my tongue into her mouth in a deep, wet kiss.

She breaks away, panting. "Do you think you can go again?"

"After that, fuck yes."

She turns to me then and leads me over to the hanging bed. Then she climbs on, and like the obsessed man that I am, I crawl after her. She's on her knees, so I lie down beside her and hold her hips as she straddles me, rubbing her pussy along my cock.

"I need you, Liam."

The way she says it sounds like it's more than just sex.

"I need you too, baby."

I take hold of her face in my hands and bring her down to me to kiss her. It's a slow but deep kiss. Open mouths, tongues tasting. Pouring how we feel about each other in every lick.

She breaks the kiss, sits up, and reaches between us, then puts me inside of her pussy. Her head drops back as I slide in deep.

"That's it, baby. Take what you need."

I take her breasts in my hands, squeezing them together.

Her hands are on my stomach for support as she rocks her hips up and down my dick. "Fuck, you're so deep. And I still feel like I need more."

I release her breasts and just move my hands up and down her body. Feeling all of her soft skin, how her body moves, the way she moans—it drives me wild, and I'm already close to coming again.

I sit up and wrap my arms around her waist, drifting my hands up her back, which is sticky from my cum, and curl my fingers around her shoulders and thrust up into her hard.

She gasps. "Holy shit."

So, I do it again, then roll my hips while I'm in as deep as I can get.

"You gonna come for me again, baby?"

Thrust. Roll. Thrust. Roll.

"I," she pants, "am so close. You feel so good." Her hands are on my shoulders, and she squeezes me. There might even be nail marks tomorrow.

Totally worth it.

I pull her down hard on me as I pump faster now. "That's it. You're mine, Alie."

"Yours," she breathes. "Oh God, I'm coming!"

She wraps her arms around my neck, pulling me into her so I can barely breathe.

Just as I feel her tightening around me, my balls tingle, and I know at any minute that I'll blow.

"Liam," she pants.

"I'm with you, baby," I say against her skin.

I erupt inside her and feel her pulsing around my cock.

We're both breathing heavy as we come down. Her arms loose around me now, her body relaxed.

"Liam, I don't want to mess this up," she says, lifting her head and looking me in the eye.

"We won't. I'm not going anywhere."

She looks down, but I lift her chin with my finger.

"Hey, I mean it. I know this is happening kind of fast, but I have no doubt about my feelings for you. I love you, Alie." I kiss her softly.

"You do?" She swallows. "Are you sure?"

"I never say things I don't mean. I think you know that about me by now. But, yes, I'm absolutely sure that I love you." I tuck a hair that's fallen out of her ponytail behind her ear. "I'm madly in love with you."

"I'm in love with you too," she says, tears in her eyes.

We stay there for a while, kissing, whispering, and listening to the sound of the ocean waves crashing onto the shore.

It's tender, trusting, and as I hold her, it feels a lot like home.

"We should probably go upstairs to bed." She starts to move off the hanging bed. "I think I need to jump in the shower first. I feel a little sticky."

"Okay, you go ahead up, and I'll grab our clothes and meet you in the shower."

She leans over and kisses me. "See you in a few."

I watch her walk away, naked. Goddamn, she's beautiful.

After picking up our clothes, finding Alie's wineglass, and bringing the monitor and my bottle in, I make my way upstairs. She's done with her shower by the time I get there, so I wash off quickly and join her in the bed a few minutes later.

She scoots closer to me and lays her head on my chest, her fingers tracing lazy circles.

"I've been thinking about something." I rub my hand up and down her arm slowly.

"Yeah? About what?"

"I," I pause, "I'd like for Sera to have my last name."

Her hand stops moving on my chest. "You do?"

I nod, even though she can't see me. "I do."

She exhales slowly. "Okay, yeah. I … I'll have to call the attorney to see what needs to be done to get your name added to the birth certificate."

"Really?" I raise my brow. That was easier than I thought it would be. I really wasn't sure how she would take my request. I mean, it stings knowing my name isn't on her birth certificate, but I don't want this conversation to turn in a different direction. We're moving forward, not back.

"She's your daughter, Liam. Of course you want her to have your name. We just need to take care of the logistics."

"Thank you." I squeeze her gently and press a kiss to her head.

"You're welcome." She lays her hand over my heart.

"I also don't want to miss any more time with Sera."

"I agree. I don't want you to either."

I pull in a deep breath. "I want to see her every day."

She shifts to look at me.

"You do see her every day now."

"I know, but I mean, I want to be there while she sleeps and when she wakes up. I want to be there for breakfast and to watch movies with her in the middle of the day."

Her expression softens.

"Liam, I'm not sure I'm ready to move in together," she says gently.

"I'm not asking you to."

"But?"

"But I don't want to go backward either."

She nods slowly.

"Well, I think after this weekend, it wouldn't be weird for her if you spent the night now."

"Yeah?" I smile.

"We can try it and see how it goes. Most nights anyway. Or at least when you aren't traveling."

The idea settles warm in my chest.

"I'd like that."

"I think we need to go slow and take our cues from Sera. Make sure she's adjusting to having you there more."

"And us? Are we still taking it slow?"

She hesitates.

"What *are* we doing, Liam? I believe you that you love me, and I do love you too. But what does this mean for us long-term?"

This isn't even a question for me.

"I'm all in," I say.

She studies me carefully. Looking for truth in my words.

"I don't want to lose you again."

"Liam … "

"I love her," I add quietly. "But I also love you."

"I love you too," she whispers, then kisses my chest.

"We'll figure out logistics when I get back from training camp," I say. "We can create a schedule and a routine that works for us. Although I feel like we're doing a good job with that already."

She nods.

"You'll be gone for four weeks."

"I know."

"We'll just have to FaceTime every night."

"Every night," I promise.

She looks up at me and smiles. "Then when you come back …"

"We build something solid." I run my thumb across her lips.

"I feel like we're in a good place right now," she whispers, sounding sleepy.

"Yeah, we are."

And for the first time in years, I don't feel like I'm chasing something. I feel like I'm finally building something. A future with my daughter and with Alie.

CHAPTER TWENTY-NINE

ALIE

Everything is quieter. Work. Home.

The couch doesn't dip on the right side anymore. The kitchen feels bigger somehow. Too much counter space. Too much air. Even the hallway light stays off because no one forgets to turn it off now.

I'm being ridiculous. He's only been gone for three days.

Three.

But the shift in our routine is immediate. There's no knock on my office door. No lunches with Sera. No giant presence behind me while I cook. No warm chest brushing my back when he reaches around for the salt. No low commentary about my knife skills. No stealing pieces off the cutting board like he's doing me a favor.

No deep voice reading bedtime stories in slightly overdramatic character accents.

And Seraphina asks for him every night.

"Daddy at football?" she says, tilting her head.

"Yes, baby," I tell her gently. "Daddy's working."

"Auntie Pwes too?"

"Yes, she's working too. She has to make sure no one gets hurt at camp."

She nods like that all makes sense.

Then she insists on FaceTiming him, and he answers every time he has his phone nearby. Even when I know he shouldn't.

The first night, he was still buzzing from drills.

The second night, he looked tired but steady.

Tonight, there's something restless in him. His eyes keep darting off-screen, like he's calculating something. Or missing something. Or both.

"I hate not being there," he says quietly while Sera runs off to grab her Walker Stallion mid-call.

"Just a few more weeks," I remind him.

"Four weeks is a long time in toddler years. Right? She's already so advanced for her age. She's saying new words every day," he adds quietly. "What if I miss something big?"

I smile softly. "She won't forget you."

"That's not what I'm worried about."

I know what he means. He's worried about missing more moments. The tiny things, the new words, new habits. Even more so because he's already trying to make up for two years. Now he feels like time is stealing from him again.

"You're doing what you're contractually obligated to do." I smile, trying to lighten the mood.

"Yeah, yeah, boss."

We sit there for a minute, smiling stupidly at each other. Not saying anything. Just looking. Like we're both memorizing this version of the other through a screen.

"And you're doing okay?" he asks.

"Yeah," I say, automatically.

But the truth is, I feel unsettled with him gone. I leave the hallway light on longer than I need to. I triple-check the stove. And I sleep on his side of the bed because it still smells like him.

It happens on a Tuesday.

I'm going over sponsorship contracts in my office when there's a knock at the door. But most everyone is gone at camp, minus me, my dad, and a few other administrative staff. And I'm definitely not expecting someone.

When I open it, Aaron is standing there with his hands in his pockets.

My stomach drops instantly.

He looks tired and a little less … polished than usual. The expensive haircut has grown out slightly. His jaw is shadowed. There's a tightness in his face that wasn't there before.

And he looks angry.

Not explosive.

Contained.

Which is worse.

"Hi," he says.

"What are you doing here?" I hold the door, blocking his entry.

"Can we talk?"

I hesitate because every instinct tells me to shut the door. But I don't.

"I called you and texted you for weeks without a response

or even an acknowledgment." My voice comes out steadier than I feel. My hand tightens on the edge of the door, knuckles pale.

"I know. I'm sorry," he says quickly. Rehearsed. Like he practiced the cadence in the car.

"You get five minutes," I say stiffly.

I hold the door, and he steps inside like he belongs here. As if he isn't responsible for detonating my life two years ago and as if he hasn't been lying to me since. As if he isn't responsible for my daughter being without her dad. As if he isn't responsible for taking my chance at something real with Liam, even if we're making our way back to something real now.

I shut the door, then move behind my desk, creating space between us.

"What do you want?" My tone is cool. Professional. It costs me.

His jaw tightens. A muscle flickers near his ear.

"You brought him here."

My pulse spikes. How dare he?

"We did, yes." I keep my chin lifted. Refuse to flinch.

"And you've talked to him?" His eyes search my face like he's looking for something. Guilt? Hesitation? Weakness?

"If you read my messages, you would know the answer to that."

"I did read them, Alie. I just want to hear the words come out of your mouth."

"What is it you want me to say, Aaron?"

He lets out a sharp laugh. "He knows about Seraphina?"

"He does."

"And?"

"And what?" I lean forward slightly, bracing my hands on the edge of my desk. I refuse to shrink. "Liam's relationship with her is none of your business."

"What did he tell you?" Aaron's jaw flexes. His fingers curl briefly at his sides before he tucks them back into his pockets.

"That you told him I didn't want to have anything to do with him and that he had no idea about the baby."

"And you're just taking his word?" he huffs, shaking his head like I'm the unreasonable one.

"I asked you," I snap. My restraint fractures. "I asked you what he said."

"And I told you."

"You lied."

His eyes flash with something cold. "I protected you, Alie."

"From what? The truth?"

"From getting hurt," he shoots back, stepping closer now. Not aggressive. Just closing space. "You think I didn't see how wrecked you were when you got back and told me he was with someone else? That he got someone pregnant? That he was probably using you because of your family name?"

The words hit because they're not entirely false.

I remember the sleepless nights. The swollen ankles. The terror of doing it alone.

But that doesn't absolve him.

"You don't get to rewrite this," I say, quieter now. Sharper. "You didn't protect me. You decided for me."

He starts pacing and running his hands through his hair.

"You were vulnerable," he insists. "Pregnant. Alone. He wasn't answering. He wasn't here."

"Because you made sure he wasn't."

He doesn't deny it.

Instead, he tilts his head slightly, studying me like I'm a problem he hasn't solved yet.

"You were barely holding it together," he says, voice lowering. "I stepped in when no one else did." He points at his chest. "I was there when she was born. I was there for the late-night feedings. I was there for the diaper changes. I was there for her first steps. First words. First tooth." His voice cracks. "He wasn't."

Aaron steps closer.

"Who are you going to believe here, Alie?" He puts his hands on his hips. "This guy you've really only known for a short time? Or someone who's been in your life forever?"

I stare at him. "You manipulated me." My hands flatten harder against the desk. I can feel my pulse in my fingertips. "You don't get credit for inserting yourself into a story that wasn't yours," I say steadily.

His expression tightens.

"And now what?" he asks. "You just let him waltz back in? Play dad?"

The way he says dad—like it's a performance—makes something inside me snap into clarity.

"He is her father," I say, each word precise. "You don't get to minimize that because it's inconvenient for you."

"I love you," he says, abruptly.

The words slice through the room.

I blink. My brain doesn't process them fast enough. "What?"

"You think I did all that because you're my friend?" he says, voice lowering. "I loved you. I loved her. I still do."

My heart feels like it's pounding outside my chest. My fingers curl against the desk to brace myself.

Love.

He says it like it explains everything. Like it absolves him.

"You had no right."

"And *he* does?" Aaron counters immediately. "Don't you think it's weird that he came here and suddenly decided he was okay with being a dad?"

"He didn't know."

"That's what he's telling you."

The crack widens a fraction.

I freeze.

Aaron sees it. Of course he does. His eyes sharpen, not triumphantly—clinically. Like he's testing structural weakness.

"You didn't hear it from his mouth back then," he continues, calmer now. Controlled. "You heard it from me. And you trusted me."

The memory flickers in my mind. The night I sat on the couch, swollen and exhausted, phone pressed to my ear. Aaron's voice firm.

"He doesn't want this, Alie. Football comes first."

"You said he didn't want her. That football was his priority."

"Maybe he didn't want her. But I think we both know football is his priority."

Tap.

"He said you never told him about her."

"Now that he's made a name for himself in the NFL, he wants her. It's just convenient—don't you think?"

Tap.

"Is that the kind of guy you want around your daughter? When it fits into his timeline? When it fits around football?" Aaron challenges.

Tap.

Doubt flickers again—sharper now.

Tiny. Unwanted.

But louder.

I think of contracts. Trades. Injuries. Headlines. The way the season swallows him whole. The way I've already learned what it feels like to be left.

"He's charming," he continues. "He knows how to win people over. He's good at saying what you want to hear."

Tap.

My chest tightens.

"That's not fair."

"What's not fair is that I was the one who was there. I stayed." His voice softens now. "I was here. Not him."

And that one lands deeper.

Because it's true. He was here. He held Sera when she cried at two in the morning. He drove us to appointments. He assembled cribs and stayed when I was unraveling.

Guilt creeps in like a slow fog.

"You're angry because he's here," I say quietly.

"I'm angry because I built something with you," he says, stepping closer again. "And you let him walk in and take it."

"I never promised you anything. We aren't a couple."

"You didn't have to."

The room suddenly feels too small.

"He's going to leave when his contract is up," Aaron says firmly. "Football will always come first."

"That's not true." But my voice lacks conviction.

"Isn't it?" he presses. "Where is he now?"

"Don't be ridiculous, Aaron. You know he's at mandatory camp."

"Exactly. He's gone."

The voice of doubt starts to creep in again, getting louder, and I'm trying to push it back, but I can't block out what he's saying. How it hits every wound I gained that night and let it fester over the last two years. I hate it. I hate that I'm giving him power like this.

"He calls every night."

"And when the season starts, and he's gone half the time? You think that won't affect her?"

I have nothing to say about that because, again, he's not wrong. Liam will be gone a lot, and Sera will miss him.

Aaron lowers his voice. "Look, I didn't lie to hurt you."

"You lied to control the outcome."

He studies my face.

"Now," I say slowly, "I'm confused because you're telling me one thing, and he's saying something different."

My pulse is racing. My palms are damp, and I hate that I feel unsteady.

I hate that he knows exactly which wounds to press.

He didn't create the doubt. He just knows how to weaponize it.

Something like victory flashes in his eyes. It's small and subtle, but it's there.

"I just don't want you to get hurt," he says gently. "Or her."

He steps back toward the door, damage done.

"I'm not the enemy, Alie."

Then he leaves, and the silence that follows nearly suffocates me.

Later that night, Liam FaceTimes us.

Sera talks to him first. She shows him a drawing she made today and tells him about snack time and playing on the field outside.

He listens like it's the most important thing in the world.

After she falls asleep, we sit quietly, not saying much to each other.

"You okay?" he finally asks.

I hesitate, and he sees it.

"What happened?"

"I, uh …" I clear my throat. "I saw Aaron today."

Silence.

"He showed up?" Liam's voice sharpens. "While I'm gone?"

"Yes."

"How convenient. And?"

I sit on the couch, doing everything I can to avoid his gaze. As much as I want to fall into this fantasy of ours, I'm aware that in total I've known Liam for a matter of months, total. All the time we have had has been in the bubble of some high-intensity moment. Hell, the night we met, I took him on some grand tour of Manhattan as if I was this wild, spontaneous spirit, and I may have been in a way, but I'll always be the woman with her guard. The one who knows risks. With Liam, I wonder if he'll stick around when we're no longer ripping each other's clothes off and tangled in sheets.

Will he want Sera when the parenting gets hard and it's more than walks in the park and pictures over FaceTime? When the bubble pops?

"He says you're lying to me."

A pause.

"I'm sorry, what?"

"He says you knew I was pregnant."

"That's insane. You know that, right?" he huffs.

"He says you're good at saying what I want to hear."

Liam exhales slowly. "Alie, he's the one who's trying to get in your head."

"But he was there," I whisper. "For everything."

"Alie, that's not fair."

"I know, but it's true."

Silence stretches. I can see his jaw tic as he takes in my words.

"I can't believe, after spending time with me this summer, you would think I would've walked away."

"I just … I don't know." I cover my face with my hands.

"Alie," he says gently, "look at me, baby."

He's hurt. I can hear it in his voice.

"You really think that's the kind of man I am? How could I not want her? Fuck, the minute I knew she was mine, I wanted her. Sure, I was angry—not about her, but about being lied to. You can't believe I wouldn't want her."

"I don't know what to think. I feel really confused and overwhelmed right now. He's been my best friend for most of my life. He was there for me when I was embarrassed and heartbroken. He was there when Sera was born. But I see you with her and how much you love her. And me," I say, and it's honest and terrible, all at once.

"I can't even talk to you in person," he says, frustration bleeding through. "I'm fucking stuck here."

"I know. I'm sorry."

"He's manipulating you."

Another long silence. I don't know what to say to that.

"Alie," Liam says, voice steady now, "look at what we've built together this summer."

"I am."

"Does any of that feel fake to you? Do you think my feelings for you or Seraphina are fake?"

No. It doesn't, but the doubt Aaron planted is there.

"I think I just need some time to process everything. The stories just don't align, and it's all jumbled in my head," I whisper, tears pricking my eyes.

"Time to process?"

"Yes."

He sniffs. "Okay."

But he doesn't sound okay.

"Just … please don't shut me out," he adds quietly.

"I won't." And I won't keep him from talking to Sera either.

We hang up without saying goodbye. Without *I love you*.

And then I sit on the couch and cry quietly in the dark, Aaron's words echoing in my mind. Liam's frustration lingering. And the worst part is, I don't know which voice is louder.

CHAPTER THIRTY

LIAM

This can't be happening.

I hang up and just stare at my phone like it might change what I just heard. But it doesn't. The screen goes dark, reflecting my face—my jaw is clenched, eyes hard, like I'm one second away from punching a wall.

Fucking Aaron. Putting poison in her ear about me. And I can't do shit about it. I'm stuck here for three more weeks. Camp isn't a suggestion. It's not optional. We're in full go mode, and I'm obligated to be here. It doesn't matter that my daughter is the team owner's granddaughter. Coaches don't care if your world is blowing up and falling apart. If you're healthy, you'd better be on the field. You're under contract; you show up. End of.

And I should be excited to be here, but what I want more than anything … is to be in New York with Alie and Sera. My family. Instead, I'm living in a college dorm room in south fucking Pittsburgh for the next few weeks, while this asshole is trying to rip us apart with his lies.

I exhale and try to calm down, but everything feels tight. Like I can't get enough air in my lungs. I need to get out of this room and take a walk.

I yank my door open with more force than necessary and let it slam shut behind me.

"Everything good, man?" Saint asks, opening his door across the hall.

"Yeah, I just need to get out of that room."

"I'll come with you. I'm feeling a little wound up tonight myself."

I really don't want to talk to anyone right now, but I also don't want to be a total dick. Luckily, Saint isn't a big talker.

We walk around the college campus in the dark. It's quiet, and luckily, no one else is around.

My phone buzzes in my pocket, so I take it out, hoping it's Alie telling me our conversation was a joke, but it's not. It's a text in the group chat. Beck telling us that Charlie's in labor. And I'm happy for them—I am. But I can't even think about anything else right now, and I don't want to sound like I don't care, so I just pocket my phone.

"Girlfriend?" he asks.

I shake my head. "No, just one of my buddies. His wife is in labor."

"That's cool." He nods. "So, you wanna talk about it?"

"I'm good. Just … life stuff."

Saint's eyes narrow like he doesn't believe me, but he doesn't push it.

Frustration builds though, and I can't hold it in.

"Timing just couldn't be worse right now," I exhale.

"What do you mean?"

Alie and I haven't really talked about how to handle the team, and I'm sure there have been some people around the facility who've noticed that Alie and I spend time together. I mean, Miss Sandy sees me every day now. It's not like we'll be able to keep this under wraps for long.

"I have a daughter," I blurt out.

"You have a daughter?" He nods. "That's awesome."

"Look, man, I'm gonna tell you something, but it needs to stay between us for now, okay? Well, Griffith knows, but that's it as far as the team."

"Yeah, of course." He holds out a fist, and I bump it.

"My daughter is Seraphina."

"As in Aliette Grant's Seraphina? The one I've known since she was born, who runs around the field?" He smirks.

"That's the one. But before you ask, that's not why I was traded here."

"I wasn't gonna ask. Not my business. But James knows, right?"

"He does now." I look at him, my brows raised.

"Oh shit. Like, recently?"

"Yeah, but that's not really the problem." I sigh. "I only found out that I had a daughter when I got here. And it wasn't a planned meet. I walked into Alie's office, and there she was."

"Oh shit."

"Yeah, turns out, my old college teammate Aaron Muldoon told her I didn't want the baby when she found out she was pregnant. But he didn't. When I asked him for her number, he blew me off, saying she didn't want to have anything to do with me, that I was just a fling."

"Okay, I gotta stop you. This is soap-opera bullshit right here. Aaron Muldoon is a piece of shit. I'm so glad he's not playing with us anymore. Sucks, just seeing him around the building. But go on …" He gestures for me to continue.

"Right? I tolerated him, at best, in college." I suck in a breath and exhale slowly. "Anyway, Alie and I are in a really good place, and Sera … she's just perfect. She has me wrapped around her little finger."

"She is a really cute kid. And now that I know she's yours, I can see the resemblance. It's the eyes." He nods.

"Yeah, that's what I noticed the first time I saw her too. So,

Aaron showed up today and started telling her lies. And I think she's confused, like she doesn't know if she believes him or not. And it sucks because they've been friends for, like, their whole lives, and I'm just coming in and trying to build a life with my daughter and hopefully with her." I run my hand through my hair.

"That's heavy. And you're stuck here for another few weeks, while he's there in her ear." He shakes his head. "That really sucks."

"I know. And it's not like I can do something stupid, like storm into Coach's office and demand to leave like I'm not some grown man, a team leader, with obligations and a career that impacts more than just me."

My words hang in the silence as we walk, looping back around to the dorm. Because what can he really say?

"Do you want my advice?" he finally says, as we approach the building.

I sigh. "Yeah, go ahead."

"I've known the Grant family for quite a few years now, and Alie's a good egg. She's smart, and she seems to have a level head about her. She'll figure it out." He pauses. "She'll realize Muldoon is an asshole. And if she doesn't, that's on her, but I don't think that'll happen. You'll work this out. You have a kid together. So, whatever happens with the two of you, you're tied for the rest of your lives."

I know he's right, but I want it all.

One restless night of sleep later, I'm on the field again, and everything feels off. We had meetings this morning in our groups, watched film, had lunch, all normal. Practice starts like always—warm-up, stretching, footwork, loosening up my arm, running routes.

Aston cracks jokes that everyone laughs at. Brody is hyper-focused on drills. Saint calls out defensive adjustments like he's creating the game plans himself. And I … go through the motions that a team leader should. I'm here physically, but mentally? I'm in New York, picturing Alie when she said she didn't know what to believe.

I feel like a man being tested. Like a man on the edge of losing something he just found. The most important piece of my life could be gone, as quickly as it came to me.

Coach blows the whistle, pulling me out of my thoughts. "Pitz! Eyes up."

I snap back. "Yes, Coach."

My focus slips again. Because I can't stop hearing the words she said.

"He says you're lying."

My hands tighten into fists. I did not lie. I didn't fucking know. I would have been there for every second if I had. I would have been at all the appointments. I would have been at the hospital, holding her hand. I would have gotten to hold Sera when she was tiny. I would've done the late nights, the diaper changes, and the exhausted mornings. I would've done it all. Because Sera is mine. And I'm already attached to this tiny human in a way I never thought possible. I'm attached in a way that makes me want to burn the world down if anyone tries to take her from me. Again.

Practice wraps for the day, and it wasn't my best performance. They're probably wondering why they traded for me. And I should be concerned about it, but I'm not.

After a quick shower, I make my way to the dining hall for dinner, but stop and take a seat on a bench to call Alie.

It rings once. Twice. Voicemail. Then I try again. Voicemail.

I lean forward and put my head in my hands.

"Come on, Alie," I mutter to myself. "Please don't do this."

I try texting her instead.

Liam: Please answer me.

Liam: Aaron is lying to you. He's manipulating you. Please don't let him get between us.

Three dots appear, then vanish.

My stomach is in knots. I can handle pressure, pain, and some of the best defensive players in the game. But I can't handle being ignored or silenced.

I try again.

> Liam: You know I can't leave camp. I feel really fucking helpless right now, Alie. But I am here. I'm not going anywhere.

I stare at the screen until it blacks out, but press the side button, showing me my lock screen picture of the three of us in Central Park. I won't lose them before we've even gotten a chance to have a life together.

My anger returns. Sharp and helpless. Because there's nothing worse than being trapped somewhere you have to be while the people you love are somewhere you can't be.

I'm so lost in my thoughts that I don't even notice the person walking toward me until I run smack into them.

"Oh shit, sorry," I say, grabbing her arms so she doesn't fall.

"Jesus H," she mutters. Then she holds my arm because whatever expression on my face must be loud.

"Liam," she says carefully. "Are you okay?"

"No, Presley, I'm not actually." I release her and pinch the bridge of my nose.

She doesn't react, just studies me.

Then she nods once. "Talk to me."

I gesture to the bench I was just sitting on, and we both sit.

"What happened?" she asks frankly.

I blow out a breath, forcing out the words before I change my mind about talking to her about this.

"Aaron showed up at Alie's office yesterday."

Presley's mouth tightens. "Of course he did."

I blink. "You're not surprised?"

She snorts. "I've been waiting for him to do something. His

silence with Alie was just too suspicious. He was plotting and planning until he could get back to New York."

My jaw clenches. "He's telling her that I'm lying about not knowing about Sera. And that I didn't want her."

Presley's expression sharpens, anger flashing in her eyes so fast that it's almost ... comforting.

"Well, that's fucking bullshit."

"I know." My voice cracks on the last word. "But he's gotten in her head, and I can't do anything about it because I'm here."

Presley leans toward me, lowering her voice. "Okay, listen." She holds up a finger. "Aaron is not doing this for Alie. He's doing it because he's selfish and he wants control."

"I'm trying to tell her that he's lying," I grind out.

"Add on the fact that he's always wanted her," Presley continues like she's been sitting on this thought for a while now.

I stare at her, mouth open in surprise.

Presley's eyes narrow. "You didn't know?"

"Alie told me when we met that they were just childhood friends and nothing ever happened between them."

"Hmm," is all she says.

I swallow hard, now thinking about my gut instincts telling me there was more to this, and here it is.

"Well, Alie would never. So, don't worry about that." Presley cuts into my thoughts.

I nod slowly, feeling unsure.

Presley leans back and folds her arms. "Aaron's motivation is obvious. He wants you out of the picture and always has. He thought you were erased, but now you're here."

My pulse hammers.

"Why?" I ask tightly. "Why continue the lie though? He knows I know the truth."

Presley gives me a look like I'm naive.

"Because if you're gone," she says, "he gets to keep playing the long game. He gets to keep playing the hero who stayed. The one who 'helped' raise Sera. The one Alie leans on, depends on."

Pure rage courses through me.

"He's hoping," she continues, "that one day, Alie will wake up and decide she owes him something. Or that they'll just be together for Sera's sake."

I see red.

"You don't do that to a kid," I say, voice low. "You don't mess with a father and daughter like that."

"I agree." Presley's tone is firm. "But Aaron doesn't play fair. He's a spoiled brat with mommy issues."

My hands curl into fists.

Presley touches my arm gently, bringing me back to the conversation.

"I know you're frustrated and you probably feel powerless right now," she says. "But you're obligated to be here. You know you have to. We need you to help this organization shine again."

"I know." I nod.

"You need to stay focused," she pushes. "Because if you get benched, or hurt, or you blow up at camp … Aaron wins."

That hits me in the chest. Because it's true. If I lose my composure, I give Aaron exactly what he wants.

I blow out a breath. "So, what do I do?"

Presley's gaze sharpens like she's already forming a plan.

"Let me talk to my sister," she says. "I'll go to Alie and make her look me in the eye and tell me what Aaron said. And then I'll remind her of what really matters."

"Do you think she'll listen to you?"

Presley gives me a fierce smile. "She'll listen to me because she knows I'm brutally honest with her. And because she knows how much I love her and Sera."

My throat tightens again.

"Thanks, Presley," I say quietly.

She nods once. "Don't thank me yet. Stay smart. Stay steady. Keep calling and texting. Keep showing up, even from here."

I swallow. "I fucking hate this."

"I know," she says, voice softening. "But love isn't convenient. And family doesn't come with a clean playbook."

She pauses.

"Also," she adds, eyes narrowing, "if Aaron is forcing these lies, there's a reason. And reasons leave footprints."

"What do you mean?"

"I mean," Presley says, voice low, "liars always slip. We just need to catch him."

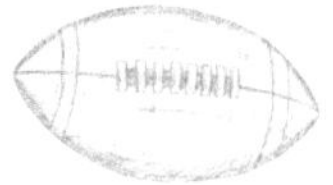

I forced myself to eat something, even though my stomach wanted to protest.

I smile and nod. Pretending to be engaged with my teammates. But underneath it all, there's something simmering and anchoring to my chest.

I'm not gonna let Aaron take this from me again. Not Sera. Not Alie. Not the future we are building.

When I get back to my room, I try calling her again, and this time, she answers.

"Hey." Her voice is cautious.

Relief hits hard, and my shoulders finally relax.

"Hey," I say, softer than I feel. "You okay?"

A pause.

"I'm … not sure."

My chest tightens again. "Alie—"

"Liam, I—" she says at the same time. "I'm really tired tonight."

"Okay, yeah. Me too." I try to keep my voice calm, forcing my frustration down. "I just wanted to say good night to you and Sera."

She sighs. "I'm sorry. She fell asleep early tonight."

Disappointment washes over me.

"Oh, okay. Can you give her a kiss for me and tell her I love her?"

"I will, and I'll tell her when she wakes up."

I clear my throat.

"I also want to remind you that Aaron is lying to you. He's trying to create doubt because he knows we can build something real."

"You can't really know what Aaron is thinking, Liam," she says, defensive.

"I can." My voice is firm. "Because he has everything to lose now. He loses his access. His influence. His place in your life."

Silence.

"I don't want this to become messy," Alie whispers.

"Oh, baby, it already is," I say. "And it's messy because of him."

She doesn't respond.

My frustration spikes, but I keep my tone steady.

"I love you," I say softly. "And I love Sera. I'm not going anywhere. And it's really fucking hard to fight this battle when I'm here."

Her breath catches, and it sounds like she might be crying.

I close my eyes, swallowing the anger, hurt, and fear.

"Just please don't shut me out," I say again. "That's all I'm asking. And don't keep me from Seraphina."

"I won't. Ever," she chokes on a sob.

We hang up without an *I love you*—again—and I'm left staring at the floor like it might give me answers.

One thing is crystal clear to me though: for the first time in my career, camp feels long. And what I'm most afraid of losing isn't a season. It's my family.

CHAPTER THIRTY-ONE

ALIE

I'm dragging at work today after a bad night's sleep. I just couldn't stop thinking about his voice and how upset and miserable he'd sounded. And angry.

What he said wasn't wrong necessarily. I'm just … I don't know. Unsure. Scared. Which is making all of this worse. And Aaron's words have weight because of our history.

But Liam's words have truth.

Then somewhere between those two things is my daughter.

Our daughter.

And that's the part that has been keeping me awake the last few nights. I'm not choosing between two men. I'm protecting my child.

My phone buzzes, breaking me from my thoughts.

Presley.

I answer the FaceTime call and see her standing on the field, wearing a T-shirt, track pants, oversize sunglasses, and an expression that says she's not here to bullshit.

"Hi," I say cautiously.

She pushes the sunglasses up onto her head.

"Where's Sera?" she asks bluntly.

"Huh?"

Presley looks at her watch. "She in the nursery?"

"Yes," I draw out.

"Okay, good. So, you're alone?"

I hold out my hands. "Yes, Pres. What's up?"

She huffs, "You want to tell me what the hell you're doing?"

I sit up straight. "Excuse me? I'm not doing anything."

"Uh-huh. And that's the problem."

I get up and close my open door.

"Presley—"

"I spoke with Liam."

I take a seat and slump in my chair.

"Okay, and?" I ask carefully.

"And he's trying really hard not to lose his mind while he's stuck in a state that he can't leave to go see his daughter and the woman he loves."

Guilt rushes through me.

Presley tilts her head to the side, staring hard.

"Aaron showed up."

She huffs a laugh. "Yeah, I know. And now you're doubting Liam."

I exhale sharply. "It's not that simple."

"Actually," she says flatly, "it is."

Now, I love my sister, but sometimes, she's so blunt and honest that it's unsettling to me. Like I'm getting in trouble in the principal's office.

"You think Aaron is doing this because he's noble?" she asks.

"Well, I mean, he was there. For everything."

"For you," she corrects. "He was there … for you."

"And Sera."

"Because it kept him close to you."

I flinch.

"You really think he was changing diapers out of pure altruism?" she continues. "Alie, you know I love you dearly, but you're not that naive."

My throat tightens.

"He told me Liam didn't want to be involved."

"And you never, not even for a second, thought that it was convenient?"

I hesitate.

"Let's line this up," she says, ticking points off on her fingers. "You run out on Liam after your amazing night together. Liam goes back to New Orleans. You're heartbroken and feel duped. You find out you're pregnant. You're scared. Aaron walks in and takes over. And you…let him. Because he's familiar."

"He was safe."

"He told you Liam didn't want the baby, Alie."

"I know. And?"

"And that meant you didn't have to risk confronting Liam yourself."

Her words land like a slap.

"Say how you really feel, Pres." I shake my head and continue, "I was protecting myself."

"And he knew that."

I swallow.

"Alie, I'm really not trying to be a dick again, but you didn't ask Liam yourself. Not once."

"I wasn't going to beg him to be a part of her life," I say defensively.

"You didn't want to be rejected. I get it. I really do."

I look away from the phone.

"And now, Liam shows up, not knowing he has a daughter, devastated that he's missed two years. And Aaron shows up to 'protect' you again?"

The pattern starts to take shape in my mind. Slowly. Uncomfortably.

"Who are you going to believe?" Presley mimics. "That's what he said, isn't it?"

My head snaps up.

"How do you know that?"

"Because, Alie, that's classic manipulation and gaslighting. Frame it as loyalty. Frame it as history. Make you feel like you owe him something."

There's a burn in my chest.

"He told me he loved me."

Presley doesn't look surprised. "Of course he did."

I stare at her.

"You don't help raise someone's child without hoping it leads somewhere," she says evenly. "And if he can't have you? Then he makes sure no one else can."

I think about what she's saying. Realizing that she's not wrong. Pieces start to click into place.

Little comments that Aaron would make over the years. Like the way he always questioned every guy I dated. The way he'd step in quickly when I was heartbroken. The way he positioned himself as irreplaceable.

I drop my head, holding my forehead.

"Fuck."

Presley releases a breath. "You see it."

I nod faintly.

"He made me feel like I couldn't trust my own instincts when it came to guys," I whisper.

"Yep, that's the point," she says. "If you doubt yourself, you cling to the person who *knows better*."

I lift my head and cover my mouth. "Oh God. He kept her from her father. Intentionally."

Presley nods once.

The realization hurts worse than the original lie because it wasn't for protection.

It was control. Selfishness.

Before I can fully spiral, I hear a knock on my door, and then it opens.

"Mommy!" Sera runs into my office, Miss Sandy behind her.

"She wanted to come see you. I hope this isn't a bad time."

I stand and pick Sera up and kiss her. "It's never a bad time for my baby."

"Just call me when you want me to come get her." She backs out of the office.

"Thank you, Miss Sandy."

I sit back down and turn Sera on my lap to face my phone.

"Is that my favorite princess?" Presley asks.

Sera waves at my sister. Then turns to me and puts her tiny hand on my face.

I hold her a little tighter than usual.

"You okay?" she asks in that small, serious voice toddlers use when they sense something's wrong.

"I'm okay," I say softly.

She looks at my sister.

"Auntie Pwes sad?"

Presley smiles. "Not at all."

Sera tilts her head. Then says something that makes me suck in a breath.

"I miss Daddy."

The words are simple. Innocent. Real.

I swallow down the lump in my throat. "You do?"

She nods. "He read story and make funny voice. He hug me big."

Tears burn in my eyes.

"Do you love your daddy?" Presley asks gently.

She nods without hesitation.

"He come home," she says confidently.

That's all it takes. I feel something settle inside me.

Because children don't calculate. They don't strategize. They just feel. And Sera feels loved and secure with Liam.

"There you go, Alie," Presley whispers.

I couldn't speak if I wanted to, so I just nod.

"Okay, girls. I have to get back to work." She turns her head as some of the players jog behind her.

I search for Liam, but don't see him.

"Hey, Pres?"

"Yep?"

"Thank you."

"Just doing my job. Making sure you don't mess up." She winks, then disconnects.

Brat.

"Do you want to stay in here for a while and play while I work?" I ask and kiss Sera on the cheek.

She nods enthusiastically. "Yes! Blocks."

I move her off my lap and get her blocks out of the closet.

"Build me something tall," I tell her.

"Okay, Mommy."

I sit on the floor and watch her for a few minutes.

My mind drifts and replays Aaron's words. Then Liam's.

Accusation. Promise.

One trying to anchor me because of history.

One trying to build something for the future.

Aaron reminded me of what he'd done for us.

Liam said he wanted to stay. That he didn't want to miss anything else.

Aaron's words were rooted in debt.

Liam's in choice.

The difference becomes more obvious, and I feel a flood of emotions. Because I know without a doubt which one feels right.

When Liam calls later that night, I answer on the first ring.

God, he looks good. It hits me how much I miss him.

"Hey," he says cautiously. Searching my face.

"Hey."

There's a pause, and I feel a blush hit my cheeks.

I clear my throat.

"My sister called me today."

"Oh?"

"Yeah, we had a good talk." I feel like I'm fumbling, nervous all of a sudden.

"And?"

I inhale slowly.

"You're right."

I look at him. The silence between us is thick.

"About what exactly?" he asks, eyeing me carefully.

"Aaron."

Another pause and a subtle nod from him.

"What do you think happened here?"

"He wanted me to doubt you," I say quietly. "And I let him. For a minute."

"Alie—"

If he doesn't let me get this out, I might cry.

"But I see it," I continue. "I see what he was doing all along."

He inhales a deep breath.

"You do?" The relief in his voice is obvious.

"Yes. And Liam, I'm so sorry."

He exhales slowly.

"Don't apologize. Let's just try to move forward."

He says the words, and I believe him, but I also feel like we need to finish this conversation.

"I do need to apologize," I insist. "Because for a second, I almost let his voice drown yours out. I let him play on my insecurities, and the truth is, he has always been there, and he was a safer bet for me because I didn't care about him in that way. He couldn't hurt me the way you could if this doesn't work out."

I see him swallow.

"Alie, I'm not perfect," he says quietly. "But I would never lie to you about this or anything. That's not who I am."

"I know."

"Do you though? I don't ever want you to doubt me again."

A sound from the hallway makes me turn my head. Sera toddles into the room with her baby doll stroller, her Stallion upside down inside. She's wearing pajamas, and her hair is still damp from her bath.

"She said she missed you today."

He goes still, and I know he must be feeling the same way I did.

"I miss her too. And you. I'm not going anywhere, Alie," he says again, softer this time.

"I know."

A slow, gentle smile stretches across his face. Something steadier settling between us now.

"I want you to know that I'm going to handle Aaron," I say firmly. Not wanting the issue to linger over us.

"You're not doing it alone."

"Okay." I nod.

A pause.

"Are we okay?" he asks.

"Yeah."

He closes his eyes briefly.

"I love you," I say, emotion thick in my voice.

"I love you too," he replies immediately.

"Mommy, that Daddy?"

"Where's my girl?" Liam calls out.

"Daddy!" She knocks her stroller down on her way over to me.

"Hi, sweetheart," he says, beaming.

"Doing Daddy?" She grabs my phone out of my hand.

"I'm at camp, working," he explains. "Tell me what you did today."

As Sera rattles on about her day, I watch him watching her.

Pure love radiates between them. And I'm angry with myself that I could have even entertained Aaron's lies for a single minute.

After a few minutes, Sera starts to yawn.

"You'd better get some rest, so you can have fun at school tomorrow," he says.

"Okay, Daddy. Wuv you. Bye." She hands me my phone and scoots off my lap to grab her Stallion.

"I'll talk to you tomorrow?" I ask.

"You know it." He winks. "I love you."

"I love you too."

After we disconnect, I take Sera to her room and tuck her in. She clutches her football in one arm and her Stallion in the other.

"Daddy call," she reminds me, even though it was just a few minutes ago that we hung up.

"Yes, baby. Daddy called."

She smiles and snuggles her Stallion closer.

"He come home."

I brush her hair back off her face.

"Yes, he will be home after camp," I assure her.

"Yes," she mumbles as her eyes start to close.

And for the first time since Aaron came back, I believe everything will be okay.

No doubt.

No fear.

CHAPTER THIRTY-TWO

LIAM

Everything seems louder when your head isn't right. Whistles feel sharper. Corrections seem personal. Mistakes amplified.

And today? I'm one bad play away from snapping.

"Let's go again!" Coach shouts.

I jog back to the line, sweat dripping from my face, trying to force my breathing into something controlled.

We're running red zone drills. Short field. Tight windows. No margin for error.

This is where I usually thrive. Precision. Timing. Execution. Leadership.

But right now, my head is in New York. To Alie's voice, telling me she loves me. To Sera's soft voice, telling me about her day.

Then to picturing Aaron's smirk when he thinks he has Alie where he wants her.

I clap my hands once. "Trips right, X slant."

Brody lines up wide left, bouncing on his toes.

I snap the ball and drop back, but the pocket collapses faster than I anticipated, so I rush the throw, making it high. Too high.

Brody leaps for the ball, but it grazes his fingertips and hits the turf.

"Fuck!" I shout, frustrated with myself.

Coach blows the whistle. "Pitz! Set your feet."

"Yes, Coach," I snap more sharply than I intended.

Aston meets my gaze across the line of scrimmage, eyes narrowing.

We reset. I overcorrect and hold on too long. Sacked.

By Aston.

Coach throws his clipboard down. "What the fuck, Pitz? What's going on with you today?"

Nothing. Everything.

I shake my head. "Sorry, Coach. I've got it."

But maybe I don't.

When Aston helps me up, he knows it too.

After practice, I rip off my pads harder than necessary. And yeah, I know it's not a good look for me as a leader.

Aston watches me from his locker.

"You gonna tell me what's going on?" he asks casually, like we're talking about the weather. "You've been off pretty much the entire time we've been here."

"Nothing," I snap.

He snorts. "That's cute. You forget that I've known you for a long time."

I ignore him.

He doesn't stop though.

"Seriously, what's going on?"

"I'm fine. Leave it alone."

"You just threw two balls like you've never held one before."

My jaw tightens. "Back off, Griff."

He stands slowly, not aggressive, but not backing down. And if it were anyone else, I'd probably be more pissed that they were butting into my business.

"This isn't about football."

I glare at him. "You think I didn't notice?" he continues. "You're distracted. And when you get distracted, it trickles down. You know how this works."

I step closer. "Leave it, okay?"

"I'm just sayin'" he says evenly, "that whatever's goin' on off the field needs to get handled. Because you don't get to spiral and drag the rest of us with you."

The truth in what he's saying stings.

I shove my hands through my hair, pacing a few steps before turning back. My pulse is loud in my ears.

"It's Alie. Aaron talked to her."

Aston's expression shifts. "Muldoon?"

"Yeah."

His whole posture changes. The casual lean disappears. He straightens slowly, hands settling on his hips as his brows knit together. "And? What's that have to do with you?"

I exhale hard through my nose."He's the reason I didn't know about Seraphina. And he's trying to convince her that I'm lying to her when it's really him lying."

Aston's face darkens. His hand curls into a fist at his side, knuckles whitening."Motherfucker."

"Yeah." I huff a laugh.

"And you can't leave."

"Exactly."

He exhales slowly.

"I get it, but you can't be snappin' at Coach like you did today."

"I know." I sigh. He's right. I know better than to bring my shit onto the field.

"You keep that up, and they're gonna start questioning your focus. And once that happens, the media smells blood. You know how this works."

"I know. I get it."

I close my eyes briefly because that's something we haven't

discussed yet either. How we're going to handle this with the media.

"This is exactly what that fucker wants," Aston says, leaning in closer to me. "You lose your edge. Look unstable. You become the bad bet."

I glare at him. "You don't think I know all this?"

"Then start acting like you fucking do. Don't let him win. Get control of yourself. Be the better man. Show her and your daughter that you're the better man."

The words land hard. Because as much as it sucks to hear them, he's right.

So, after a good night's sleep and a few texts with Alie this morning, I'm ready to reset this whole experience at camp.

Today is hot, and I'm exhausted after endless reps. And by the time we're on the last sprint, my legs are burning.

Brody false starts next to me, and Coach blows his whistle.

"Reset!"

Brody mutters something under his breath.

I look over at him and snap, "Lock in, Vaughn!"

He looks stunned. "Oh, now you want to join us?"

"I'm ready. Let's go!"

He glares at me.

I see Coach watch us out of the corner of my eye. He's watching us closely to see what we'll do.

Saint steps between us subtly. "All right, everyone," he says firmly, "breathe."

I step back, hands up.

Coach studies me.

"Get it together, Pitz and Vaughn."

"Yes, Coach," we say together.

But I don't miss the assessment. And I can't afford that. Not now.

After we finish running our drills, I'm in the cold tub when Presley walks in. I'm not surprised she strolls in here as if there aren't men in various states of undress at every bay.

"Hey, Presley," I say, feeling slightly awkward.

"Hey." She props a hip against the tub.

"Make yourself at home."

She rolls her eyes. "Oh, please. I see you guys naked all the time."

"I'm not naked."

"It wouldn't matter to me if you were." She lifts a brow.

Okay, then.

She crosses her arms. "So, I talked to Alie."

"I know. She told me. Thank you."

She nods slowly, studying me. "You know, Sera said something while we were on the phone."

I sit up, listening.

"She said she misses you."

My heart thumps. "I know. Alie told me."

"That kid," Presley murmurs. "She cuts through all the bullshit. She's the priority."

"I know that." I pause. "I really want to confront Aaron, but do you think Alie and I are good now?"

I hate to ask her sister, but I've been feeling out of my element the past few months.

"I think … there's a long road ahead," she cautions. "But you're not drowning either."

"And Aaron?"

"Alie wants to handle it. And I think you should let her."

"Not gonna happen."

She glares at me. "Alie needs to do it, Liam."

Silence stretches between us.

"Look," she says carefully, "you need to stabilize."

"What are you talking about?"

"This is bleeding into your conditioning."

I drop my head back. "Fuck. I know."

"Saint told me. And I saw you out there."

I blink. "Saint did?"

Interesting.

"The team is worried."

I exhale sharply. "Awesome."

"Don't be offended. It means they care. They need you out there."

That hits.

It's not the pressure. It's the responsibility.

"You're the leader," she continues. "You don't get to implode."

"I'm trying."

I feel like she sees inside my mind or something. Presley is way too observant for my comfort level.

"I know you are."

She softens. Just a little.

"She loves you," she says quietly.

I close my eyes. "And I love her. I love them both."

"Then act like it," she says. "Not like a guy who's about to self-destruct."

I laugh once, humorless. "You're brutal."

"Not really. Just honest."

I shake my head slightly.

"Thank you."

"Don't thank me yet," she says. "Just be the guy I think you are."

I should ask what she means by that, but she scares me a little, and I'm not sure I can handle the answer right now.

She stands and starts to walk out.

"Oh, and Pitz? You should probably get out of the tub before your balls fall off."

I bark out a laugh. "You got it. Doc."

She whips back around and glares at me.

Which only makes me laugh again.

CHAPTER THIRTY-THREE

LIAM

The next morning, I show up early. I'm in the film room alone. And it's quiet as I rewatch yesterday's throws. I analyze my foot placement. My release timing. Study the defensive alignment. And force myself to focus. Because Presley's right, and so is Aston. Aaron doesn't get to take football from me too.

And today, I'm going to man up and apologize to my team for being an asshole the past few days and tell them about Sera and Alie. Not all the details, but I want everyone to know they're mine.

I walk over to Coach, my helmet in hand.

"Coach, if it's okay with you, I have something I want to say to the team, before we start."

He nods approvingly, then blows his whistle. Then, when everyone looks our way, he gestures to me.

I release a breath I didn't realize I was holding.

"First off," I begin, scanning their faces, "I owe everyone here an apology."

A few brows lift.

"My attitude the past few days has been piss poor. Uncalled for. Unprofessional." I shake my head once. "That's on me. You deserve better from someone wearing this jersey. You deserve a leader."

I glance around the circle again, making sure the words don't just fall flat into the air.

"We've got too much talent on this field to waste time on my bullshit. I'm proud to play with every one of you."

There are a few nods.

"We didn't get this far to just show up. We're gonna dominate this season." I put on my helmet. "I promise each and every one of you that I will give you everything I have this season."

Everyone claps, and a few hell yeah's are heard.

"Let's fucking go! Titans on three." I clap my hands once.

"One…two…three. Titans!"

I mean every word I said. This is my team, my responsibility on this field. And we're gonna win.

Once practice starts, I lock in.

First rep in the red zone. Snap, drop back, set my feet, deliver a perfect spiral.

Brody snags it clean in the back corner, then points at me. "That's what I'm talking about!"

I don't react, but I nod once.

And we run it again. And again. Each rep cleaner and sharper than the last.

Then movement behind them catches my eye.

At first, it barely registers.

Just another body near the sideline.

But then my brain connects the shape. The posture. The face.

Aaron.

He's leaning against the fence with a clipboard tucked under one arm, talking casually to one of the assistants like he belongs here. Like he didn't destroy years of my life with one lie.

My jaw tightens as I stare at him across the field.

All I can see is Sera's face. Her tiny hand wrapped around my finger. The way she laughed the first time I lifted her onto my shoulders.

And then another image pushes in behind it. Every birthday I missed. Every scraped knee. Every bedtime story I should have been there for.

All the years I didn't know she existed.

Because of him.

Something inside my chest twists hard.

"Let's run it one more time," I say, my eyes still locked on Aaron. "Brody, go left fade, on two."

We line up, and I call out, "Blue eighty."

I catch Aston's eye and see him inching toward the left side of the field.

"Blue eighty."

I give a subtle nod.

"Set - hut!"

My arm moves before my brain can second-guess my actions, and I intentionally overthrow the ball, missing Brody, and it hits Aaron right in the face.

His head snaps sideways, his clipboard flies from his hand, and skids across the turf.

And then I see Aston barreling into him, and he hits the ground hard.

For half a second, the entire field goes silent.

The grass blurs beneath my cleats as the distance between us shrinks.

Then chaos erupts.

Shouting. Whistles. Cleats pounding.

Someone behind me calls my name.

"Pitz!"

I don't stop.

Aaron looks up when my shadow falls over him, his hand covering the eye I hit.

His expression flickers from pain to confusion to recognition.

"Liam—"

I hold my hand out for him to take. "My bad. Ball gets a little slippery sometimes."

For a split second, I see Sera again. The way she clung to Alie's leg when she first saw me. The way her voice sounded when she said Daddy like she'd been waiting her whole life for it.

All the time I should have had with her.

Gone.

Because of him.

The last thread of my restraint snaps, and I let go before he can stand, making him fall again.

"Jesus, Liam!" Presley yells, then bends down to look at Aaron's face.

Aston grabs my arms, holding me back before I can lunge forward.

"Pitz, what the hell!" Saint comes running up to us.

But my chest is heaving, adrenaline roaring through my veins.

"You lying son of a bitch!" I shout.

Aaron pushes himself up onto one elbow, snatching a towel from Presley's hand, eye already puffy and blood blooming along his lip as he stares at me in stunned disbelief. "I don't know what Alie told you. That woman is a liar."

"Excuse me," Presley says and stands with her hands on her hips, outraged.

I lean down and grip him by the collar. "Utter Alie's name one more time and I'll end you."

"Liam I—"

"You told her I didn't want my daughter!" My voice cracks through the air, louder than I intend. "You let her believe that!"

The field goes quiet again.

My teammates freeze.

Coaches stop mid-step.

Aaron's face drains of color.

"You kept me away from her," I continue, the words ripping out of my chest. "Years, Aaron. Years I didn't even know Seraphina existed because you couldn't stand the idea of losing Alie."

No one speaks.

The truth hangs heavy over the field.

I shake off Aston just enough to step forward again, my gaze locked on him.

"If you ever come near me again," I say, my voice dropping low, lethal, "or Alie, or my daughter ..."

My hands flex at my sides.

"I swear to God I will end you."

Aaron doesn't answer.

He just stares up at me like he's finally realizing what he did.

Behind me, Coach's voice cuts through the silence.

"Someone want to tell me what the hell is going on here?"

My chest rises and falls as I look around at the team.

At the confusion.

At the shock on their faces.

They deserve the truth.

So I drag a hand down my face and say it.

"Some of you may have seen me around the complex with Alie Grant and her daughter."

A few guys nod slowly.

"Well ... they're mine."

Silence falls again.

"Seraphina is my daughter," I say, my voice rough now. "And Alie ... she's the love of my life. I just found out about my kid when I got to New York because of him," I say, jerking my head toward Aaron. "Because he told Alie I didn't want them."

Murmurs ripple through the group.

"He made her believe I chose football over my own family," I continue, my voice rough. "So yeah ... I lost almost two years with my daughter."

I swallow hard.

"And I lost years with the woman I love."

The words hang there for a second.

Presley touches my arm. "I think you made your point."

I look over at Coach and see his jaw tighten.

He turns slowly to Aaron, who's now standing again, wiping blood from his mouth.

The look Coach gives him is pure ice.

"You done here?" Coach asks.

Aaron opens his mouth like he might argue.

Coach doesn't give him the chance. He steps forward, his expression carved in stone.

"Get off my field."

The words are quiet.

But final.

"Now," Coach continues, stepping closer, "or you'll be escorted out by security before you can blink."

Aaron looks around, realizing no one here is on his side.

Coach jerks his head toward the parking lot.

"Go, Muldoon."

Aaron hesitates for half a second.

Then he picks up his clipboard and walks.

No one stops him.

Then the gate slams shut behind him.

"The fuck," Coach says under his breath. "Did you know about this?" he says to the OC standing next to him, who shrugs and shakes his head.

"Thank god that this was a closed practice today." He huffs.

"Alright, show's over. Hit the showers," The offensive coordinator barks.

Aston clamps a hand on my shoulder. "Let's go, buddy."

I take a few deep breaths and nod. Then I jog off the field, feeling steadier than I've felt all week. Not because the problem is gone. But because I'm not letting it own me.

I shower and make it back to my room in record time. I'm

anxious to talk to my girls, and I know the late-night calls are hard with bedtime for Sera.

Alie answers on the second ring, a little breathless. "Hey."

"You busy?"

"No, I just left my phone in the kitchen, so I had to run and get it. I was in Seraphina's room."

"Ah, okay. Do you want to call me back?"

"No, no. We're good. As long as you don't mind sitting in on bath time."

"Not at all. Where is my girl?"

Alie's eyes go soft. "She's right here," she says when she walks into her room.

Sera's twirling around her room, listening to some music that I can't make out.

"Daddy's on the phone."

Sera spins. "Daddy!"

"Sera!"

That makes her giggle.

"Daddy's going to talk to us while you take your bath."

"Yay!"

Sera holds the phone and rambles on about her day while Alie grabs what she needs from the room.

"Okay, let's go." She walks out of the room, and Sera follows with the phone. I nearly get motion sickness as she walks with it.

Once she's in the bath and distracted with her toys and bubbles, Alie props the phone on the counter.

"So…I talked to him again today," she says.

"A—" I start to say, but she puts her finger to her lips.

I look at her, confused, but then she points to Sera. Probably best that I not bring up my little incident with Aaron right now.

"Okay, and?" Wondering if it was before or after I hit him in the face with the football.

"It was interesting."

"Interesting how?"

"Well, I've been avoiding his calls, but after you and I talked, I answered today."

"So what did he say?"

"He admitted more than he meant to, I think."

My jaw tightens.

"He said he didn't want to lose me. Or Sera."

I inhale sharply.

"And I told him that keeping a father from his child isn't love."

My eyes close, and I rub them with my palms.

"Alie—"

She stops me. "I'm sorry I doubted you."

I shake my head. "You can ask me anything. Talk to me about anything. Just don't let him interfere in our life together again."

"I won't."

She bites the inside of her cheek and looks at Sera, then back at me.

"How was practice today?"

I scoot back on the bed and lean against the headboard. Internally debating whether or not I should tell her for a split second.

I'll tell her later.

"It was better today."

"Good, I'm glad."

We're quiet for a moment.

"Camp feels really long this year," I admit.

"It feels long for me too."

"I really hate not being there with you two."

"Me too. But we're okay, right?"

A few days ago, I was the one asking this question.

"Yeah, we're okay."

Now, I feel it, believe it.

"I love you, Alie," I tell her.

"I love you too."

After I say goodbye to Sera, we hang up, and this time, I don't feel like I'm crawling out of my skin.

I feel more focused than I have the whole time we've been here.

Aaron tried fucking with the wrong man. But what he didn't count on was that pressure makes diamonds too. And I'm not breaking.

CHAPTER THIRTY-FOUR

LIAM

The second the plane lands, I hop in the new car that I had delivered to the airport so it would be here when I landed. I don't stop for food or even go check my apartment. I go straight to the complex to see my girls.

Four weeks of FaceTime, controlled breathing, and trusting that what we're building won't crack under distance or pressure has nearly made me lose my mind. And I need to see them like I need air.

I walk into the facility, twirling my keys around my finger.

A few staff members nod and say hello.

"Welcome back, Mr. Pitz. You ready for Sunday?" someone calls out.

"Always," I answer automatically with a smile.

But my focus is on one thing. Alie's office.

Instead of waiting for the elevator, I take the stairs two at a time. My pulse is already racing by the time I reach her office. I can hear her from the hallway, and also a male's voice.

And then I freeze. Waiting just outside her door.

Aaron.

"Now he's trying to ruin my credibility. And you see what he did to my face! Do you really want your daughter around someone who can't control his temper?"

"Aaron, that's enough," she hisses.

"Alie, I don't know why you're believing him. Have I ever given you a reason to think I'd lie to you?"

"Aaron, just stop," she pleads.

He laughs. "He wasn't here. I was."

My fists clench, my blood boils.

For a split second, all I see is red thinking of—his smug face, the years he stole, the lies he let her believe.

"You lied to both of us," she says. "You kept us from being a family."

"I did what was best."

"For who?" she demands, her voice rough with anger.

"For you! For her!" he snaps. "He left."

"He went back to New Orleans because he had to. And I left him that morning, not the other way around. I should have stayed and asked him instead of making assumptions."

"Still, he wasn't here." He goads.

"He didn't know I was pregnant!"

He huffs. "You think this ends well? Football always wins for him. And it always will."

"That's not true. And you don't know him at all," she says.

"You want stability for her?" he presses. "Or do you want headlines and uncertainty?"

That's it. That's the manipulation. The *for her sake* angle.

"Stop," she says, firmly.

There's a pause.

"I've trusted you for most of my life," she continues. "How could you lie to me?"

"I've protected you."

"No, you tried to control me," she corrects.

Silence.

"And you can't ever be in our lives after this," she says, voice shaking.

"Alie—"

"No," she says calmly. "Anything athlete-related from here on out can go through my dad. We're done."

"You're making a mistake," he claims.

"No," she says quietly. "I already made the mistake of trusting you. I won't do it again. I stand by Liam and his word."

"Alie, this isn't over," he mutters.

"Yes, it absolutely is. You need to leave." She demands.

I've had enough.

Knocking on the door frame dramatically, I stroll into her office, and I see Aaron standing by the window with his back to me, Alie behind her desk. And Sera's sitting on the floor coloring.

The air shifts immediately.

Alie looks up first, and relief floods her face.

"Liam," she gasps.

Sera spins around. "Daddy!"

She drops her crayons and runs straight to me.

I scoop her into my arms instantly, burying my face in her hair, breathing her in.

God, I missed this.

"I missed you so much," I murmur.

She kisses my cheek dramatically. "You gone long."

"I know. I'm sorry. I had to work."

Only then do I look at Aaron. And whatever calm I had left from camp evaporates.

He folds his arms, cool and controlled, like he didn't just try destroying my life.

"Back early," he says with disgust.

"Looks like I'm right on time, actually."

Alie moves closer to me.

"Aaron was just leaving."

She wraps her arms around my waist, and I bend my head to

kiss her. It's not the kind of kiss I had pictured on my way here, but it'll have to do for now.

"Mommy, Daddy kiss!" Sera claps her hands.

"Why are you even here?" I ask him.

He doesn't move. Because of course he doesn't.

"I represent one of the rookies," he says smoothly. "I have business here today."

"You don't have business in her office, and we just got back. So no. You don't." I snap.

Aaron's eyes flick to Alie. "She asked me to stop by."

Alie gasps. "I did not!"

I set Sera down gently. "Can you color a picture for me?"

She looks at Alie.

"Go ahead. Color, baby," she says softly.

Sera can probably sense the tension, but she sits back down on the floor with her crayons and paper.

I step closer to Aaron.

"You need to stop," I say, voice low and dangerous.

"Or what?" he asks quietly.

"Or I'll forget we're in a professional building."

Alie steps between us, her hand on my chest. "Okay, let's just stop this here."

I look at her.

"He's the problem, Alie. Not me. "

She looks up at me, curiously, and maybe a little proud.

"Did you really do that to his face?" She tugs on my shirt.

"Ball was slippery, baby. Let's call it an equipment malfunction."

"Uh, huh. Right." She smirks.

I wink at Aaron and give him a big ol' fuck you smile.

He steps toward the door like a petulant child, muttering something under his breath.

I look at my daughter and see her looking from Aaron to Alie.

Stepping forward, I point at the door. "You heard her. Out."

He huffs like the little pussy he is, slams the door behind him, and immediately the room feels lighter. Like someone finally opened a window after years of stale air.

"Unc mad?" Sera asks.

Alie crouches beside her. "It's okay, baby. I promise." She smooths Sera's hair back from her face, pressing a kiss to her temple.

I reach for Alie's hand and pull her to me.

"Are you okay?"

She nods slowly.

"God, I'm so sorry," she whispers.

"Alie, stop apologizing. He manipulated you." I tug her in closer, needing to feel her in my arms.

She exhales shakily.

"Hey," I lift her chin with my finger.

Her eyes are glassy.

"I love you," I tell her quietly. "I love her."

She nods, tears in her eyes. "Are you going to be able to forgive me?"

I don't hesitate. "Yes, I already have."

Her breath catches.

"But we need to move forward," I add. "No more letting people interfere or define us."

She nods again. "We move forward."

"And I think we should start with you two coming to my place tonight."

Alie looks at Sera, then me. "I think we can do that."

"Good. Now kiss me."

I slide my hands into her hair and drop my mouth to hers. Giving her the kind of kiss I had planned on before Aaron ruined the reunion.

We lose ourselves in each other until I feel a tug on my T-shirt.

"Daddy, go home?"

I lift her in my arms, but keep the other around Alie.

"Yeah, sweetheart. We can go home."

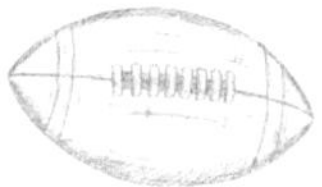

We make a stop at Alie's place first so she can get some things for herself and Sera to spend the night.

Once we get to my place, Sera insists on exploring every room like she's inspecting a castle. A small castle.

"Big couch," she announces.

Alie laughs. "I'd say she's excited for her first sleepover here."

"It won't be her last," I reply.

I ordered pizza on the way here so we didn't have to think about cooking. It's not exactly on my meal plan, but I think we're all too tired to think about it.

We eat. Sera spills juice. We clean it together. It all feels so normal.

After her bath, we're lying in the guest room, reading her nighttime story, and I'm mentally calculating how to get this room ready for her. To make it hers.

She falls asleep, clutching her Stallion and football.

Alie and I stand in the doorway, my arm around her waist, watching her sleep for a minute.

"She's perfect," I whisper.

"She is," Alie agrees.

"You ready for bed too?"

She nods and looks up at me. "I bet you're pretty tired. It's been a long day for you with traveling, and now this, having us here."

"I am tired, but I need you."

She lifts up on her toes and kisses me. "Then let's go."

I pick her up, my hands gripping her ass, and her legs wrap around me. We kiss as we walk toward my room.

"I don't want to lose this again," she says against my lips.

"We won't."

She kisses me first this time. It starts soft, like she's relieved. Like we're reconnecting instead of feeling desperate. Our hands exploring each other slowly, reverently.

Every breath. Every kiss. Every touch is grateful. Intentional.

When I carry her over to the bed, I set her down and slowly peel off her clothes. It's not chaos or urgency. It's a closeness I've never felt with anyone but her.

I want to take this slow. I want to make love to her.

Her fingers tangle in my hair as my mouth moves along her skin between her neck and shoulder.

She says my name like it's a prayer.

When she reaches for my clothes, I stand and undress. Her eyes watching my every move.

Once I'm naked, I crawl between her legs, settling my body over hers. She slides her hands up my abs and chest, making her way to my neck, guiding my mouth to hers.

"Liam, kiss me."

I tease the seam of her lips with my tongue. Slow, deliberate. I glide my tongue along hers, and we savor each other.

"I need you," she moans.

"You have me, baby." I pull her bottom lip into my mouth and suck.

I push up so I'm leaning over her, my arm bracing my body.

Her hand snakes between us and wraps around my dick,

sliding up and down, squeezing my tip, making precum coat the head.

I lean down and lick the tip of her nipple before wrapping my lips around it. When I bite down on it, she runs her hands into my hair, holding my head in place.

"That feels so good," she moans.

I move to the other, then release it with a pop. "Fuck, you're perfect."

I sit up, leaning back on my heels, and look down at her swollen pink pussy. She's spread wide for me, and I could easily lose control. But I want to take my time.

I move my hands up her thighs and reach under to grab her ass. Then I bring her hips down to meet my cock and slide it through her slit, soaking my shaft with her arousal.

My cock reaches her opening, and our eyes meet when I slowly push into her. I let out a breath, then swallow her moan with my mouth.

I push into her to the hilt. Our eyes still connected.

"You're mine, Alie."

"I'm yours. Always," she whispers.

I release her legs and pull out just long enough to straighten my body over hers, bracing my arms on either side of her head. I push in again, slowly, our eyes locked.

"More," she whispers.

I push into her harder, circling my hips, and she gasps.

"You like that?" I lean down and lick her bottom lip.

"So good." Her hips meet my rhythm, and we kiss, tongues tangling, tension building.

My orgasm is getting closer as our hips thrust together. And I can feel her starting to pulse around my dick. So, I pull back from our kiss to catch my breath and bury my head in her neck, licking and sucking.

"Are you getting close?" I ask against her skin.

"Yes," she breathes, her hands finding my hair, tugging. "Don't stop."

Her pussy starts milking my cock, and my control snaps, and I drive into her harder, trying to make her come before I lose it.

My mouth hovers over hers, our breaths joining, lips brushing. "Come, baby. I can't hold it much longer. You feel too good. Choke my cock with your pretty pink pussy."

"Oh God! Come with me, Liam," she says, breathless. Her hands grab my ass, pulling me into her deeper as she starts to come.

Her head tilts back, and she moans as she spasms around my dick, and I … come harder than I ever have in my life.

The connection we have, the way our bodies know each other on a deeper level than just physical satisfaction, is everything. There's no doubt in my mind that this girl was meant to be mine.

I pull out of her and roll to my side, stretching my arm under her head.

She tucks into my arm and rests against my chest as we catch our breath.

"I've been thinking. I don't want Sera growing up in just apartments," I say quietly.

She looks up.

"We can keep your place in Manhattan. Especially with your parents there," I continue. "But I want a house not far from the complex."

"With a big yard," she murmurs.

"Yeah, with a big yard," I agree. "Somewhere she can ride a bike. Have some normalcy in this big life we live."

Alie smiles. "This all sounds pretty permanent."

"Because it is. I"—I pause—"am permanent."

She studies my face.

"Okay then. I guess we start house hunting?"

"Really?" I ask, excited. "You want to do this with me?"

"I do. After being apart these last four weeks, I realized that I want to spend our days and nights together. Be messy together. Watch movies. Sleep in late. All of it."

"I'm all in, baby." I kiss her forehead.

She leans into me, and for the first time since all of this started, everything feels … steady.

Messy. Loud. Complicated.

Perfect.

And I wouldn't trade this life for anything.

CHAPTER THIRTY-FIVE

LIAM

It's the first game of the regular season. I wake up before my alarm. Game days are always like this for me. My adrenaline is spiked, and I'm anxious to get on the field. And this game is special because I get to play against the Cowboys, which means I'm playing against Archie. I can't wait to see him, and I'm even more excited for him to meet my daughter and Alie.

What makes it even more special is that this is the first time my daughter will get to see me play in person. It's also the first time she and Alie will stand on the field with me before kickoff. The first time we'll take photos publicly. And it's the first birthday I'll get to celebrate with her.

I decided to stay at my place last night, just so I could get centered. Alie's having a party planner at her place this morning to set up a birthday party for Sera after the game, so it'll be hectic over there soon.

I sit on the edge of my bed, thinking about all the changes that've occurred in the last six months. Six months ago, I didn't know she existed. Six months ago, Alie was a memory. Now … I can't imagine breathing without either one of them.

I pick up my phone and shoot Alie a text.

Liam: You guys up?

She responds immediately.

Alie: Yep. Sera's been up since six asking if it's Daddy's football day.

I grin.

Liam: I'm getting ready to head out now. You'll bring her down early?

Alie: Yes, I will. We'll see you in a few hours.

Liam: Love you.

Alie: Love you too.

I close my eyes for a second and breathe. This—*this*—is what I'm playing for now. It's not about the fame. I want my daughter to be proud of me. I want to provide for my family. And the truth is, football won't last forever. But my family will always be here.

When I get to the field, I get dressed and taped. I don't usually talk much before games. I try to get locked in and visualize plays, routes, and think about the opposing teams defense.

Once I'm ready, I make my way out onto the field. The stadium is humming with electricity when I step out of the tunnel. It's still a little early, but the stands are already filling. The grass is still clean and sharp. And music is blasting through the speakers.

I jog toward midfield, but then I see them, so I change direction.

Seraphina and Alie are standing near the rope barrier. She

has a tiny #4 jersey on, and her hair is in pigtails, and I swear my heart skips a beat. And Alie's wearing a custom jersey with my name and number on it. Goddamn. They light up my life.

Sera spots me instantly. "Daddy!"

She tries to duck under the rope, but Alie holds her back.

I walk over to them, kiss Alie, and lift Sera into my arms.

"I wear your shirt!" she announces proudly. "And I gots a 'adge."

"I see that! And a badge too," I say, trying not to choke up. "You look better in it than I do."

She turns in my arms to show me the back. "Wook."

Instead of my name on the back, it says *Daddy*.

I look at Alie, and she smiles at me, her eyes soft.

"What does the back of yours say?" I ask Alie.

She turns, and I see my last name on her back. And, fuck me, I love it. She looks good with my name on her. Come to think of it, I've never had anyone important to me, outside of my immediate family, wear my jersey.

Now, *she* is my family.

"People are taking pictures of us. I guess we're really doing this." She laughs.

"We really are." I kiss her forehead.

"You ready for today?" she asks quietly.

"Not really. Just anxious to get out here and play. I'm excited to see Arch too."

"You're going to be amazing." She puts her hand on my arm.

Sera grabs my face with both hands, bringing my attention back to her.

"You win?"

I laugh. "That's the plan."

She nods seriously. "Okay, Daddy. Win."

A photographer walks over to us and interrupts. "Can I get a photo, Liam?"

I look at Alie, and she hesitates for a half second, but nods. I know she's stayed out of the spotlight for most of her life, and she's kept Sera out of it too—for which I'm grateful—but I want the entire world to know that these are my girls.

"Yes, that'd be great."

Sera's nestled between us, already grinning.

Alie moves to my other side and slips her hand into mine naturally.

The camera flashes, and it makes Sera giggle.

"Thank, Liam. Ms. Grant." He nods to her.

Sera kisses my cheek. "Daddy play now?" she asks.

"Yeah, sweetheart. Soon."

"I cheer," she says, clapping.

I kiss her on the forehead, then turn to Alie.

"I'll see you after the game." I kiss her lips, lingering for a minute longer than I should on the sideline.

"Be safe," she whispers against my lips.

"Always."

"And win." She pats me on the ass.

"Yes, ma'am." I wink.

Alie reaches for Sera.

"Come on, baby. Daddy needs to get warmed up."

"Bye, Daddy!" she says, waving as Alie turns to walk away.

"See you later." I wave back.

As I turn toward the field, one of my favorite reporters intercepts me.

"Liam, can I grab you for a minute?" she asks.

"Yeah, of course."

I lean down so I can hear her over the growing noise.

"This is a big opener for you today. Are you feeling the pressure of being the new quarterback for the Titans?"

"There's always pressure, but I'm excited. I'm ready to get out there and play. Give the fans a winning season."

"You know I gotta ask. You were just with Alie Grant, and I assume her daughter, who hasn't been in the public eye. Is that why you came to New York?"

I look toward Alie and Sera and watch them as they near the tunnel, Alie straightening Sera's jersey.

"Not a story I'm going to share with you today, Carissa, but that's my daughter and the love of my life. They're my reason for everything."

She blinks, mouth open.

"Well then, congratulations!"

"Thanks." I smile proudly and jog off before she can ask anything else.

"Good luck today, Liam," she shouts after me.

I throw a hand over my shoulder and wave.

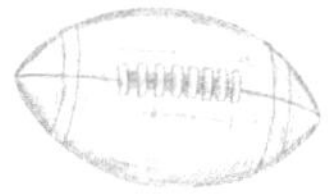

The stadium is vibrating with energy.

There's one minute and twelve seconds left, and we're down by four with the ball on the twenty-two-yard line. The red zone always feels smaller than it looks on film. Everything happens faster. Windows shrink. Lanes collapse.

I press my palms over the holes in my helmet so I can hear my coach through the headset over the noise of the crowd.

"Second and seven," I mutter. We don't need a field goal. We need a touchdown.

Coach's voice crackles. "Trips right. Z Dagger Y Cross. On one."

I jog to my huddle, clapping once to get their attention.

"Gun, gun. Trips right."

We all clap once, then get into formation. I have one wide receiver alone on the left boundary. Trips bunched to the field—my other wide receiver is wide, the slot stacked just inside, Brody tight to the formation. My back offsets to my left hip.

I see their defense shift with us. Moving their two safeties high, their corner, and my friend Silas Arbuckle, covering my wide receiver playing soft, then their nickel shaded on the inside.

My eyes travel slowly, studying them. The middle linebacker, also known as the Mike, hovers at five yards, feet bouncing. He's the key.

"Fifty-two's the mike!" I point, resetting protection.

I step forward, my hands out.

"Blue eight! Blue eighty!"

The safeties don't roll. Two-high shell.

Cover two? Maybe they rotated late.

I can see my wide receiver. Silas, covering him, is giving a cushion. The twelve-yard comeback is there if I can take it. It's safe and efficient. But safe doesn't win games down four.

I clap. "Set! Hut!"

The ball snaps clean into my hands. Three-step from gun. My tailback crosses me, and I scan for pressure.

No blitz.

My eyes snap to the safeties. They widen with my wide receiver's vertical release. The outside receiver eats up the sideline, forcing Silas to turn and run. The deep half safety opens his hips. Ready.

Now I find the mike.

He hesitates, and that's all I need.

Brody releases clean, angling across the formation on the

deep cover. Slot pushes vertical, then plants hard, cutting into his dig at fifteen.

The mike drifts with the crossing tight end. And there it is.

My window opens for half a second between the sinking hook defender and the backside safety.

I hitch once. Then the pocket tightens.

The right guard gets walked back into me, so I slide left to keep my base under me. Don't drift. Don't fade. Reset.

The dig opens behind the linebackers.

I plant my back foot and let the ball fly. It leaves my hand in a perfect spiral. Time slows in the way it only does in moments like this. The noise of the crowd disappears, and it's just leather and air.

Slot settles in the void, numbers square to me, and the safety drives late. Too late.

The ball hits him in the chest, and he turns upfield.

Contact explodes at the five.

He spins, legs moving, dragging a defender to the three before they haul him down. Then the stadium erupts when we get first and goal.

I sprint down the field, getting in his face. "That's what I'm talking about!"

The defense scrambles to line up. They're gassed. And we won't give them air.

Forty-five seconds with the clock running.

I run back to the huddle.

"Same formation," I say, voice steady. "We'll kill it if they zero."

We line up again, trips right. Their defense crowds the line this time. One safety creeps down, single high. Man-on-man coverage.

I smile, then lean toward my wide receiver. "Win inside."

He nods once.

I glance at my back. "Check release. If they bring six, you're on."

He taps his chest.

The corner over my other receiver presses tight.

"Blue eighty!"

Linebackers inch closer.

"Blue eighty!"

Nickel blitz showing off the edge.

There's my play.

"Set! Hut!"

The snap hits, and the defense explodes toward us. Zero blitz.

I take a step back and plant my foot. No time for a full progression with men across the board. It's win or lose.

Brody bursts off the line, pushing the defender's hand away and angling hard inside before bending back across the goal line.

The safety tries to undercut, but slips.

I throw high toward the back pylon.

Brody elevates above the crowd of bodies, arms extended.

The ball drops over his outside shoulder.

He secures it as a linebacker crashes into his ribs, and they tumble across the goal line. Then the official's arms shoot straight into the air. Touchdown.

The sound of eighty thousand people cheering detonates, and it shakes the stadium like an earthquake.

I don't remember running to him, but I'm pulling Brody off the ground as the rest of our line piles on. We're screaming, laughing, helmets smashing together.

Thirty-eight seconds left on the clock.

After this field goal, they won't have time to make it down the field.

I jog to the sideline and watch the replay on the Jumbotron.

We get the field goal, punt, and then game over.

I walk out onto the field, looking for Archie and Silas, who I've gotten to know pretty well. He married Beck's sister and also played for Walker with my friends and Aston and Ace Griffith after I left.

I see Archie first and wrap my arm around him.

"Well done, brother." Archie slaps my back. "Helluva play there at the end. Finding your groove with these guys?"

"Yeah, I feel pretty good about the season."

Aston walks over, and Silas is behind him.

Archie and Aston hug, and Archie lifts him up, as a big brother would.

I grip Silas's hand and pull him in. "Great game, man."

"Today wasn't our day, but it was good to see you. Settling in here okay?"

"It's been great. You coming to my place tonight? I'd love for you to meet my girlfriend and my daughter."

"I can't. I don't have the same freedom as Griff here has," he says, putting a hand on Archie's shoulder.

"What can I say? I'm like a favorite child. Coach loves me." Archie pats his own chest.

"Fuck off." Silas laughs. "I'll see you guys later. Good to see you both." He hugs Aston one more time, then fist bumps me and walks off to go say hi to a few of my teammates.

"You feeding us, Pitz, or do I need to grab something before I head your way?" Aston asks me.

"What the fuck do you think?" I laugh, shaking my head.

"Just checking, asshole," he chides.

"Okay, I'll see you guys later. I need to go say hello to a few people," Archie says.

We break apart, and I stop to give a few interviews.

"Congrats, Liam. Great start to the season. How do you feel after that win?" The reporter holds the microphone up to my face.

"It feels good. I couldn't wait to get the season going, and it's always good to win the first game."

"What do you think the difference is between last season and this one?"

I glance up, looking for my family.

"My priorities." I don't elaborate.

"Thanks for your time, Liam. Congrats."

I nod. "Thanks."

After a few more interviews, I head back to the locker room and clean up fast. I want to get to my girls and get home so I can finally be there for my daughter's birthday.

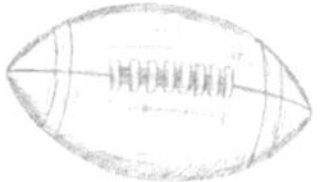

We're at Alie's place in Manhattan. It's a small party, including her parents and sister. Archie holds Emma's hand while she has their newborn son, Tucker, strapped to her chest.

There are pink balloons everywhere and streamers that say 2. And lots of sugar.

Archie's kids, Lainey and Duke, are running around with Sera like they're on sugar fumes, and the cake hasn't even been cut yet.

Aston shows up late, of course, holding a stuffed unicorn that's almost as big as Sera.

"For the MVP," he says.

She beams. "Fank you!"

"God, Pitz. She looks just like you," Emma says warmly.

"She really does," Alie agrees. "It's not fair that we do the cooking, then they look like their dads."

I wrap my arm around her. "Maybe the next one will look just like you."

"Next one?" She looks at me with her brows raised.

We haven't talked about more kids, but I want as many as she'll give me.

Instead of answering, I lean down and kiss her.

"This is … insane. Much more hectic than her first birthday party," she murmurs.

"Good insane though?"

"Yeah, she's having a blast with them."

We eat some food, visit, and the Grants get to know my friends. Having Archie and Emma here to meet my girls and celebrate my daughter means the world to me. I've really missed them.

When it's time for cake, everyone sings, and she squeezes her eyes dramatically before making her wish and blowing out the candles.

"What'd you wish for?" Aston asks her.

"Secret." She grins.

Smart kid.

The party winds down, and Alie's parents and sister are the first to leave. Everyone else leaves soon after because Archie and his family have an early flight back to Dallas tomorrow.

Sera's crashing hard from sugar and a full day of excitement.

After her bath, she tries to convince us to let her wear my jersey to bed, but it has smeared cake and … unidentifiable stains.

She holds onto her football and Stallion like she doesn't want to let go.

"Daddy stay?" she asks.

"Yes, sweetheart," I say immediately.

"Mommy, baby story," Sera says.

"Baby story?" I ask.

"She likes it when I tell her about the day she was born." Alie sits on the edge of the bed.

Sera grabs my hand as Alie starts.

"Two years ago today, I knew it was your day to arrive. After working really hard to get you out of my belly, I heard the tiniest cry."

"Me!" She points to herself.

"Yep, it was you. And when the nurse brought you over to me, I fell in love instantly. As soon as she put you in my arms, you stopped crying." Alie traces a finger down her cheek. "You had chubby, rosy cheeks, the most perfect little mouth, and your eyes … were wide and curious, like you were studying everything around you. There was a puff of brown hair on your head, and no matter how many times I tried to smooth it down, it wouldn't lay flat."

Sera pats her hair.

Alie smiles at me over Sera's head.

"I wike that," Sera says with a yawn.

"I like that story too," I whisper.

We watch her fall asleep, then close the door behind us.

The apartment is quiet as we make our way over to the couch.

"Today was perfect."

"It was." I sit next to her and take her hand in mine.

"You were amazing today."

"Thanks, baby." I brush my thumb along her jaw.

She curls her legs on the couch and leans into me.

"I want more days like this," I say, feeling content.

"We'll have them," she says, tilting her head to look at me.

I kiss her slowly, wanting her to feel my love and commitment to her and our family.

The season just started, but for the first time in my life, so has the rest of it.

EPILOGUE

ALIE

Christmas in New York is pure magic. If I hadn't grown up here, I would almost say it seems staged. Like someone turned up the saturation on the entire city and shook a snow globe.

Lights drape across Central Park, and carriages roll past, wrapped in garland. The air smells like roasted nuts and cinnamon.

Tonight, we brought Seraphina to Wollman Rink to ice skate. She looks adorable in her tiny white coat and pink knit hat, cheeks flushed from the cold air.

We lace up inside the warming tent. Liam helps Sera with her tiny skates like he's handling fragile glass. He's so gentle and careful with her. And there's an undercurrent of awe in everything they do together. Like he still can't believe she's real.

The rink glows under white lights strung around the perimeter. The skyline glitters behind it.

We step on the ice slowly, Sera gripping both of our hands.

"Mommy, twirl," she demands, tugging on my hand.

Liam lets go of her other hand, and I take her hands in mine and spin us slowly in a circle.

Liam stands beside us, hands shoved into the pockets of his coat, watching the rink like he's memorizing the moment. He looks calm. Almost … too calm.

"You sure you want to be doing this?" I tease. "We're in the playoffs, and you can't get injured."

He smirks. "Baby, I'm an elite athlete."

"You're a football player."

"Exactly. Elite." He winks.

Sera tugs on his hand. "Daddy skate!"

He looks down at her like she's his world. Because she is. We both are.

"Okay, but if I fall, don't laugh." He looks at her with a brow raised.

She covers her mouth with her hand, giggling.

"No laugh, Daddy." But she shrieks when he pretends to wobble dramatically.

"Daddy fall!"

"I'm not falling." He laughs, steadying her.

I watch them for a moment. Seeing the way he bends slightly. The way she trusts him without hesitation. It makes my chest tighten.

Just six months ago, this was fragile at best.

But now … it feels solid. We're solid.

We skate together in a slow circle around the rink, Sera insisting on trying to glide on her own. But she only makes it three seconds before Liam scoops her up mid-wobble.

"I got you," he says softly, kissing her cheek.

After a while—*two laps*—Sera gets tired and wants hot chocolate. We find a bench. Liam comes back with our hot chocolate and sits with Sera between us. Just like the scene on a postcard, snow starts to fall. It's big, soft, puffy flakes. Sera leans forward and catches snow on her tongue and giggles when she gets one, then takes a drink of cocoa.

Liam brushes some of the snow off her hat.

"You having fun, sweetheart?" he asks her.

She nods excitedly, whipped cream mustache on her lip.

Liam isn't teasing Sera about the whipped cream mustache. He isn't cracking one of his usual jokes. He just keeps looking at me like he's memorizing something.

"You cold?" he asks me.

"No, I'm okay," I say, shaking my head, then taking a sip of my own cocoa. Since it's snowing, it's fairly warm for a New York winter evening. Plus, I'm wearing my red coat tonight because it's Liam's favorite.

"Are you sure?" he asks again.

"Yes … "

Then he stands and holds out his hand. One for me, one for Sera.

"Come with me, girls."

Sera looks at me, then at Liam.

"Okay, but I'm not done yet." I lift my cup.

"I'll get you another one."

The air suddenly feels quieter, like the whole rink is holding its breath. My stomach flips. I don't know why, but something feels different.

Liam doesn't joke the way he usually would. His hand tightens around mine, and he keeps glancing between Sera and me like he's making sure we're both right where he wants us.

We step onto the ice, snow falling around us, glittering against the lights.

"Liam," I whisper, feeling suddenly nervous, "what are you doing?"

He takes my hands in his and looks at me with pure love.

"I've spent most of my life chasing things," he says quietly. "Wins. Contracts. Being the best."

I swallow.

"And then I found out I'd already missed the most important thing."

My hands start to shake.

"Sera," I whisper.

"And you," he says, pulling me closer.

Everything seems too quiet, and I swear I can feel my heartbeat in my ears.

"I can't get that time back," he continues. "But I promise not to miss anymore."

Tears sting my eyes.

"I won't miss another Christmas. Or another birthday."

I lift my gloved hand and wipe at my falling tears. "Liam…"

"I love you," he says firmly. "I love you in a build-a-life way."

My breath leaves me in a shaky exhale.

Then he drops, shakily, to one knee on the ice.

"You okay, Daddy?"

Leave it to a child to change the tone, making us both laugh.

I faintly hear someone nearby gasp, but I don't look. Because all I can see is him.

He pulls off his gloves and takes a small velvet box from his coat pocket, then opens it. The ring catches the lights, making it sparkle.

"I want to marry you, Aliette Grant," he says. "I want to be your husband every day for the rest of my life."

His voice softens, like he's trying to hold in his emotions.

"Will you marry me?"

I'm full-out crying now, and I can't stop it. And they aren't pretty tears. They're overwhelming, shaking tears.

"Yes," I breathe.

He blinks like he's trying to make sure he heard me right.

"Yes," I say again, louder.

The rink erupts in applause when they see him remove my glove and slide the ring onto my finger.

It fits perfectly.

He stands quickly and pulls me in for a kiss. Soft at first, then turning deeper. And when we finally pull apart, it's because our daughter is tugging on my hand.

She's watching us, wide-eyed and curious.

I laugh through my tears and show her my ring.

"Pwitty!" she gasps.

Liam kneels down to her level. "I have something for you too."

He pulls out another box and opens it to show her.

"Mommy and I are going to get married," he says, watching for a reaction.

She smiles and blinks.

"But I want to make a promise to you too, sweetheart." He pulls out a dainty gold necklace with three hearts inside one another.

"I promise that you and Mommy are always in my heart, every day, even when I have to go away for work."

She throws her arms around him, then me. And then somehow, we end up on the ice in a messy, mittened group hug while strangers clap, probably recognizing Liam at this point, and take photos we'll possibly see on social media.

Once we turn in our skates, we walk through the park with Sera bundled between us.

I can't stop staring at my ring as it glitters under the streetlights.

"You planned this, didn't you? To do this here?" I ask.

"I did."

"At Christmas."

"Felt … like the perfect place and time, don't you think?"

He stops walking and faces me.

"I've never been surer about anything in my life."

Sera interrupts, tugging on his hand, "Daddy, carry me."

He leans in to kiss me before picking her up effortlessly.

I watch the way she rests her head on his shoulder and his ease with her.

This is ours.

"Hey/" He takes my hand.

I look up at him.

"Merry Christmas, Vixen," he whispers.

I smile.

"Merry Christmas, Blitzen."

Snow keeps falling, and everything feels like it's exactly how it's supposed to be.

A FEW DAYS LATER

LIAM

The first thing I notice when we walk into the facility on Monday is that everything looks the same. Same building. Same routine. Yet everything feels different.

I have Sera in my arms, and Alie's hand in mine. I can't help but rub my thumb over her ring every few minutes. Just to make sure it's there. That this is real.

We drop Sera off at the nursery, and then I walk Alie to her office and linger a little too long with a kiss that could cause some trouble. She eventually shoos me out, and I make my way down to the locker room and drop off my bag.

The minute I walk into the weight room, I notice Aaron

talking to one of our linemen, who's also his client. We've avoided him for the most part, and Alie was serious when she told him that any communication would be business only, and not through her. Her father has honored that request, too, and from what I've heard in hushed conversation, the family friendship between the Grants and Muldoons has been strained. Sera has asked about him a few times, but she's still so young, so I'm not sure that she'll have any memories of him at all.

I wanted to bring Alie down later and make an announcement to my teammates together, but having Aaron in the room, I'm feeling like now's the perfect time to announce our engagement. Just to dig that knife a little deeper into his heart.

Aston spots me and walks over to me. "Well? Did you do it?" he asks.

I nod, and a slow smile stretches across my face. "I did."

"That's all I get? I want the details. I saw a few pictures on social media, but you need to give me a play-by-play," he says, waving his hand toward him.

I made the mistake of telling Aston about my plans to propose. He insisted on helping me look for rings and wanted in on the plan for how I was planning to propose. But he actually turned out to be a big help. And I know he's excited for me, us.

"Hold up. I'm going to make an announcement, and then I'll tell you." I nod toward Aaron, and Aston follows my gaze.

"Vicious, man. I love it." He holds out a fist to me.

I put my fingers to my mouth and whistle.

Someone turns the music down.

"Hey, everyone, I have an announcement to make."

My teammates stop what they're doing and turn their attention to me.

"Some of you may have seen some pictures of me on social media with Alie and Sera." I look around and see some of the guys nod. "Well, Alie and I got engaged this weekend!" My smile is genuine because I'm a fucking sap when it comes to her and Sera.

Congratulations are called out, and a few guys come up to hug me, including Saint and Brody.

"I'm happy for you, man. Congrats," Saint says, slapping my back.

"Thank you. We're really excited."

"Congrats, Pitzy," Brody says. "When's the wedding?"

"We haven't really talked about it much yet, but ... " I pause to see if Aaron is listening. Petty? Yes, but the fucker deserves it. "We want to get married as soon as possible. Likely this spring before the draft."

"Doesn't give you guys much time, but I guess when you have the kind of money the Grants do, anything is possible." Brody laughs.

I just laugh and shake my head. "Yeah, I mean, the sooner the better." I might say that part a little louder than necessary.

Aston claps me on the back. "You gonna stand around and gossip, or are we gonna work?"

"I thought you wanted to hear about it?"

"Oh, I do. I want every detail, but I also have plans later and want to get this done."

"Plans with who? I'm your only friend here." I point to my chest.

"That's not true. Brody and I hang out sometimes," he explains.

"So, why didn't you just say you were hanging out with him later?" We walk over to one of the benches.

"Who are you, my dad?" He huffs a laugh.

Now I really want to know, but I won't push. Today.

We get started and make our way around the weight room, and I give him every detail of the engagement. Loudly, just to make sure Aaron can hear me clearly. Especially the parts about Sera being excited.

By lunchtime, we're wrapping up, and Alie walks in and comes toward me. She spots Aaron and flinches, but she keeps the smile she has on her face.

I see him walk out of the room with his client a minute later and notice them going into one of the meeting rooms across the hall.

Some of my teammates make their way over to Alie to congratulate her on our engagement. Watching her shine and show off her ring makes me possessive and so goddamn proud to call this woman mine.

When I've had enough of sharing her, we walk out of the weight room, and I pull her into one of the meeting rooms, locking the door behind me.

I lift her in my arms, and she automatically wraps her legs around my waist, making her skirt bunch, and set her on the desk at the front of the room.

"What are you doing? I thought we were going to go have lunch with Sera," she says, wrapping her arms around my shoulders.

"We are, but I need to fuck my future wife first. Watching you show off your ring, knowing Aaron was in the same room, makes me feel like I need to claim you. Make you mine all over again." I pull down her V-neck sweater low enough to expose one of her breasts.

"Liam! What if someone tries to come in?"

"That's why I locked the door, baby. I want everyone to know you're mine, but I'm the only one who gets to see you." I say, then drop kisses from her neck to the top of her breast.

I pull down the cup of her bra because I need more.

"You're so perfect. Pretty rosebud nipples begging to be sucked," I say, leaning down and taking her nipple in my mouth, sucking.

She moans and moves her hands into my hair, holding my head to her breast.

I continue sucking, licking, and biting her nipple, but move my hands to the hem of her skirt, pushing it up to her waist.

"As much as I want to taste you, we don't have much time if we're gonna have lunch with our little girl."

She takes the waistband of my shorts and pushes them down far enough for my dick to spring free. Her hand wraps around me, and she pumps me once, twice. But I've been hard for her since we walked into this room and her legs wrapped around me.

I grab her ass and pull her to the edge of the table. Then I spit on two of my fingers, pull the thin strip of lace to the side, and push them inside of her pussy, but she's already wet for me.

"You need me as much as I need you, baby?" I pump in and out, stretching her.

"Yes, I love when you get like this, " she breathes, her hand still stroking my cock. "When you look at me like you're about to lose control."

She releases me and grabs my hips so my erection lines up with her pussy.

I remove my hand, then guide my dick inside her tight heat.

Her arms wrap around my shoulders, and her head drops back as I thrust in.

"This is gonna be hard and fast. Can you handle that, baby?"

I take hold of her thighs and spread them as I pump in and out of her.

She nods, biting her lip. Then she releases her hold on my shoulders and leans back, bracing her upper body on the table with one hand, and the other working her clit.

I look down and watch our bodies come together. This is pure fucking. Fast and frantic.

"That's it," I praise her. "You look so pretty like this. Working your clit, my cock sliding in and out of your pussy."

"Liam," she starts to pant.

"You gonna come for me, baby?" I lean forward close enough to kiss her, but I don't. Then I slowly pull my cock out.

"What are you doing? Don't stop," she says, eyes wild.

"Beg me to let you come." I push the tip in, teasing her.

"Please. Please let me come."

She tilts her hips up, trying to get me deeper inside, but I hold back, keeping just the head at her entrance.

"I'll let you come if you scream my name. Scream it loud so *he* can hear you. So he knows you're mine."

"I'll do anything. Just make me come."

Not able to hold back any longer, I answer by thrusting into her hard. My fingers digging into her thighs.

Her body starts to tremble, and her pussy contracts around my cock. Her hand stills on her clit as she comes, her chest heaving.

"Oh my God, Liam!" she yells. Loud. "I'm coming!"

And I fucking love it. Because she's mine and I want everyone to know it.

I let go a second later, burying myself deep inside her as I come, and then hold her close, my cock covered to the hilt by her pussy. I look down at us joined, and, fuck me, that's hot.

I can't wait to put another baby in her. I'll keep that thought to myself for now though.

We hear noise outside the door, likely guys leaving for the day.

"Oh shit," she says, pushing at my chest. "We'd better go."

I pull out, watching my cum leak out of her, and adjust her thong back in place.

She looks around. "Crap, there's nothing in here for me to clean up with."

I shake my head slowly, smiling. "Leave it. I want to know that my cum is dripping out of you, soaking your panties when we walk out of here."

And if we happen to see Aaron … that'd be a big fucking bonus.

"Liam … " She looks at me and rolls her eyes, but there's a smile on her face.

"You love the idea of it too." I lean in and kiss her.

"You're right … I do," she says, nipping my bottom lip before pulling away.

I lift her off the desk and fix her sweater and straighten her skirt, before planting a soft kiss on her lips.

"I love you, baby."

"I love you too, fiancé." She kisses me again. "Now let's go get our baby for lunch."

I unlock and open the door, touching her back as she walks out first.

She's pulling at her skirt and straightening her sweater. Her cheeks are pink, and there's no doubt what we were doing in that room to anyone passing by.

The door to the room next to us opens, and Aaron and his client come out of the room.

He glances over at us, face scrunching with disgust, and shakes his head, then walks toward the elevator.

Yeah, I think he heard us.

Good.

Asshole.

I hope the image of us, flushed and fucked, is burned in his mind.

Alie smiles at me. "That might have been a little petty, but totally worth it."

Then another door opens down the hall, and we turn our attention toward it and realize it's Presley's office.

Saint comes out a minute later, walking backward and smiling. Then he leans back in, but we can't see anything because of the doorframe.

A second later, we see him backing up into the hall, this time an arm pushing him out. Then Presley steps out, hand still on Saint's chest. And she's ... smiling. In a way I haven't seen her smile before.

The kind of smile you have after getting thoroughly fucked.

She doesn't notice us and turns back to her office.

But Saint does see us. He smirks and winks at us. Then holds a finger to his lips. "Shh ..."

Holy shit.

I look at Alie, and her mouth is wide open in shock. Then she turns her head slowly and looks at me.

"Did I just see what I think I saw?" she asks.

"Yeah, baby. I think we did."

Then we burst out laughing because everything suddenly seems lighter.

Aaron is out of Alie's life.

The season is starting.

We're engaged and moving into a house. As soon as we find one …

Seraphina is smothered in love by both of her parents.

And my life isn't divided between football and everything else.

It's all finally come together as one.

The same team.

Want to see what Alie and Liam are up to now? Read their **bonus chapter here**!

Next up in the Gridiron Legacy world is **Presley and Saint's** book! **Preorder The Pact**.

BONUS CHAPTER

TEN MONTHS LATER

ALIE

The stadium is still buzzing from our win tonight. The echo of the crowd, the lights, the music, and the fans linger in hopes of getting an autograph. And my husband just played one of the best games of his career. I think we have a shot at making it to the Super Bowl this year.

Sera and I are waiting in the executive suite for him to come up. And we were able to get his parents here for the game. They're getting more comfortable with the idea of flying now that they have a granddaughter. My parents have brought them into our family with ease, and our fathers became fast friends. Having them all here tonight was important for me because our family of three is about to grow.

My fingers press lightly against my stomach, a subconscious move that feels familiar, yet new. It's still surreal. Since we've been together, it's been a whirlwind, but in all the best ways. I can't wait for this next chapter.

Then the door swings open, and there he is. His hair is still wet from the shower, but he's glowing from the win. He looks a bit exhausted, too, but breaks out into a smile when he sees me.

Mine.

Our eyes lock, like they always do, and something squeezes in my chest, and butterflies take over in my belly. Then Sera runs to him, and he catches her as she leaps into his arms.

"There's my girl," he says, placing a kiss on her cheek, making her giggle.

She squirms when she sees my sister walk in. So, he sets her down, and she runs to Presley.

He lifts a hand, saying hello to everyone else in the room, but walks over to me.

"Hey," he says, wrapping his arms around me and planting a soft kiss on my lips.

"Hi," I answer when he pulls back. "Good game," I manage to get out.

"Thanks." His voice shifts—less post-game high, more focused. On me. Always on me. "You, okay?"

I nod too quickly. Which is apparently my tell, because his brows pull together immediately.

"What is it? Something wrong?" His eyes roam over my face, then my body.

Dammit. I had a plan. Something cute and memorable. Something that didn't involve me standing here speechless, trying not to cry in front of my husband and everyone else.

"Come over here." I take his hand and lead him over to one of the couches.

"Baby, you're making me nervous here. Are you okay?" Concern etched across his face.

He sits first and pulls me down onto his lap, his arm wrapping around me, anchoring me to him.

"Talk to me," he murmurs.

I exhale, but it's not steady.

Then—

I laugh.

Because of course I do.

Liam blinks at me. "Why are you laughing?"

"Because I had this whole plan," I admit, covering my face with my hands. "I was going to tell you in some cute, Pinterest-worthy way. You know—something adorable and perfect."

His mouth twitches like he's trying not to smile, but is also confused.

"But here we are," I continue, my voice shaky, "and you just played the game of your life, and I'm about to drop a few bombs."

His hand cups my face before I continue. "Hey. Whatever it is, we got this."

He always does this. He has a way of centering me, calming me.

"Alie," he says again, softer. "What's going on?"

I swallow. Then I take his hand and place it against my stomach.

He looks down at our hands, then quickly back to my face. "Alie—"

"I'm pregnant."

I feel it in his hold—the exact second it hits him. The moment his world tilts.

"Say that again," he breathes.

I smile through the tears that are now running down my face. "I'm pregnant, Liam."

A disbelieving sound leaves him as his hand presses more firmly against my stomach, like he's trying to feel something that isn't there yet.

"Are you serious right now?" he asks.

I nod. "Very."

He takes my face in both of his hands, his eyes shimmering with tears.

"Alie," he says softly. "We're having a baby?"

Emotion swells in my chest. "We are."

He lets out a full-bellied laugh, and I feel it through my whole body.

"Yeah," he says, more steadily. "Yeah, we are."

He leans back, studying my face, his thumbs brushing under my eyes.

"You feeling alright?" he asks. "When did you find out? You didn't go to the doctor without me, right?"

"I found out for sure today when I took a test before we came to the stadium. I have to say ... it was torture not telling you when I saw you on the field before the game." I huff a laugh. "And no, no doctor yet. We'll do it all together this time."

His gaze softens in a way that makes my heart melt.

"Another baby," he says with awe. "And this time I'll get to do it all— the ultrasounds, hearing the heartbeat for the first time, late-night feedings, first steps ..."

I nod. "Felt like the right time to change your life again."

He smiles and shakes his head slightly. "This is bigger than football. You could have told me before the game."

"No, I couldn't. I needed you to stay focused." I laugh.

He kisses me with a tenderness I feel all the way to my toes. So much love pouring into this kiss.

I take his wrists in my hands and pull back.

Because I'm not done.

"There's something else," I say quietly.

His posture changes. "What is it?"

I stand, walk over behind the bar, and grab my bag. I sit next to him when I get to the couch, and pull out the folder I've been carrying around since yesterday.

His gaze falls to it, and recognition and understanding register.

"The paperwork?" he asks.

I nod, tears falling again.

For our daughter. For putting his name on her birth certificate.

"I was going to do this yesterday, but when I suspected I

might be pregnant, I felt like … everything should happen all at once."

He stares at the folder, like it might undo him.

"Alie, thank you," he says, voice rough.

I shake my head. "You don't have to thank me. She's yours, and you should have been on there from day one."

Emotion flickers across his face—raw and unguarded.

I set the folder down, then lace my fingers through his, squeezing. "You're her dad. And now…" I glance down at my stomach, then back at him. "Our babies will have your name."

Silence.

I hand him the folder, and he doesn't hesitate to take it.

Liam pulls out the paper and brushes one of his hands over her name. It's not the first time he's seen this; he did have to sign it. It's just official now.

He puts it back in the folder and sets it on the other side of him. Next thing I know, I'm in his lap, his arms wrapped around me, one hand spread over my belly.

"Our family," he whispers against my lips.

"Our little family," I say, then kiss him.

He pulls back. "Wait, do I get to pick the name?"

I blink. "Um, no. We'll do that together."

"Look, I love Seraphina's name, but I didn't get to be a part of any of it. I want it all this time."

"You can help," I snicker.

"Okay," he nods seriously. "So I'm thinking something strong. Legendary."

"Liam—it could be a girl."

"Maybe after me," he continues, ignoring me completely. "Liam Jr. has a nice ring to it."

I laugh. "You're too much."

He laughs with me, but pulls me into him again.

"Yeah," he murmurs, "but I'm yours."

"That you are." I agree.

"And their dad," he adds quietly, his hand spreading over my stomach again.

This man makes me melt.

He kisses me again, deeper this time.

And I don't care that our families can see it. I'm sure they can tell something is going on.

We'll get to the announcements in a minute.

But first…

I'm going to stay locked in this moment because it's the only one that matters.

Read more books by Ava Sutton.

www.amazon.com / author / avasutton

avasuttonbooks.com

WALKER UNIVERSITY STALLIONS

Counter Play - Beckham & Charlie

Zone Protection - Archie & Emma

Strong Side - Casey & Noelle

Silent Count - Bo & Chelsea

Lockdown Corner - Silas & Brooke

GRIDIRON LEGACY

The Trade - Liam & Alie

The Pact - Saint & Presley (May 2026)

The Secret - Aston Griffith (July 2026)

TDB - Brody Vaughn (September 2026)

TDB HOCKEY SERIES

TDB - Aiden Griffith (January 2027)

FLORIDA JAGUARS

TDB - Ace Griffith (TBD)

ACKNOWLEDGMENTS

To my family, thank you for your support. You're my reason for everything. I love you all, eternally.

Compass Press, thank you for walking me through the author journey.

Jovanna Shirley, once again, thank you for your patience and expertise. I sort of made my deadline. YAY!

Jeannine Colette, what would we do without you? Seriously. I'm honored and privileged to have you on this journey with me. This one is for you. Your favorite guy.

Sarah Sentz, from cover to page, your feedback is so incredibly valuable. You stay right along by my side, and Autumn's, and you never complain when we (Autumn 😉) gives you more to do! Just a reminder … you can't escape us. Ever.

Sam R, thank you for reading early. Your voicemails and feedback mean the world to me. Thank you for everything you do for me and for cheering me on since day one.

Rickie, thank you so much for reading early, and your feedback helped me pull some loose strings together. Thank you for everything you do for me, and I adore every post you make for me.

To my ARC Team and all readers, thank you for reading more of my words! Your reviews, edits, and just knowing you're reading still blow my mind. Thank you, thank you!

Wordsmith Publicity, Autumn and Roxie, thank you for helping me reach readers and for your guidance and support!

Ava Sutton is a sports enthusiast and author of spicy college and professional sports romance.

When she's not writing, you can find her nose in a book, scrolling social media or planning dream vacations she someday hopes to take. She lives in Dallas, Texas with her two dogs.

Connect with her on Facebook, Instagram, and TikTok.

www.ingramcontent.com/pod-product-compliance
Lightning Source LLC
LaVergne TN
LVHW100512110826
845146LV00002B/605

* 9 7 9 8 9 9 4 6 3 4 1 5 8 *